The Ancient Magus' Bride

❖ The Silver Yarn ❖

THE ANCIENT MAGUS' BRIDE: THE SILVER YARN

Seven Seas books may be purchased in bulk for promotional,
educational, or business use. Please contact your local bookseller or the
Macmillan Corporate and Premium Sales Department at 1-800-221-
7945, extension 5442, or by
e-mail at MacmillanSpecialMarkets@macmillan.com.

Follow Seven Seas Entertainment online at
sevenseasentertainment.com.

TRANSLATION: Andrew Cunningham
ADAPTATION: Jessica Cluess
COPY EDITOR: Ysabet MacFarlane
COVER DESIGN: Nicky Lim
INTERIOR LAYOUT & DESIGN: Clay Gardner
PROOFREADER: Jade Gardner, Kris Swanson
ASSISTANT EDITOR: Jenn Grunigen
LIGHT NOVEL EDITOR: Nibedita Sen
DIGITAL MANAGER: CK Russell
EDITOR-IN-CHIEF: Adam Arnold
PUBLISHER: Jason DeAngelis

ISBN: 978-1-64275-001-0
Printed in Canada
First Printing: March 2019
10 9 8 7 6 5 4 3 2 1

The Ancient Magus' Bride

❧ The Silver Yarn ❧

Table of Contents

War at the Walshes'

YUICHIRO HIGASHIDE

"A HOME IS A PLACE to which people return, and a place they protect."

As always, Elias was giving the girl an impromptu lecture.

"That's true," Chise said, nodding. "Home" had meant a place where she could feel safe at one time. But she could no longer return to that place.

That was a long time ago.

Now she had a place where she belonged, a place to protect. People there waited for her return, people to whom she could say, "I'm home."

Then again, while she knew she could return, she wasn't sure how much protection it could offer her.

"The line between home and the outside world is a type of barrier. Humans cannot live on their own, yet they desire a place where they can *be* alone. Isn't that right?"

Chise nodded. This made sense to her. Being alone all the time was quite lonely. Humans craved connections with others. But at the same time, it was human nature to seek private spaces where they wouldn't need to interact with anyone.

A room of your own. A place where you could be by yourself.

"So, in a broad sense, the rules inside your home are different from the rules outside it. And if the rules are different, the beings born and raised there are also different."

Elias took a small bottle of water and poured it out, tracing a line.

"There was a home here once," he said.

"There was?"

Chise blinked and looked around. Indeed, now that she was paying attention, she noticed remnants of a stone wall; patches where the grass grew differently; signs that something large had once rested here in this field.

But unless you were actively looking for it, you'd see only grass.

"So, did...?" she began.

Did the people who lived here fall prey to something uncanny? Elias guessed her thoughts. "No, nothing like that. The people who lived here simply moved away in the usual fashion."

Hypothetically, a family of six might have lived there. A grandfather and a grandmother; a mother and a father; a brother and a sister. The grandparents had made up their minds to live out their lives in this house, and their children had done the same. But the youngest generation longed to see more of the world and left for greener pastures.

The grandparents vanished, and the parents followed in time. No one remained in this place. The brother and sister talked it over, divided up the belongings, and tried selling the house. But the remote location and awkward design dissuaded anyone from buying it. Gradually, the house deteriorated—and neither of the children really cared.

Under those conditions, a home could fall apart in no time at all.

"But can a house fall to pieces so easily just because nobody lives there?" Chise asked.

"It depends on the house. This one had a house faerie—a Brownie, you see."

"Like the Silver Lady?"

"That is the house faerie in *our* home. Like I said, each house has different rules and different beings living within."

"Right."

Chise didn't really get it. Silky was the only house faerie she knew. Other kinds probably existed, but Chise knew nothing specific.

"They do not haunt the people, just the house. They delight in mischief but also help with the housework. However..."

Elias picked up a pebble from the remains of the house and held it to his brow.

"If people abandon the house, there's no point in mischief or housework. And if a faerie's actions no longer carry meaning, they cease to be themselves."

The water mingled with the dirt, forming mud. The mud was like a boundary line, seemingly marking a front door.

"So this home's faerie...transformed into something else?" Chise asked.

"It did."

Elias stood, brushing the dirt off his clothes.

"As I was saying, there are different rules for every house. Another person's home is like another world, albeit a very small one."

Chise had visited any number of these other worlds, so she had an idea of what that meant.

"So you must always be careful when stepping into

someone else's home. We hold no sway over the rules of that house, for those who live there decide the rules."

"R-right."

"That said, this should settle things. Now they can build a new home here in time."

"Was it cursed?" she asked.

"Not exactly, but I suppose it was something like a curse. The remnants of failure lay here. The voice of a former Brownie, rejecting all but the ones who had once lived here."

Nobody can come in.

No one can set foot here.

This is our domain.

"Remnants..."

"Curious?" he asked.

Elias's question caught her off guard. "Maybe a little."

There was a Brownie living in Elias's home, one who waited patiently for their return. So what were house faeries in other homes like? What type of house faerie imprinted itself on the ground like a curse?

Chise had to admit she was interested.

"Fair enough. Perhaps it would do you good to get a taste for how terrifying it can be to enter someone else's home."

Elias placed his finger on Chise's forehead.

"Don't worry. I'm simply sending your mind into the past, allowing you to view the memories held within this place," he said.

"Understood."

Chise closed her eyes. Immediately, she felt like she was falling. It was surprising but not enough of a shock to make her cry out. Elias had said not to worry, and Chise always trusted him.

These were far and distant memories.
The story of two Brownies, imprinted on the land.

❧

Brownies have no names. However, as a Brownie develops a personality of its own, it becomes more than just a house faerie. It must be called something.

The Walsh family Brownie was often called Gray Walls on account of the house's imposing walls of gray stone. But people rarely used that name in a positive sense. If he was referred to by name, it was only when he'd played a particularly awful prank on a human, injuring them so badly the other Brownies were gossiping about it.

"Gray Walls did it again!" they'd say.

Humans and faeries were different creatures with

entirely different goals and reasons for living. When they met, good or bad things could happen. Sometimes they lived together in harmony, and sometimes they didn't.

Brownies were a harmonious type. They helped with the housework and pulled pranks. Without both of these qualities, they would no longer be Brownies. So, to the other Brownies, Gray Walls was downright bizarre.

He didn't hate humans. He didn't hate them, but his "pranks" were cruel. He didn't spill things on the floor or break plates; nothing that tame. He left nails sticking out of the floor. He weakened planks on the stairs. He made the bathroom floor slippery. These tricks were less mischievous than malicious, tormenting the residents of his home.

Above all, Gray Walls' pranks could be fatal to those who lived there.

This house is haunted.

The head of the Walsh family said those words before he disappeared, leaving no sole heir. Normally the house would be sold and another family would move in, but the Walshes refused to sell.

Perhaps that was their way of getting revenge on the Brownie.

If you hate humans that much...
We'll destroy the reason you exist.

Who knew what the Walshes were thinking? They merely left the house to rot.

They departed one day without warning, leaving all the furniture, clothing, even their food, behind. At first, Gray Walls believed they'd simply gone out, that they'd come back eventually. He considered this a great opportunity to ready his next prank.

One week passed. Gray Walls thought it was a long vacation.

One month passed. Gray Walls wondered if they'd gotten sick.

One year passed. He knew the other faeries were laughing at him now.

Oh, poor, poor Gray Walls. A Brownie whose people ran away!

Gray Walls shook his head.

They hadn't run away.

They would never do that. They couldn't have. They'd left all their furniture behind. Humans would never go away without taking all their belongings!

Ten years passed.

The house's neighbors forgot anyone had ever lived there.

The walls deteriorated so badly that the name Gray Walls no longer made sense.

But Gray Walls waited patiently.

In time, someone new would live here. When they did, he could pull pranks on them again. This idea had passed from conviction to obsession.

The other faeries feared what he'd become and no longer gossiped about him. No one spoke to him, no one even saw him. All except for one Brownie.

🍂

That Brownie was called Rust Eyes.

Faeries cared little for physical attractiveness, but a human would have considered him much less appealing than an ariel or a vodyanoi. His appearance was sinister enough to send a chill down anyone's spine.

He had eyes the color of rusted iron, making it impossible to tell from the outside if he could even see. One arm was long and gnarled, making him look like a faerie who worked with wrought iron rather than one who did housework.

In fact, he'd earned the nickname Rust Eyes because the family he lived with, the Elgars, were blacksmiths.

With the exception of dwarves, faeries hated iron as a rule. Only the strangest Brownies would ever choose to live with a smith. But Rust Eyes was a very strange Brownie. Brownies had many personality types, but "diligent" was the best word to describe Rust Eyes.

Now, "diligent" was the last word anyone would use to describe your average faerie, but this Brownie was quite unique. He did so much housework, but his pranks were scarcely ever mischievous. The only prank he ever pulled was to carefully turn the stacks of china upside down.

This amused the Elgars. To Rust Eyes, it was his signature prank.

Children born in the Elgar family, especially those who could see faeries, thought all Brownies were diligent, kind, and helpful. Rust Eyes never considered trying to change that impression. He simply couldn't abide seeing anything out of place and acted accordingly.

Whether the Elgar family fortunes took a good turn or a bad one was of no importance to him. When the Elgar family baby died of pneumonia, Rust Eyes turned the plates upside down. When their daughter was married, he turned the plates upside-down.

He had no interest in human affairs, and that disinterest

showed itself in the piles of upside-down china.

Time passed, each day the same as the one before. As the times changed, so did the routines of those around him. But Rust Eyes refused to change. If tomorrow wasn't the same as yesterday, he couldn't bear it.

Thanks for your help!

The letter left on the pile of upside-down plates did nothing to change his mind. The clumsy handwriting indicated that the Elgars' only daughter had written it.

Humans had begun seeing Brownies as creatures of legend rather than close neighbors. Rust Eyes learned this from the daughter's letter. As the house became modernized, people forgot about faeries. Drunk on their own arrogance, the cities changed around them.

So she'd wanted to thank the faerie that helped keep the house clean as if nothing had changed.

The letter explained all this. Rust Eyes slipped it into the box of treasures he'd hidden in the eaves. The letter didn't make him work any more or less diligently.

To him, rules were essential. If he had cleaned a room, then he would turn all the plates over. That was the rule Rust Eyes had made for himself, and sticking to that rule gave him all the pleasure he needed.

As such, receiving the letter didn't change his actions. Further letters awaited him on the stacks of china, letters which gave updates on the family or on life at school, but Rust Eyes' behavior didn't change at all.

But he read the letters.

She'd meant them for him, so he felt it was his duty to read them. The letters weren't terribly interesting, mostly making a big deal out of ordinary events—how she'd managed to write twenty lines describing a boy throwing up at school, he could not say—but Rust Eyes wouldn't treat any gifts poorly.

Rust Eyes ignored other faeries as studiously as he ignored the humans around him. Since the house dealt with iron, other faeries rarely came anywhere near the Elgar home, or anywhere near Rust Eyes.

If they thought of him at all, they thought of him as that strange faerie who didn't hesitate to work with iron. Nothing more.

So Rust Eyes paid little attention to anything outside his territory.

But he knew that a Brownie named Gray Walls lived next door, in the house the Walshes had let fall into utter ruin.

He knew the Brownie's extreme pranks had brought about tragedy and broken the heart of the home's owner.

And he knew the Brownie was still waiting for the owner to return.

This wasn't normal behavior. Rust Eyes may have been a strange Brownie, but he still dwelt within the acceptable range of faerie behavior. But Gray Walls' obsession went beyond that.

Just as there were limits on the pranks a Brownie could pull, there were limits on how long a Brownie should wait. No contract bounded the Brownie; he hadn't been summoned and shackled, Gray Walls was just waiting for his masters to return. Despite all the awful pranks he'd pulled, he was certain of their homecoming. It felt almost sinister.

Rust Eyes caught a glimpse of him two or three times a year.

He wanted nothing to do with Gray Walls, and Rust Eyes assumed Gray Walls was the same. So he ignored him.

In hindsight, the very fact that he ever caught a glimpse of him at all was odd.

As Rust Eyes went through his daily routine, something unexpected happened...

Petra, the Elgar girl who had sent him all those letters, went missing.

❦

Petra Elgar's mother had told her there was a Brownie in their house when she was only five years old.

It had been meant as a warning: *Don't let the faerie surprise you. Don't try to talk to it. It might be dangerous.* And so on.

He lived in the same world as them but followed different rules. She had to think of dealing with faeries like staying over at a stranger's house. Petra wouldn't want anyone jumping on her bed covered in mud, would she? Well, that was her mother's explanation for how to deal with faeries.

Outside the house, Petra did just as she was told. Even if she saw faeries, she ignored them, not even listening to their whisperings. But no child could be satisfied with just that, not when a real Brownie lived in their own house.

He (or perhaps she) didn't like showing himself to people, but he helped with the housework. Petra often found rooms clean when she knew for a fact nobody had cleaned them. Things she believed she'd lost would show up on her desk.

Every time this happened, her mother would put some warm milk on the mantle.

"This is how you show gratitude. Make sure you don't drink it, okay?" Her mother laughed, happily.

Once, the milk had looked so good that Petra snuck a sip of it. The next day, someone had dumped all the garbage in the house out on her bed. After that, she never drank any of the Brownie's milk again. Of course, even though it had been her punishment, the garbage was all dry dust and bits of paper. He hadn't dumped anything smelly there, so Petra was sure this Brownie was nice.

When had she first heard about the Brownie next door?

The house next door had been a ruin as long as she could remember. She'd somehow known something haunted it. Her grandmother, grandfather, father, and mother had all warned her never to go there, over and over.

At ten, Petra's mind balanced uneasily between discretion, curiosity, and common sense.

Discretion—don't go into someone else's house without permission.

Curiosity—something she had never seen before lived in the ruined house.

Common sense—faeries might not really exist.

Petra's curiosity and common sense teamed up to defeat her discretion. If the house's gray walls had still existed, discretion would have won out. But that barrier was long since gone. Two thirds of the walls had collapsed, and Petra easily stepped over them onto the house's grounds.

She was sure there was nothing there, but this would satisfy her curiosity.

She secretly filled a backpack with chocolate, cookies, jerky, a leather canteen filled with water, a candle, and some matches. She was totally prepared, and her parents had no idea.

As had been already said, Rust Eyes was disinterested in the world outside. He took pleasure in his routine, as always.

But because of his very monotonous nature, he alone noticed Petra's odd behavior. Petra wasn't doing what she always did. Human behavior had some random elements, but it was unlike her to fill a backpack with chocolate and jerky while humming happily to herself.

Not a picnic. No one else in the house is talking about it. She's hiding that bag from everyone else.

This is important enough for her to stop herself from eating the chocolate immediately.

This can't be good for the family.

Rust Eyes knew all of this but thought no more on the subject. He never involved himself in human affairs more than was strictly necessary.

The next day, the girl left the house. Rust Eyes had watched her go.

Petra didn't come home that day. No one left warm milk for Rust Eyes on the mantle.

❦

The Walshes' Brownie, Gray Walls, was obsessed.

He had to protect this house. Someone had to live here, to accept this home as their own. Brownies were house faeries, but you couldn't have a house without humans. More importantly—and this was far, far, far and away the most important thing to Gray Walls—without humans, he couldn't pull pranks.

This was his sinister idea of fair trade, though it was neither fair nor a trade. It was more like a one-sided plunder.

Gray Walls had arrived at this horrifying idea three years earlier. He'd begun using the broken-down walls to tug at the neighboring children's curiosity. "There's gotta be something in that ruined house," they'd say, and others would agree. The grown-ups who knew better all warned the children, but they could do nothing to stop their curiosity.

And at last, the Elgar girl became the first to enter the Walsh family grounds.

It was a cloudy day. Backpack on her shoulders, Petra stood outside the house. She normally didn't even dare look directly at it. She swallowed.

It hadn't seemed this bad from far away, but up close, there was a sinister air to the place.

It didn't seem to be whispering, "Stay away." Quite the opposite, and that was what scared her.

Something seemed to be calling for her.

Something terrifying.

Maybe the Brownie had long since gone. This place had been a ruin since before she was born, since her father was a little boy. Surely the Brownie had left. It must be safe.

Petra stepped over the wall.

"Hello!"

The main entrance of the house was tightly locked, the double doors wrapped in chains. Petra wandered around to the back, but there were chains on those doors, too. She was already at an impasse, her plans dashed.

"Huh?"

Not about to let this chance slip away, Gray Walls made a sound, drawing her to her destruction.

The sound had come from beside her. When she turned, Petra found a window whose glass had long since fallen out.

"Does that mean come in?" she asked.

It seemed like it did, and this cheered her up a bit. She was clearly being welcomed. The Brownie that lived here wanted her to enter. Who could blame her for dreaming? No one should expect a ten-year-old girl to sense malice so easily.

The longer humans live, the more likely they will be exposed to true malice, whether it be human or faerie in nature. And sometimes that malice lures children in, like sugary sweets.

Petra was shocked by the amount of dust inside the house. She'd imagined a Brownie would have kept the place clean.

"Hello?" she said.

Only silence answered. Petra hadn't expected the Brownie to reply, so she continued exploring. The house was very old, and the piles of dust made her skin crawl. Even the air was unpleasantly damp.

She checked every room on the first floor, but all she found was dust; nothing worth seeing. Petra already wanted to go home but felt if she didn't explore a little longer she'd be a coward. It was a two-story building, so maybe there was something upstairs.

She climbed the stairs and found three doors. One of them moved with a loud creak. Petra ignored the fact that no wind could have moved the door.

As if beckoned, she headed straight for it.

Petra had never known real malice. Everyone she'd ever met had looked on her kindly, and she had many friends.

Her house was old and comfortable, but her family wasn't rich. The community around her was close-knit, everyone watching each other all the time. But she was such a thoroughly average girl that she sparked no envy and earned no grudges.

But here...

In this house, in this room, in this ghastly place she should have never entered...

For the first time, she encountered true malice and was overwhelmed by it.

"What...is this?"

This room had once been the owner's study, his pride and joy. The big oak desk at the center of the room was still there...but the place had been thoroughly trashed.

Vicious claw marks marked the walls. Every single book had been yanked off the shelves and torn to pieces. The desk was so gouged with scratches that no one could ever work upon it again. A coat rack stood in the center of the room, books precisely impaled on every spoke like proudly displayed hunting trophies.

Petra couldn't put this horror into words. Even so, she understood.

This was *bad*.

Whether a human or a faerie was responsible for this, they were clearly a being she shouldn't be anywhere near.

Fear welled within her, and, just before it exploded, Petra clapped both hands over her mouth. She was afraid if she screamed, something would notice her.

She'd lost her appetite. She summoned all her strength and forced herself to stand. But just before she began down the stairs, she froze.

The stairs lay broken in places, pointy bits of wood sticking out of them. It was like something wanted her to impale her feet.

Something clearly did. Now that Petra had witnessed

evil, she could feel it. This was a "prank." The Brownie was still here and trying to trick her.

"Uh..."

She moved carefully, one step at a time, praying the stairs wouldn't break under her. She moved slowly. The stairs creaked beneath her weight, making her even more nervous. The boards felt like they could snap in two at any moment.

She wanted to pray to God, to beg someone to come save her. But fear and regret invaded Petra's mind. She would never oversleep again. She'd help with the housework all the time and help look after the neighbors' babies even without the promise of candy in reward.

Offering up these prayers, she made it halfway down the stairs.

"Ahh!"

Something grabbed her ankle. She lost her balance and toppled forward. A jagged wood spike waited for her.

Instinctively, she twisted to avoid it and succeeded. Her backpack was so big and heavy and full of candy and jerky that it shielded her fall.

"Eek!"

She tumbled the rest of the way down but avoided serious injury. She'd managed to get far enough down the stairs that the fall didn't hurt much. The fright of having her ankle grabbed had done more damage than the fall.

Her little heart beat a mile a minute.

Something had grabbed her. She'd definitely felt something grab her ankle. Petra got up and scrambled toward the window through which she'd entered.

The window, the window, the way out! Have to get there, have to get out, gotta get to the window!

But she soon stopped in her tracks. She'd been in this room before. When she'd climbed in the window, she'd seen this china cabinet. She remembered being disgusted by the dust piled on those plates.

But now, the window was gone.

No, it was here. It was still here, it was just sealed up. Wooden boards covered the window completely.

She was trapped.

That simple, horrifying truth finally made Petra scream.

❦

That evening...

The Elgar's only daughter should have long since been home. Her father and mother ran around, checking wherever they thought she might be: friends' homes, nice neighbors, homes with cats, anywhere she might have gone.

But the girl had vanished. None of them had seen her today, which meant she'd been missing since she left the house that morning.

Rust Eyes watched them frantically trying to decide what to do. He'd performed his usual trick, but neither of them had even noticed.

Well, can't blame them, Rust Eyes thought. Their daughter was missing. Had someone kidnapped her? Had she run off somewhere? The possibilities spun in circles that led nowhere good.

Only Rust Eyes had noticed Petra's odd behavior the day before.

If she'd gone to the woods, someone would have noticed. Besides, nothing really popped out of the woods this time of year. There was little to no chance any faerie would lure her there anyway. Petra's body smelled strongly of iron, and, while it wasn't fatal, faeries found that odor repulsive. Most faeries would be reluctant to even speak to her.

In the end, Rust Eyes didn't think that scenario very likely.

Which meant...

Only the worst possibility remained. Rust Eyes went into the fireplace and scrambled up the chimney, staring across the roof at the house next door.

Gray Walls' house lay wrapped in silence.

But Rust Eyes was a Brownie, and he could tell: the Brownie next door was *delighted*.

I did it! Thanks to you, I can play pranks again!

Rust Eyes could see Gray Walls' excitement. Human eyes never could have picked up on it, but nothing could fool a Brownie's eyes.

Petra was trapped in the Walsh home.

Rust Eyes was sure of it.

❦

The girl pounded on the windows for a while. She knocked on the doors. She screamed and screamed, and then screamed some more.

But the doors and windows remained stubbornly shut, and not a soul answered her calls.

Petra sat down, sniffling, then discovered something lying next to her that hadn't been there a moment before.

A broom lay at her feet, exactly like one a witch might ride in a faerie tale.

Petra racked her brains. If the Brownie had given her a broom, did that mean it wanted her to clean?

She stood, wiped her tears on her sleeve, and picked up the broom. Maybe if she cleaned, it would let her go. Maybe if she cleaned, she could leave.

She had to believe that.

She took a handkerchief from her backpack, covered her mouth and nose, and began sweeping the floor.

Sweat poured down her face. The house was huge, and the broom heavy; but cleaning was her one escape. Pausing only to eat some chocolate and drink some water, she swept the entire great hall.

"Next..."

Next came the bedrooms? Dreading it, she stepped out of the room. A moment later, something made a noise, and Petra spun around to stare in horror.

It was back. All the dust she'd swept into the dustbin and thrown away was back, scattered across every surface.

She hadn't made the Brownie mad or hurt its feelings. No, it had done this deliberately.

"Oh."

At last Petra understood what this Brownie wanted.

The Brownie didn't just want her to clean. It wanted her to clean so it could make the place dirty again. That was its idea of a prank.

And that meant...

"I...can't ever leave."

Petra Elgar would never get out of this house.

Too dejected to hold on to it, she let the broom fall to the floor with a clatter.

❦

No one in the Elgar family had slept that night. Petra wasn't in the forest, she wasn't in any homes nearby, and no body had been found floating in the river.

She'd completely vanished. Some people even suggested that the faeries got her, but the Elgar father rejected that idea. His daughter wasn't the type to let herself be spirited away.

As the day passed, Rust Eyes found he couldn't control the disturbance in his heart, the irritation that had welled within him.

This day wasn't following the rules.

There was no milk. They hadn't even noticed his prank. Banshee-like wails echoed ceaselessly through the house, both the mother's tears and the father's lamentations. A faerie, or something else, had taken her? Either way, the girl was gone. Gone without a trace, as if she'd fallen in a pit somewhere.

Rust Eyes felt this family wouldn't last long. He doubted the parents would ever have another child. This deep despair would end their family line.

And disrupt his rules.

With his reason for being a house faerie gone, he would have to find a different house. Which was fine; creating a whole new set of rules was a choice he could make. But this family always gave him milk. They pretended not to notice him. They never tried giving him clothes to replace the rags he wore.

Would he be lucky enough to find another house like this one? Rust Eyes felt the chances were low.

So what should he do?

Should he step outside his comfort zone and do something?

I'm thinking. I'm thinking about it. I'm considering something I normally never would. I'm thinking about what that would entail, about what I'd need to do. I'm formulating a plan. I just need to make a decision.

One step. One crucial step.

Maybe, just maybe, everything would work out better than he imagined. Or maybe it would be far worse, and he would no longer be himself.

Rust Eyes thought about it.

He hated iron, hated steel, didn't care about humans at all. But this wasn't a bad house, and that was reason enough to take this step. Reason enough.

He should do it.

Not for anyone else. He had to step into Gray Walls' domain for himself.

Rust Eyes stopped thinking and took that step.

❦

Petra cleaned, Gray Walls pulled a prank. She cleaned again, he pulled a prank. She cleaned again, he pulled a prank. She cleaned again, he pulled a prank. She cleaned again, he pulled a prank. She cleaned again, he pulled a prank, she cleaned again, he pulled a prank, she cleaned again, he pulled a prank, she cleaned again, he pulled a prank, she cleaned again, he pulled a prank, she cleaned again, he pulled a prank.

It never ended.

No progress, no future, no hope. No one was coming to save her.

She swept the dust from a bedroom and collapsed onto the bed, exhausted. But she couldn't sleep. She wasn't hungry or thirsty either. She was scared. The Brownie here saw her as just another part of the house.

"Huh?"

Petra rolled over and glimpsed something between the bed and the night table. She reached out and picked it up.

It was a note. The paper was yellow and wrinkled, but she could read the writing.

She recalled the nightmarish study.

Hesitantly, Petra began scanning the note.

The spirit in this house is not a Brownie but a devil.

My son will never run again. That thing made him fall down the stairs, and that was it. He didn't slip. That thing grabbed his feet and tripped him.

My wife will never go outside again. The fire in the hearth suddenly sparked on her clothes.

I know this is that faerie's, that horrible Brownie's, idea of a prank.

We're abandoning this house, this country. We won't look back. Why should we? Curse that faerie. Stay here waiting for a new master until you die.

Die, die, die, die, die, die, die!

If this Brownie had been behind those horrible accidents...

Rage and frustration filled this note. How could these horrible occurrences be pranks?

She'd just finished crying, but tears welled up in Petra's eyes again. She was so scared, so tired, and so sad. She'd heard sadness could make your heart feel like it was being ripped in two; Petra understood that feeling now.

She read the note again. The man who wrote this must have been deeply miserable. These pranks had ruined his life and forced him to leave his home, his country.

The same thing was going to happen to her. Losing a leg would probably hurt immensely. Losing her hands would probably be awful. Never seeing the sky again would be downright lonely.

She wished a mage would come to save her. A good mage who could grant her every wish, teach her to fly away from this place.

If faeries existed, then maybe mages did, too.

There was a loud crash.

Petra turned to the door. Faint hope soon gave way to despair. A broom and a wet cloth had been placed there for her.

This time, he wanted her to wipe down the corners, too.

"No," Petra whispered. "I won't! I don't wanna! I can't do this anymore!"

As if in response, a noise came from the ceiling, like an angry stomp.

But Petra was only ten and couldn't control her outburst that easily. She just kept yelling "no."

Gray Walls picked up a vase, ready to throw it at her.

"That's enough, Gray Walls."

A low, growling voice made Petra's every hair stand on end.

❧

How long since he'd gone outside? Rust Eyes didn't remember. He barely had any sense of time to begin with. To him, the repetition of days was comforting, not tiresome. This felt like the third day he'd ever lived.

On the first day, he found a new master.

On the second day, he lived his daily routine.

And on the third day, he protected that routine.

He didn't open a window; rather, he smashed it. Outside air rushed through the shattered barrier like it was entering a vacuum. The humans around them had long since fallen asleep; the night was so silent one might think all life had vanished.

"Why are you here?" Gray Walls asked Rust Eyes, a dire threat in his voice.

Rust Eyes wore the same rags as Gray Walls. The

tattered clothing fluttered in the night breeze. The rusty eyes that were his namesake gleamed. Rust Eyes lifted his abnormally long arm, and in his hand he held a jagged wooden spear.

He'd brought a weapon.

"That child belongs to my house, Gray Walls," he said in measured tones.

Perched on the stairs railing, Gray Walls flew into a fury. "What a load of crap, Rust Eyes! She's the new master of *this* house! My new master!"

"Wrong," Rust Eyes said. "What do you expect from a child of ten? As your master, do you think she can make this house new again? Impossible. You'll only ruin her."

"So?" Gray Walls' lack of concern was terrifying. He considered the girl to be his master. As his master, it was her job to clean this place so he could pull pranks.

That was all that mattered to him. The toll it took upon her was of no consequence.

"I see. That's the way you are."

"You need to shut the hell up, Rust Eyes. You're a much stranger Brownie than me!"

"So?" he said, a deliberate mockery of Gray Walls' earlier response.

"How dare you?!"

"You disturbed my domain first, Gray Walls. That's the only reason I've invaded yours. You will give the child back to me."

"Shut up!"

At Gray Walls' howl, Petra screamed.

"Shut the door!" Rust Eyes yelled.

A few moments later, he heard the door slam. Her gaze had unsettled him, so this was a relief. Now there was no turning back. Not that he'd ever planned to lose.

"You'll pay for this, Rust Eyes," Gray Walls seethed.

"I never thought you'd just give her up. That's why I brought this."

Rust Eyes hefted the spear in his long arm.

House faeries rarely fought among themselves. Their role was to protect their own domains. Only humans fought to the death or to prove superiority. Faeries had no need of such things.

But when their goals conflicted, it was a different matter. They approved of damage done in the name of protection; to protect what was theirs, they would go for the throat.

Their bodies were at most a few feet long, but they attacked like ferocious beasts. Sharp, strong claws that could easily split a human's skin swiped at each other, fangs that could snap bones in two lengthened.

Unlike wild beasts, they had no fur. Their skin was exposed. Like their names, Gray Walls had gray skin, and Rust Eyes' hide was the color of rusted iron.

And Rust Eyes held a weapon in his hands. A sharp, wooden spear, strong as iron and every bit as cold.

"You think you can beat me in my own home?!" Gray Walls cried.

"I do."

The calmer Rust Eyes was, the greater Gray Walls' fury grew. And now, it erupted. "I'll rip you apart!"

"Go ahead and try!"

A small but ferocious war began.

Brownie claws were sharp, hard, and dug deep.

Gray Walls didn't hesitate to try and rip Rust Eyes open, but the wooden spear easily pierced his palm.

"Gaaargh!"

He screamed like a Banshee. Blood flowed, and pain shot through him. His screams echoed throughout the house. Shut in the bedroom, Petra could hear the muffled shriek. Rust Eyes hoped she wouldn't panic and come running out.

The two Brownies flew around the great hall. Though

the wooden spear weighed him down, Gray Walls wielded his claws deftly. They ran across walls and ceilings—clash and retreat, clash and retreat. Rust Eyes sneered, taunting Gray Walls.

"That human is only ten, Gray Walls. She could never be your master," he said.

"Shut up!"

They clashed again. This time, Gray Walls' anger won out.

But Rust Eyes didn't stop to stare at his injury. He attacked again. Gray Walls knew Rust Eyes wouldn't stop, and, with a slash, severed the fixture holding the tattered chandelier in place.

Rust Eyes had landed directly underneath it. "Aah!" Unable to dodge in time, the chandelier pinned one of his arms. Gray Walls spied a chance and went for Rust Eyes' throat.

With no other alternative, Rust Eyes threw the spear. While Gray Walls dodged it, he yanked his arm free. The arm was no longer usable, and his spear had been snapped in two, but he was free once more.

Howling with rage, Gray Walls threw the broken spear aside.

"What do you know? I haven't had a master in decades! She came to this house, she's mine now!" he yelled.

"Humans aren't things. You've become far too twisted, Gray Walls."

They clashed again.

Rust Eyes picked up a piece of his spear, using it like a club to pound Gray Walls' arm. But Gray Walls stepped back, and the spear struck a candlestick. Gray Walls had lived so long in this house to easily know where everything was.

"Ouch!"

Rust Eyes' shoulder split open. It wasn't a fatal wound, but it came dangerously close.

"This house is mine! I kept it clean! This house was my pride; it was everything to me! But they looked at me, and they pitied me!" Gray Walls cried.

Oh, that made sense.

Brownies loathed human compassion, and they despised sympathy. It filled them with unfathomable rage and usually drove them from the house. Rust Eyes knew why. It was a feeling fueled by inferiority. Humans built the houses; all faeries could do was move in.

They didn't want to be *allowed* to live there or for humans to think they were *letting* them stay. They helped out around the house to *earn* their keep.

That made them even, yet the humans pitied them for it.

Anger at their pranks, small gestures of gratitude—

these were all part of the order of things. Compassion was not. To a faerie, pity was like poison. Most would just leave under such circumstances. But on rare occasions, they'd react like Gray Walls had.

Rebel against that scorn, that cold gaze.

Rage, anger that shook the body, fury, and madness...

"But you know this is a mistake. You know that perfectly well," said Rust Eyes.

"Shut up!"

Gray Walls never could have predicted what happened next. Ignoring the bleeding gash in his shoulder, Rust Eyes grabbed the heavy *iron* candlestick and swung it at Gray Walls' head.

"What?!"

Rust Eyes also found the cold iron horribly unpleasant, but he gritted his teeth and endured it.

The candlestick dented the side of Gray Walls' head. He slammed into a wall, emitting a gasping groan.

"Ugh. Ugh. Uggghhh."

Gray Walls didn't want to leave this place. He didn't want humans to pity him. His cruel pranks had given the Brownie a strange delight. Why was it so much fun to hurt those who had hurt him?

"I am sorry, Gray Walls. But I have to protect what's mine, and I have to follow my own rules," Rust Eyes said.

Brownies were small, quick faeries who helped with the housework, thanked with a small saucer of milk. Though they wore rags, they must never be given clothes.

"Then...what... What am I?!"
Unable to leave the house, unable to live with humans, Gray Walls was no longer a Brownie, no longer any other type of faerie. Gray Walls had become unique, unlike anything else. The price was that no one would ever care about him again.
"You aren't anything, not anymore."
Rust Eyes spun the candlestick. The top of it had a jagged spike on which to hold a candle. The spike gleamed in the light.
Gazing at it, Gray Walls whispered forlornly, "I'm nothing?"
"The gray walls are long since gone."
And, without hesitation, Rust Eyes swung the candlestick.

With a click, the door opened.

Petra had been shivering and hiding under the covers. She poked her head out. The great hall was dark, and she couldn't see a thing. But she knew something was there.

After a long silence, she whispered, "Are you there?"

"I am."

The voice wasn't very nice; it was rather curt. But she knew immediately this wasn't the thing that had trapped her here.

"Um, can I leave now?"

Silence. Petra took this as a yes and softly slid to the floor, nearly losing her balance. Her legs felt weak, but she slowly made her way out of the bedroom.

A breeze was blowing. It felt like freedom, though a little cold.

"Oh."

The front door stood open. Its chains had been shattered.

Outside, darkness stretched as far as the eye could see. There was a light in the distance—her house.

"The door's open. Do what you like," the voice said.

Petra turned around.

There he was.

He stood in the corner of the hall, hidden in shadow. He was here, but her human eyes couldn't make him out.

"Um, thank you. Really."

"No need."

A curt response. Petra took it to mean he wanted nothing to do with her. Yet his words and voice felt so warm to her. She wondered why.

"Don't come back here," the thing in the corner said.

Petra gulped, and nodded. She knew better, even without this warning. She would never play explorer again.

"Um," she said, worried about one thing. "The, uh, faerie here?"

What had happened to the faerie that trapped her?

"It won't go to your house."

These words had the ring of truth to them and a deep sadness beneath that.

Had it died? Vanished? Either way, she believed him.

"Go."

Petra ran.

"Mummy! Daddy!" she yelled. Her family heard her cries and burst out of the house.

Sobbing, she flung herself into her parents' arms.

A human would have wept at this reunion, Rust Eyes thought. Gray Walls had vanished. As Rust Eyes had said, he was no longer a Brownie. Rust Eyes didn't know where he'd gone. There was no point in wondering where a faerie went once they vanished.

His hand still stung from where he'd touched the iron.

Humans could never grasp the true nature of a faerie, nor could faeries truly understand humans. But Brownies became Brownies only when they lived with humans.

That had been true for Gray Walls too, though Rust Eyes had destroyed him. Rust Eyes himself was now likely something other than a Brownie.

The story of the girl's adventure, and the faeries' little war, were both over.

Only the empty house remained.

That, and a single strong wind that tried to blow everything away...

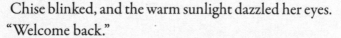

Chise blinked, and the warm sunlight dazzled her eyes.

"Welcome back."

Elias seemed to have finished his work. He stood by her side, looming over her. For a strange moment, she saw in him a trace of the much smaller Rust Eyes.

"I saw," she said.

"And? How was it?"

She thought about Silky, waiting in their home. Silky said almost nothing but always anticipated their return.

She, too, was a Brownie. Silky always let Elias and Chise see her, as if it were normal. Perhaps that in itself was a small miracle. Normally, humans and faeries didn't live alongside each other, and faeries never revealed themselves.

The vast majority of humans lived their lives without ever knowing that faeries existed.

"Um, is the curse lifted? The Walsh curse?" Chise asked.

Elias looked puzzled. He shook his head.

"The Walsh home and Gray Walls are long since gone. You saw how Rust Eyes destroyed them both."

"Er."

Chise blinked, taken aback. Then, suddenly, it made sense.

"This curse came from the Elgar family Brownie. It appeared when their home fell to ruin."

He'd protected it.
He'd lived there in peace.

But his feelings for the place had been so strong, so stubborn. Like forged steel.

"Elias, how long ago did those events take place?"

Elias glanced up at the sky, thinking.

"I believe they were over a hundred years ago. I don't remember for sure."

"I see."

Come to think of it, the glimpses Rust Eyes had given her of the smithy, forging metal pots and hoes, would be unusual in the modern world. Those scenes came from a long lost age.

Still, she hadn't imagined the house itself would disappear.

"What happened?"

Elias had no answer for her. She'd known he wouldn't. He'd come here merely to lift the curse, with no way of knowing what had caused that warm, peaceful household to turn into this empty lot.

"I doubt it was anything," he said, at last. Nothing in particular. No disasters, no strange events, nothing shocking or tragic. Just a peaceful end.

Rust Eyes had watched it happen. Watched as their lives fell to oblivion. Had he been frustrated? Had he resigned himself, accepting the inevitable? Remnants were only remnants. There was no telling what he had ultimately felt.

"What do you think?" Elias asked.

Chise considered, then said, as if to herself, "I think he only half-accepted it."

He'd accepted the destruction as inevitable but had grown angry and left, his frustration seeping into the ground. Every issue had two sides. This was the path the rust-eyed faerie had chosen.

❧The End☙

Natural Colors

MEGUMI
MASONO

I**T WAS EARLY SUMMER**, and white and pink roses
filled the garden. Many of them were in full bloom,
round bursts of color that perfumed the air with their scent.

A gray stone house stood at the back of the garden.

This is the place, right?

Standing outside the low hedge, Kyleid felt depression
wash over him. He sighed.

This had all begun two weeks ago. He'd visited his
master, Kai, to ask for a favor after a long absence.

Two years had passed since Kyleid had become a magus craft artificer and started his own workshop.

"I think it's high time I completed an original device
and made a name for myself. Can you help me?"

Kyleid had spoken with passion, and Kai had nodded
as if he understood. Kai was an experienced mage, and

while he was certainly very old, he appeared to be in his mid-twenties. He had blond hair and blue eyes—a strikingly handsome man.

"I know just what you mean," Kai had said.

"Then you'll help?"

But just as Kyleid's hopes rose, Kai's smile turned evasive. Kyleid knew Kai well enough to see the signs. This sort of smile meant he was searching for a reason to refuse.

Shortly after Kyleid's parents had died in a traffic accident, Kai had entered his life. He'd claimed to be a friend of Kyleid's father. Kyleid had never met him before, but it seemed his parents had often turned to Kai for advice about their son, so Kai knew everything about Kyleid. He said, "You have the potential to be a mage. Would you like to be my student?"

Kyleid had no idea what made him accept that offer. He simply nodded, without hesitation. In hindsight, his grief and loneliness had been so great that Kai's cheery disposition had seemed like the sun breaking through the clouds. They'd lived together for over a decade before Kyleid finally set out on his own.

Kyleid knew his teacher well. He wasn't surprised when, after a long silence, Kai said, "I know someone better suited to help you."

Unable to simply ignore his master's suggestion, Kyleid had come here to see the individual in question. Feeling extremely reluctant, he made his way up the path through the roses to the front door.

He was reluctant for several reasons, mainly that he'd never met the person who lived here. Kyleid wasn't the most socially adept, and it took a great deal out of him to meet new people...especially if that person was a woman. Kyleid had actually never met a female mage before.

He stood outside the door, looking in vain for a doorbell.

Do I just knock, or...

Uncertainty always annoyed him. He directed the bulk of his frustration at Kai. Couldn't Kai have just accepted Kylcid's request?

He was always like that. Always ready to give up, always foisting his work off on others. Kyleid knew he was just lashing out, but he couldn't silence the thoughts.

Here, at the last step, his courage abandoned him. He stood uselessly at the door for an incredibly long time until the person inside finally opened it for him.

The woman who answered the door had brown hair and pale brown eyes. She looked around thirty. Her long, fluffy hair was bound loosely at the back. She smiled, but her eyes were piercing. There wasn't a trace of hesitation to be found in her expression. She seemed very strong-willed.

Unprepared, Kyleid completely failed to think of anything to say, but the woman didn't wait.

"How long did you plan on standing there?" she said, without so much as a "hello." "If you've got business with me, spit it out."

Her hostile tone irked him, but he *had* been dithering.

"Hi. I'm Kyleid Fein."

Kai had often told him that good manners were the best answer to hostility. Kai had never been a stickler for manners himself, but this rule alone he'd stuck to firmly.

"Kai sent me. Is Elda here?"

"That'd be me." Still smiling, she looked Kyleid over. She was on the small side, with her head only coming up to Kyleid's shoulders, making her glance up to meet his gaze. "You're very tall," she said, as if this were his fault somehow.

"Not especially," he said. She was just tiny. Pointing that out would be rude though.

"Come in," she said, relenting. She moved aside and waved him in.

Inside, the smell of roses only grew stronger. She led him into the living room, where they sat opposite each other on a pair of couches.

"I got the letter from Kai yesterday," Elda said. "Said

he'd sent his student my way, so I should help however I could. But he didn't bother writing a damn word about what exactly you required."

"Only yesterday?" Kyleid said, surprised. He'd spoken to Kai nearly two weeks ago. What had taken the mage so long?

"In other words, I'm to hear what you have to say. If I'm not interested, I'm free to turn you down." Elda grinned at him. She seemed to be deliberately provoking him, testing his reaction.

Kai sent me to her! Why didn't he at least explain?

Kyleid directed his anger at Kai again. Kai was Kyleid's polar opposite, always cheerful and outgoing, very good with people. However, he also couldn't say no to a woman and was frequently careless with his words and actions. Whenever Kyleid asked him for something, Kai never just did it; he'd put it off or forgot completely. Perhaps the fact that he'd remembered his promise this time was worth celebrating, but if this introduction didn't pan out, then he'd been useless. Kai's careless attitude was both irritating and exasperating. He'd sent Kyleid all this way, and now Kyleid might have to leave empty-handed. But then a thought occurred.

Well, if she turns me down, that'll give me an excuse to make him help.

This thought calmed him considerably.

"I asked my master for help first. He said you'd be better suited for the task, so here I am."

Right. Just state your business clearly.

His mind made up, the words flowed easily enough.

"I'm a magus craft artificer. I'm working on a certain device and recently completed a prototype. To test its functionality, I need to expose it to magical activity."

"What sort of device?" she asked. Elda didn't bother hiding her skepticism, but she was at least hearing him out.

"I'm trying to make a device that measures how much magical energy is expended when magic is performed."

Kyleid removed a dark brown leather bag from a small trunk. Inside was a brown wooden box, twenty centimeters tall and forty centimeters across.

"It's merely a prototype. I'm currently calling it the measuring device."

He opened the lid. Inside was a smaller pouch made of the same leather as the bag. Kyleid removed the contents and laid them on the table.

They were long, thin rods made of semi-transparent stone, five in total, each a cylinder with a rounded tip. All were the same shape but of different lengths and thicknesses. The smallest was only five centimeters long, while the longest was nearly ten. The shorter ones were much thinner. The longer they got, the thicker they became.

"I made these by shaving down several types of minerals and combining the dust. I'm calling them Vibration Crystals. These crystals react to magic energy by vibrating and releasing light. Charting their reactions allows me to measure how much magic energy is being used. If I can prove the Vibration Crystals respond to magic properly, I intend to make a more elaborate version next. But to do that, I need to be present when magic is being used, performing experiments and gathering data."

"You're a mage. Why not try them on your own magic?"

"I've done that any number of times, but only three of the five ever vibrate. The results are always quite similar. I need to find out if this is my own limitation or a flaw with the device. To do that, I need the help of an experienced mage."

"Why did you decide to make something like this?" Elda sounded baffled.

"If we know exactly how much magic energy is expended for each spell, I believe that could solve many problems. At the least, it would eliminate the risk of overusing magic."

"I don't think that's something we particularly need. Such a risk would be much more common among alchemists."

Kyleid shifted uncomfortably. He felt like she'd seen right through to what he was really trying to accomplish.

"Perhaps a mage of your talents has no need of it, but it could be quite helpful to someone in training," he said.

"Would it?" Elda considered this. "I guess I'm just not that interested in something I wouldn't use myself."

Looks like I failed to convince her of the importance of my work... Kyleid was disappointed. He'd explained it clearly, yet he'd failed to make her at all curious. That definitely hurt.

But the mischievous, mocking smile on Elda's face transformed into a more pleasant one.

"You have very beautiful eyes. I can't remember the last time I saw such a deep blue," she said.

"Huh?"

Kyleid blinked at her. Where had *that* come from?

"I love beautiful colors," Elda said, like this was incredibly important. "Very well. It's a request from an old friend after all. Stay as long as you like, but don't expect too much from me."

"Um, you mean..."

"I mean I'll help with your little project, but I won't change the way I work. If you agree to that, then you're free to do as you like here."

"Got it. And, thank you," Kyleid said, not really sure what to think.

He was relieved she hadn't sent him packing, but part of him felt like he'd have been better off if she'd refused outright and forced Kai to help.

Kyleid had tried and failed to have Kai explain why Elda was better suited for the task. After meeting her, Kyleid still had no real clue. She didn't seem like the most helpful soul, nor the type of person who would let Kai shove his work onto.

The guest room was comfortable, but Kyleid had trouble sleeping.

When he woke the next morning, the first thing he saw was the unfamiliar ceiling.

"Uh," he groaned, taking the alarm clock from the bedside table. It was nearly noon.

Crap! Kyleid jumped out of bed.

He opened the curtains, discovering that the cloudy skies of the last few days had given way to clear blue.

This is bad... He'd been nocturnal for a while now and always had trouble waking up in the morning. Even in someone else's house he'd turned off the alarm and gone right back to sleep. He was all set to run out of the room when he realized he was still dressed in his pajamas.

Right, calm down.

He took a deep breath and quickly changed.

In the hall, the smell of roses had grown even stronger. He followed it and found himself in the kitchen.

Elda was wearing a cream-colored, knee-length dress, and a grass-colored apron. Her hair was loosely bound at the back, and she carefully watched a pot on the stove. The pot was filled with water and rose petals in all shades of pink and white.

He was about to speak to her when she switched off the flame, held her hands above the pot, and began chanting a spell.

Argh, I blew it.

He was mad at himself. He'd been in such a hurry to get down here he'd forgotten to bring the measuring device. It was too late to run and fetch it now. Here was his chance, and all he could do was stand and watch.

Elda pressed her palms together. Something like dark pink threads began growing between her clasped hands.

The threads wound themselves around her slender frame. They interwove to form a single, thin cloth about twenty centimeters long. The pink became even more vivid. Something flimsy, like a silk shawl, fluttered around Elda's shoulders.

What is *this?*

Kyleid had never before seen colors like this used in magic. He tried looking closer, but the whole thing suddenly vanished without a trace.

Only then did Elda leave the pot, turning toward Kyleid at the door.

"Morning," she said.

"Good morning."

"It's almost noon, you know." She grinned. He felt sheepish, but curiosity overcame his embarrassment.

"You were using magic?"

"Yes, making something for a client. Lotion infused with rose water."

"I saw something that looked like pink cloth."

"Yeah, mages can see it," she said, dismissively. But she caught the question in his look and shrugged. "If you wanna know, I can tell you. When I use magic, I always pick a color I think would be appropriate. It's like I've got threads of all colors, and I pick them out one at a time. One thread after another until they're all woven together into a single cloth. It looks like a cloak, so people call me the Colored Cloak, or just Colors."

"Fascinating."

This meant he could easily know when she was starting a spell and when she was done.

Maybe this is why Kai said she was suited for the task? Because it's easy to tell?

But it was a real shame he hadn't been able to measure this spell.

"Don't suppose you'd be willing to use magic again?"

"Nope. I've got nothing else to do that needs it."

He'd figured it was useless to ask.

"Um, what time do you usually get up?" he murmured.

"Hmm. Usually around five, I guess?"

"Got it."

Five...

The very idea was depressing, but he'd have to put up with it to complete his measuring device. His emotions must have shown on his face because Elda was clearly trying to repress a smile.

"No need to force yourself to match my schedule, you know."

"But I need to be around when you're ready to use magic," he said firmly. "As long as I'm here, I'll match your schedule. I'll wake up at the same time as you tomorrow."

"Suit yourself," she said, laughing. Then, as if she'd just remembered, "Sit down. Time for lunch."

She sliced up a baguette and made cheese and tomato sandwiches. Perhaps she thought this wasn't enough food for two, so she also put some egg salad on sliced bread.

"Tea? Black or herbal?" she asked.

"Black will be fine."

Elda put some tea leaves and hot water in a large tea pot and set it on the table. "I generally don't get fancy with meals, but if it's not enough, just say so."

He could tell she was being hospitable, but the way she said things was always so domineering it made him shrivel up. He forgot to even answer, just watched her expression.

"What?" she asked.

"Oh. I wondered if you were angry about something."

She looked genuinely surprised. "No. Why would you think that?"

"I just...feel like you're giving orders or scolding me."

"I sound that bossy?" She grimaced, then nodded. "Come to think of it, the locals also make faces sometimes when I'm talking. Maybe that's why. I'll have to watch for that."

"No, I apologize for speaking out of line."

"Oh? I always feel much more relaxed when people state things clearly. I was just thinking you were a man I can talk to."

Elda didn't seem angry, which was a relief. To avoid letting anything else untoward slip, he took a big bite of the baguette sandwich. As he did, someone pounded furiously on the door. The sound was so loud and close that he jumped, almost dropping the food.

In addition to the hallway door, there was a door in the kitchen that led to the garden. The knocking continued.

"Come on in! Who is it?" Elda called. As she stood, the door opened. A young woman ran in.

She had short chestnut hair and big eyes—very cute. But right now she was white as a sheet, and quite beside herself. Closing the door behind her, she said with a weak voice, "Elda! Please! Find my ring!" Tears flooded her emerald green eyes.

"What happened, Claire?"

Elda put an arm on her shoulders and led her to the chair. Elda took a small pot from the shelf, made some tea, and gave Claire a cup. The smell was sweet, yet clean and crisp.

"Drink this first. It'll calm you down."

Claire took a sip.

"It's good," she said. Only then did she look at Kyleid, sitting across the table from her. "Who is this?" she asked.

"Student of a friend. Staying here a few days for work. Don't worry about him. Where'd you lose your ring?"

Claire's eyes wandered for a moment, but she answered, softly, "In the forest. You know, by the river where I always used to go."

"I told you that place was dangerous and that you shouldn't go there anymore, remember?"

"But...but I knew nobody else would be there..." Claire covered her mouth with both hands, fighting back tears.

Elda grabbed a chair and sat down next to the girl. "This ring is important?"

"John gave it to me when I saw him in London last month. We're engaged, but I haven't told my parents yet. We're going to tell them when he's here on his next vacation. He told me not to let anyone see the ring, but I was just so happy! I went to the forest alone to try it on in secret. The way it caught the light was so beautiful, I was overjoyed. Oh, I should never have done that."

Claire bit her lip, hanging her head.

"I took the ring off to put it back in the box, but there was a loud splash. I jumped, then took a step closer to the bank. I suddenly tripped on something and fell, and the ring went flying. I looked everywhere but couldn't find it. Maybe it fell in the river!"

The tears were flowing now.

"I don't know what to do! If I've lost my engagement ring, how can I ever face John again?"

With that, Claire put her face on the table and sobbed.

"In the forest, by the river bank. You sure pick the worst places to lose things," Elda said. She looked a little put out but gently patted Claire's back. "That's enough crying now. It'll be okay."

Claire looked up and grabbed Elda's arm.

"Please, Elda. Find my ring!"

"Hmm." Elda seemed to be thinking this over.

Desperate, Claire began babbling. "Of course, I'll pay you a reward! You don't want money for problems like this, right? I know what you like. It's a little early still, but once they're in season, I'll bring you strawberries and raspberries from my uncle's farm every week. Please, help me!"

Not even trying to wipe her tears, Claire pleaded with Elda. Elda met the girl's gaze with sadness in her eyes. After a long, long silence, Elda freed her arm and took both Claire's hands.

"Okay then. I'll do it."

Claire's face lit up. "Really? Thank you!"

"It's too soon to thank me. There's no telling if it'll work or not. Tell me something: Did the ring have a gem?"

"Yes, a sapphire. My favorite."

Clutching her handkerchief, Claire got to her feet.

"I've skipped out on work. I'd better get back."

Once she was gone, Elda sighed deeply, as if trying to expel something toxic from her body.

"Sounds like a tough one," Kyleid said.

Elda looked as if she'd just remembered he was there.

"Oh, this is no problem at all. I was thinking about something else entirely."

Kyleid must have appeared puzzled, because she shot him a wry smile.

"I've lived here five years now. Sometimes, like today, I get asked for sneaky things, things people want kept secret. I don't take all those jobs, but I sometimes wonder if my presence here causes more harm than good."

"Um, that's a tough question. I'm not even sure why you'd ask it."

"I can't really explain. But if a mage like me weren't around, Claire would have never asked for help finding her ring. She'd have searched for it herself, over and over, and if she couldn't find it then she'd tell her fiancé what happened and apologize. Maybe that would be better than to handle it all in secret. Maybe I should have turned her down, but I just felt so sorry for her. Whenever I take a job, I kinda regret it."

"I don't think you need to regret helping those in need." Kyleid didn't really get what was bothering her. "I'm sure if she told this John fellow she'd lost the engagement ring, it would be a huge shock. I'd feel sorry for both of them. It's clearly better if you can find it."

"Maybe."

"Definitely! I'd say refusing to help when you can do something is...cold-hearted."

"Oh, good point. I didn't really think of it that way." Elda nodded and then gave him an awkward smile. "I've traveled on my own for so long, maybe I forgot how to relate to other people. It's good to get outside opinions every now and then. Thanks. That really helped."

"No, not at all. I didn't say anything that insightful." He'd just said what he thought and felt embarrassed to be thanked for it.

"Then I'd better get ready."

With that, Elda left the kitchen.

She returned a few minutes later, having changed into a white shirt, blue cardigan, and jeans.

"Sooner I get this over with, the better. I'm off to the forest. You coming?" she asked.

"I am. Just a minute."

Kyleid ran to his room and grabbed the bag with the measuring device.

Elda walked out the kitchen door and into the backyard.

The backyard was much larger than the front. Many types of flowers grew there, though the only roses were some small, double-flowered, yellow blooms that grew alongside the walls.

Kyleid recognized a tree with small white flowers—an

elderberry. But that was the only tree he knew. Never one for horticulture, he was unfamiliar with much of the garden. Shrubbery fenced in the perimeter, and beyond that was a gentle slope covered in soft green grass.

It's blinding.

The sunlight itself wasn't actually all that bright, but Kyleid felt momentarily dizzy. How long had it been since he'd ventured outside on a bright, sunny day? He'd spent the last few months cooped up in his workshop, slaving over his prototype. He'd basically only gone out to get groceries.

Elda made her way through the garden and out a small wooden gate nestled in the hedge. Turning, she headed into the trees.

Sunlight bled between the branches of the oaks and beeches, brightening the forest. Low-lying underbrush was all around, but plenty of paths were wide enough for human use.

Elda moved quickly, with purpose. Kyleid could barely keep up; he had to scramble to catch her a few times. After a while, he saw the river flowing through the trees. Elda left the path, stomping over the underbrush to the bank. The river itself was about five meters across, and the forest continued on the other side. The water wasn't particularly high, but it flowed fast and clear.

At last Elda stopped, and Kyleid was finally able to catch his breath.

"Really? You're winded from that? You really ought to walk more," Elda said, shaking her head.

"I...clearly could use more exercise... Is this the place?"

"Yeah. Claire loves it. Often comes here alone. When she proudly displayed a sapphire ring, they must have thought she was showing it off. Highly likely a neighbor pulled a prank on her."

With that, Elda began chanting under her breath. Dark blue threads emerged from her cardigan, wrapping themselves around her.

Kyleid hastily took the measuring device out of his backpack. To ensure he didn't drop it, he attached a thick leather strap to the box and hung it from his neck.

He opened the lid and took out the pouch with the vibration crystals inside. Then he loosened the bottom layer of the box, flipping it over to display the five hooks he'd fixed there. He hung each of the vibration crystals on these hooks in order from smallest to largest and was ready. The crystals dangled from a piece of string, swaying in the breeze.

Much like the first time he'd seen Elda do magic, the threads multiplied around her body, eventually forming a single blue cloth.

Strange... Glancing from Elda to the device, Kyleid was baffled. She was clearly using magic, but the vibration crystals weren't responding at all.

Is she too far away?

He'd never tried using the device outdoors. He was standing two or three meters from her, trying to stay out of her way. Maybe that was the problem.

Kyleid moved closer to her from behind, a step at a time. The two smallest crystals began vibrating. Each gave off a soft, throbbing light. The crystals' reactions always came in stages; as the magic energy increased, they not only vibrated, but began glowing. The longer they glowed, the stronger the magic they detected. The smallest of the crystals responded to the faintest magic, and at the highest volume the device could detect, all the crystals would be vibrating. Then the light wouldn't pulse at all but instead shine brightly.

Elda's shawl left her shoulders, drifting away as if carried by the wind.

At last, the shawl vanished into the river.

A few seconds later, a dark blue pillar of light rose from the water about a meter off the bank. But this shone only for a moment before vanishing in the blink of an eye.

Elda's magic stopped, and the crystals stilled. Kyleid

took a notebook out of his pocket, recording the results of the measurement. For now, he could only roughly guess the numbers, but if he could prove these stones measured magical energy accurately, eventually he'd be able to connect them to a meter that would be more exact.

"Seems like she definitely dropped it in the river," Elda said, turning around. "Well? You manage to measure me this time?"

"Yes, thanks. What was that spell?"

"I was calling to the sapphire in the ring. A spirit responded, telling me where it was. Now the question is how to get it back."

She folded her arms, staring at the water's surface as she thought. Kyleid had nothing helpful to add, so he just watched.

Suddenly, all five vibration crystals began shaking. Light pulsed out of them several times like a camera flash. Not only that, each crystal swung wildly on its hook, as if trying to smash into the others. Kyleid had never seen them move like this.

"What the... You aren't using magic, so how..."

"Quiet," Elda snapped, stepping protectively in front of him.

A horse appeared before them, soaking wet as if it had

just risen out of the river. Water dripped from its mane and tail. Kyleid could tell immediately this was no ordinary horse. Its eyes shone with clear intent, staring directly at them.

"It's a Kelpie. It lives in this river. Rarely shows itself, but it looks like it's after something today. They're dangerous, so don't provoke it. Just back away. And do something about the noise that device makes, if you can."

"I'll...try..."

The five crystals still flashed violently, hummed loudly, and spun on their hooks.

The crystals react to neighbors as well?

Was the Kelpie using magic? Or were the stones reacting to its very existence? He wasn't sure. Unfortunately, he'd never considered how to stop the crystals' reactions.

Oh. Distance. I can just move away.

Remembering how the device hadn't reacted to Elda's spell at first, Kyleid took the strap off his neck. He held the device behind him and began slowly backing up. But the Kelpie shook itself as if to stop him, stamping its hind legs on the ground.

Certain it was gearing up to attack, Kyleid froze.

Compounding the threat, the Kelpie bared its teeth and let out a loud whinny. Satisfied that Kyleid had completely stopped moving, it turned to Elda.

"You want to recover the ring? I could give you a ride," it said. Its voice was chillingly cold, a low rumble from the bowels of the earth.

When Elda said nothing, the Kelpie pressed her for a reply.

"Or should I fetch it for you? Doesn't have to be you. I could take that human there. Would take no time at all."

Kyleid had never met one before, but he knew about this water horse. Anyone who climbed on its back would be dragged under the surface and drown.

"Thanks for the offer. I'll figure something out on my own," Elda said.

The Kelpie wouldn't take no for an answer.

"You think the river faeries will give it up that easily? They love pretty things."

"Pretty things? Well then, this might be worth a try," Elda said softly. She addressed the Kelpie, speaking clearly. "No matter how many times you offer, I won't accept your deal. I cannot give you what you desire."

The Kelpie stamped its forelimbs in frustration. It said nothing more but neither did it look ready to leave.

"It knows we're mages," Elda whispered. "Given that it spoke to us, I don't think it intends to attack. But stay on your guard, and don't take your eyes off it."

With that, she moved back to the riverbank. She held

her arms out before her, placed her palms together, and began chanting a spell.

Each finger moved in turn, as if reeling something in. One thread after another appeared: Red like roses, orange like the setting sun; yellow like the rapeseed flowers that bloom in the spring, and purple like the lavender that flourishes in summer; blue like the sky on a sunny day, indigo like the deep sea; green like young shoots budding. All types of colors twined around Elda's body.

The threads moved like they were alive, twirling in the air. They began gathering together, winding around each other, finally forming a giant cloth that covered Elda's entire body.

The resulting cloak was of a brilliant pearlescent hue, the colors shifting wherever the light hit it. At first it looked silver, and then as the yellow flourished, it turned gold, then pale pink. It shifted from one soft color to the next.

With her glittering rainbow robe, Elda appeared to be bathed in divine light.

How beautiful...

Kyleid couldn't take his eyes off her.

But the moment couldn't last forever.

When Elda began her magic, the crystals' vibrations intensified to the point where he had to keep a tight grip to avoid dropping them. Kyleid put the strap back on, hanging the device from his neck. He then used both hands to steady the box, but the vibrations running through it were like nothing he'd ever felt before. His arms shook violently. The crystals had been flashing rapidly, but now all five shone with a steady light, spinning constantly. The strings seemed poised to break.

Kyleid tried subduing the crystals' reactions by distancing them from Elda. The moment he started moving, the Kelpie looked away from Elda and glared at him. Once again, he froze. He'd just have to put up with it until her spell was done.

Elda reached her right hand out toward the river's surface. The pearlescent gown left her body, drifting through the air and falling into the water. Glittering in the light, the current caught it, and the gown vanished, melting into the river.

Ah...

Kyleid sighed despite himself. Those colors had been so beautiful. Now that they were gone, he felt a profound loss.

Then, the water changed where the robe had vanished. A whirlpool spun itself up, growing to nearly a meter across, increasing in speed. Walls of water formed around it, with the center plunging into the depths like it was trying to drill a hole in the riverbed.

Elda knelt on the riverbank, put her hands side by side, and pushed toward the whirlpool. A ring popped out of the center, drops of water trailing in its wake as it drew nearer, and landed right in her open palms.

A moment later, the whirlpool disappeared. The river went back to normal.

Elda took out a handkerchief, and carefully dried the ring off. She checked it over, studying it from every angle before wrapping it up and stuffing it in her pocket.

"Looks like they chose your side, Colors," the Kelpie said, having watched all this in silence. It spoke in even tones. Kyleid found it impossible to guess its thoughts.

"Yes. I need not disturb you any longer," Elda said, choosing her words carefully.

With her magic gone, the crystals' movements weakened slightly, and the lights began pulsing again. They still spun on their hooks though.

Doesn't look like they'll stop until the Kelpie's gone.

As he thought this, Kyleid looked up, and their eyes met. The Kelpie's attention had been on Elda during the spell, but at some point its focus had shifted.

The gray horse had stayed perfectly still this whole time. Now, with a clatter of hooves, it charged right for Kyleid.

It all happened so fast he had no time to run. He just stood rooted to the spot.

"Kyleid!" Elda shouted. She took a few steps toward him, appearing to move in slow motion. The Kelpie was enormously fast.

Just as Kyleid thought he was done for...

The Kelpie kicked the ground right in front of him and jumped, easily clearing Kyleid's head. It turned and said, "It went well this time, but don't give yourself airs. We aren't always that nice. This is a warning. We can attack you at any time."

"I would never dream of underestimating you," Elda said. "But if you would harm us, remember that we have means of protecting ourselves."

The Kelpie snorted derisively and vanished into the water.

"Whew..."

The tension had drained out of Kyleid. The moment the Kelpie vanished, the crystals fell silent. They had definitely reacted to its presence.

But Kyleid's relief only lasted a moment.

With a shrill whine, the smallest vibration crystal shattered, its pieces falling to the ground.

"Agh!"

Kyleid let out a little shriek, but it sounded like someone else's voice.

As if his scream were the signal, the crystals each broke

in turn and in order of size, until the largest hung covered in countless fractures. For a moment, Kyleid hoped against hope that this one would at least survive, but it turned to dust and covered the grass at his feet.

All his energy left him. He slumped to his knees.

"This...this can't be happening."

He felt Elda's hand on his shoulder but couldn't speak. He stared hopelessly at the broken shards.

Elda watched in silence, but at last she undid the strap around his neck and took the box from him. Opening the lid, she found the crystals' pouch and gathered up the shards, pouring them inside.

Kyleid watched, unable to think, unable to do anything.

The pieces were so tiny Elda could only gather so many of them herself, so she chanted a spell softly. Several white threads appeared, weaving a piece of cloth so tiny it was almost a string. It vanished, and, as it did, the translucent fragments rose as if snared by the wind, formed a line, and poured themselves into the pouch.

Elda placed the pouch in the box and hung it from her own neck. Then she took Kyleid's arm and pulled him gently to his feet.

"We'd better get home."

She pulled Kyleid's hand, and he stumbled after her.

As they walked through the forest, he gradually recovered and his brain began functioning again. Frustration and self-pity overwhelmed him. If he opened his mouth, he believed he would scream.

Perhaps she picked up on this, because Elda didn't say a word.

He was so focused on controlling his raging emotions that he barely remembered getting back to Elda's house. He suddenly found himself sitting on the couch in her living room.

She left him alone for a while and returned holding a mug.

"If the smell doesn't bother you, drink this. It'll calm you down."

The mug smelled faintly of mint. He took a sip and found it a little sweet; she must have put some honey in it. He wasn't sure what other herbs were mixed in, but it definitely warmed his belly.

"You're still quite pale. Once you drink that, you should sleep a while," she said.

"Sorry. Didn't mean to make you look after me..."

"I wasn't planning on meddling, but...I guess I just can't leave well enough alone. You seem pretty unstable."

He wished he could deny it, but he currently lacked the energy to argue.

Elda sat opposite him but said nothing more. She just stared into the distance, seemingly lost in thought.

Kyleid put his cup down. He took out the leather pouch filled with the vibration crystal shards that Elda had gathered for him. He poured a few out into his hands, but couldn't bear to look and quickly put them back.

Nothing I can do with these… They'd shattered, much like his dreams and hopes. He'd seen a clear path to finishing the device; so clear it made the downfall even harder. It was his own fault for not considering their durability, but an even bigger problem was that they'd reacted to the appearance of the Kelpie at all. That meant this device wouldn't have been able to accurately measure magic energy in the first place.

His mind wandered uselessly from problem to problem. Growing fed up with it all, he muttered under his breath, "Guess I'm back to square one."

Elda's gaze snapped back to him. "It was a prototype, right? It was supposed to discover flaws. Seems like you were really rushing to finish it. Any reason why?"

"I was rushing?"

This surprised him. No one had assigned him to this task; there was no deadline. He hadn't intended to rush at all. But looking back, there had been a part of him in a hurry to finish as soon as possible, and he was all too aware of the reason why.

He was hesitant to tell her though. She didn't really seem to expect an answer anyway. Elda just gave him an indifferent stare, like this had nothing to do with her. Yet he felt like her concern was genuine, if only because he'd sensed warmth and care in that cup of tea.

"This device is for an alchemist friend of mine," he said, making up his mind to tell her. It felt like a cloud hanging over his heart began to lift.

Chris—the alchemist in question—had been Kyleid's friend since they were children. They were close as could be. But ever since Chris had entered the alchemists' academy, they'd grown apart, meeting once a year at best. Shortly after Kyleid left Kai and began his own workshop, Chris had come to visit.

"I heard you went out on your own, so I figured I should drop by."

The years seemed to have taken their toll on Chris. There were dark cycles beneath his eyes.

"You okay, Chris? You look exhausted."

"Do I? If it's that obvious, maybe I really am overdoing it," Chris said with a self-deprecating grin. "Research is an endless cycle of hypothesis and experimentation. I try to pace myself, but before I know it, I've used too much magic. Maybe there's a disconnect between how much magic I think I'm using and how much I actually expend," he said.

"Don't be silly! You were a star student at the academy! Seriously, if you overdo it you could really hurt yourself."

"Yeah. You should take that advice yourself, now that you've got your own business."

They'd parted all smiles, but what Chris had said stuck with him. This was the first time Chris had sounded defeated. That conversation had given Kyleid the idea to create a device that could measure magical output. He'd wanted to make something original now that he had his own workshop, and by making the device himself he could address his own self-doubt.

Chris had earned a reputation at the academy, and Kyleid had always felt inadequate in comparison. They weren't equals, and that thought had bothered him for years. But if he could complete this device, he was certain Chris and his colleagues would recognize his talents as an artificer. Best of all, the device would help Chris.

But Kyleid hadn't wanted to tell anyone he was making it for a friend. He thought that was too much information and faintly embarrassing. The more he'd buried himself in creating the thing, the more scared he'd felt.

Chris was a proud man and not one to accept help easily. If Kyleid admitted he'd made it for him, Chris would undoubtedly insist he didn't need it. He'd been so anxious at the thought that he'd avoided seeing Chris ever since.

But if I show Chris the completed device, I'm sure he'll want to try it out.

He'd convinced himself of that anyway.

"But I wasn't rushing for Chris. I'm sure I was trying to finish it quickly so I could earn myself some accolades."

Kyleid bit his lip. When the vibration crystals shattered, the first thing that had popped into his mind wasn't his friend, but his own happiness, which now seemed very distant indeed. He felt even more pathetic.

"This isn't just a matter of the heart. Even physically, I'm not cut out to be an artificer. I've spent months working on the measurement device, and lately I get tired so easily and get too sleepy to work. I can't make the progress I should be making, and that frustrates me. I'm sure the crystals broke because of my own lack of focus."

Kyleid hung his head, staring at his hands.

"Stop blaming yourself." Elda's voice no longer sounded gentle. "If a thing breaks, it can be made again, but people don't work the same way."

Kyleid looked up in surprise.

Elda appeared genuinely concerned.

"You've had a nasty shock today. That takes its toll on both body and soul. You need to be conscious of that and pamper yourself."

"I know that, but how?"

"Go straight to bed. You're absolutely exhausted, I'm sure. Even if you can't sleep, stay in bed a while. I'll bring some food up later."

"Okay."

She had a point, so Kyleid went to bed.

Alone in his room, the fatigue washed over him. As he told her about Chris, Kyleid had realized he wasn't terribly altruistic. Deep down, he wondered if he was really making this device for himself.

"I think it's high time I completed an original device and made a name for myself."

He'd told Kai that because he didn't want to admit the truth, but perhaps that really had been his motivation all along.

Enough! I don't wanna think about this anymore... He forced himself to change his clothes and lie down. Almost instantly, he was asleep. He woke up several times, but never felt like getting out of bed, and eventually drifted into a deep slumber.

While he slept, Kyleid felt someone enter the room.

He kept his eyes firmly shut until he heard the curtain flung back, and the morning light struck his eyelids.

Ow...

He slowly opened his eyes and found Elda standing by his bedside.

"How do you feel?" she asked.

Kyleid sat up.

Hmm? I fell asleep in the afternoon...yet it's still light out?

He felt like he'd been asleep a lot longer though. Elda saw the confusion on his face and shrugged.

"I didn't think you'd sleep straight through till morning," she said.

"What? What time is it?"

"Seven. I was getting worried, but you look okay. You must be starving. Come down to the kitchen."

I slept that long?

He was surprised, but his head felt much clearer. He was in a far better mood than the day before. Still, months of hard work had gone down the drain, and he was a little mad at himself for being able to sleep so soundly. Everything felt so suddenly meaningless that he almost wanted to laugh out loud.

He changed and went downstairs to find breakfast waiting for him. He had no appetite, but Elda stared so shrewdly that he began forcing it into his mouth.

"Oh, what happened with the ring?" he asked.

"I guess Claire couldn't stand waiting. She showed up here shortly after you went to bed. I gave her the ring, so I'm sure she's relieved. She burst into tears the moment she saw it. Surprised the hell out of me."

"I'm sure those were tears of joy. Good thing you took the job."

"Yeah. You were right about that," Elda said.

He finished eating. Elda had clearly been anticipating this and brought him out into the backyard.

"What do you think of this garden?" she asked.

Kyleid was confused.

"I guess...it's well looked after?"

"I didn't mean that..." Elda said, annoyed. "What do you feel when you look at the flowers here?"

"I don't really know much about plants, so... I mean, you're growing herbs and stuff here? They must come in handy. You're incredibly organized."

"Agh, you intellectuals. Always thinking with your head first."

Elda let out a deep sigh and pulled a brown medicine bottle from her pocket.

"This is an oil made of rosemary, Saint John's wort, and two or three other herbs."

She poured a small amount of the oil into her palm

and then rubbed her hands together. When the oil was evenly coated, she held her hands out to Kyleid.

"Close your eyes and smell this," she said.

Kyleid did as he was told, closing his eyes and inhaling deeply through his nose. He smelled something faintly bitter with a crispness quite different from mint. He took a few more sniffs, and his breathing improved considerably.

Elda may be using magic here, but it felt so good he didn't have the urge to check.

At last, the smell faded, and she spoke again.

"Now open your eyes and look at the garden."

It appeared the same as it had before.

Elda pointed at the plants growing closest to them, chanting their names like the words of a spell.

"The herbs here are mint, rosemary, and yarrow. The one with the reddish-purple flowers is common sage. Rue is the one with the green center and yellow petals. These are less common, but I also have some hyssop, with the pink flowers, and some chamomile."

She moved through the garden, repeating this process.

"The ones shaped like torches, all fiery red, are strawberry candles. The white ones are lace flowers, and the pale purple ones are Canterbury bells. The light blue ones with gauzy petals are blue poppy."

As Elda called each name and pointed out its corresponding flower, Kyleid slowly began registering all the colors and shapes.

Yesterday he'd thought the elderberry's blooms were white, but today he could tell they were softer, more of a cream.

Then he looked past the flowers and realized the leaves were all different as well. He hadn't registered them as anything but green before, but there were so many different shades of green, some bright, some dark. Now that he'd noticed it, he could no longer see the plants as all the same.

"I had no idea there were so many colors here."

"Not just here. The world is filled with all sorts of gorgeous colors."

Elda's words led him to look up at the sky. How long had it been since he'd really noticed that blue? He remembered how much it had once meant to him. His heart skipped a beat, and he felt ready to cry.

The trees and flowers that swayed in the breeze were so full of life. Life flourished all around him, its power dazzling. This was why each color seemed so fresh and clear, so filled with beauty.

"How did I not see how vibrant all this was?" he asked.

This newfound sight made it seem like his old world

had been black and white, all dull shades of gray. Just being in a place this beautiful, this resplendent with color, filled his heart with joy.

"You just forgot," Elda replied.

"Is this magic?"

"In a sense. That oil did sharpen your senses a little. And by drawing your attention to each in turn, the plants here led you to perceive all the colors around you again. That was all it took to remind you of nature's beauty. This magic isn't mine, it's from the flowers themselves. Truth is, before I even met you, Kai's words had bothered me."

"He said something about me?"

"Yes. He said he wanted you to look not at the numerical representation of the magic you were using but directly at the phenomenon occurring before your very eyes. But he felt this would be difficult for you to do after so much time locked up in a workshop, cut off from nature. Just now, you felt the beauty of the world, and it touched your heart. Don't forget that feeling. Even if you complete your device, don't ever look at magic as being by the numbers. That's my wish as well."

"I understand." Kyleid was surprised by how deeply Elda's words affected him. He felt light, like a burden had fallen from his shoulders.

Elda took a long look at his face, then smiled.

"You look much better. When I first saw you, I was instantly worried. You were so pale and gloomy!" she said.

"I was?"

"You didn't know? Do you think Kai sent you here because he couldn't be bothered?"

"No... Well..."

Kyleid wasn't sure of the answer.

"Knowing him, that may well be part of it. But he had another reason. You may not have known it, but, when you first arrived, you were suffering. You didn't look like someone filled with hope, excited about creating something new. Kai was very worried about you. He said you're a workaholic and you get so wrapped up in what you're doing you forget to sleep and eat. He asked me to make sure you got some proper rest here."

"He did?"

Kyleid was amazed. The entire time they'd lived together, Kai had never once said anything like that to him.

"He's hardly the type to admit what he really feels. But if he was willing to ask me for something like this, you must be very important to him."

"I never even stopped to wonder."

Rather than be glad his teacher was concerned about him, he felt sorry for all the things he'd never stopped to notice.

"If you wish for him to know how grateful you are, just show him how well you're doing. It doesn't have to be for long, but forget about your work. Relax here a while." Elda winced. "I'm giving orders again, aren't I? Um... I meant, you *can* relax here, okay?"

"Sorry, that's my fault. You don't need to be so worried about the way you say things," Kyleid said.

He now regretted having said that to her. If he'd known her better, he'd have never brought it up.

"I'm glad you told me. It made me stop and examine myself. I'm just trying to say that I'm not forcing you. If you want to leave, I won't stop you."

Given the broken measuring device, it made sense that he'd want to get back to his workshop as soon as possible. But for some reason, he really didn't feel like it.

"I won't get in your way?" he asked.

"A little late for that!" Elda laughed. Reassuringly she added, "I'm a loner by nature, so I never considered living with anyone else. But that doesn't mean I don't enjoy having friends drop in for a stay."

Kyleid took Elda at her word, and, for the next five days, he didn't think about his job at all. At first she dragged him around the garden, and he helped collect rose and elderberry blossoms. Once he began taking walks of his own accord, she stopped meddling. He didn't go any-where near the river, but he did walk around the forest, savoring the colors and scents of the trees, touching their trunks and enjoying the feel of their bark on his palms.

As the days passed, he began thinking about the mea-suring instrument again.

First, I have to make it more durable.

And he had to stop it from reacting to faeries.

Which means starting over from scratch.

But this thought no longer pained him as the energy to make that fresh start welled up within. The shattered crystals and the need to create the device again gave him a chance to reevaluate himself.

He still wished to have his skill acknowledged, but now it wasn't everything. The desire to help his friend was definitely still present in his heart.

And now, reminded of the world's beauty, he wanted to be someone who lived a life without shame.

He returned from his walk, entering through the back door into the kitchen. On the kitchen shelves he saw a stuffed rabbit. It was wearing a black tailcoat, like a char-acter from a children's story. At nearly fifty centimeters tall, it was hard to overlook.

"Has this stuffed animal been here the whole time?" he asked.

"No, I just brought it down from my room." Elda reached out and took it off the shelf. "I had a colleague of yours make this for me a long time ago. He's named Phil. He'd guarded my house for a very long time, but a few months back he stopped working."

"Oh. Is that why you don't have a doorbell?"

Elda stroked the rabbit's head fondly.

"I wanted to send it out for repairs, but the artificer has passed on. I didn't know who else to ask."

"So you were thinking about asking me?"

"Basically, yeah." Elda winked at him. "Of course, only if you feel like it. I just wanted to bring it up before I forgot."

"I don't have my tools with me, so I'd have to bring him back to my workshop."

"Please do."

Kyleid took Phil and looked into his red eyes.

Had this white rabbit once run around the kitchen and garden, letting Elda know visitors had come? Or had he led guests to the parlor? Kyleid could imagine him doing both. It must have been a lonely day when he stopped working.

He felt a sudden urge to fix Phil right away, so he made up his mind.

"I'll be leaving tomorrow," he said.

Elda didn't look surprised. "Off to make another measuring device?"

"I think I probably will, but that won't be my only task. I'll make sure to do other jobs along the way and develop that device at its own pace. I think it'll take a while, but I don't want to just give up."

"Then let me offer you a piece of advice: Get your friend to help you. When things aren't working out, ask him for advice. You may well find a way to solve your problem," Elda said.

"But..." Kyleid hesitated. "If Chris says he doesn't need it, I..."

Even now, he was frightened of Chris's rejection.

But like a mother watching her child, Elda smiled. "Is this friend of yours incapable of understanding how hard you work? How you feel? Is he the type of person to trample all over good intentions?"

"No, he definitely isn't." The strength of his own denial surprised Kyleid.

Elda nodded. "Good. Then you'll be fine."

How much had his own fears and inferiority complex tied his hands? He was now aware of how much they'd prevented him from making the right choices.

He hung his head, frozen to the spot. Elda gently put her arms around him.

"Don't worry. I know you can do it," she said.

Kyleid couldn't respond. He buried his face in her shoulder. He'd even forgotten how it felt to rely on someone else.

"Now then. Keep your head up and get ready for your trip home!" she said, slapping him on the back.

When Kyleid left the next morning, Elda walked him to the front gate.

"You've been such a help. I can't thank you enough," he said. He was so grateful his chest felt ready to burst, but he couldn't put this feeling into words.

Elda smiled and nodded, as if she understood everything going through his mind.

"Take care of Phil for me, and come visit again sometime. Bring Kai with you, if you like."

"I'll make sure he knows the offer stands."

Part of Kyleid didn't want to leave, but he brushed that thought aside. *This isn't the end. I can see her again whenever I like.*

With that, he quickly walked away, thinking about the future.

When he got home, he had a mountain of work to do. But before any of that, he needed to write a letter to Kai, one that would subtly express his gratitude and let his master know he was all right now.

To my beloved teacher:
Color has been restored to my world.

The End

Children of the Battlefield

CHIKASHI
YOSHIDA

"What is possible will not do. The safe and obvious approach will not be satisfactory. We must employ difficult methods, improbable methods, even methods deemed entirely impossible. The eyes of the world are upon us."

—WINSTON LEONARD SPENCER-CHURCHILL
ENGLISH PRIME MINISTER
DURING THE WAR WITH GERMANY

1

SUMMER, 1940—
The British Empire faced the greatest threat in its history.

Nazi Germany had swept through France. Now, with England as their next target, they stretched out the evil hand of invasion, with the Luftwaffe standing at the forefront of these efforts. Nightly airstrikes dropped bombs on military airports and radar stations alike.

The RAF fought desperately, but theirs was a losing battle. If the Germans gained control of the skies, their panzer divisions would land on British soil.

And England had no means to stop them.

First, England's weapons were vastly depleted. Operation Dynamo had successfully retrieved most of the BEF from Dunkirk, but they'd been forced to leave the bulk of their heavy weaponry behind. Scarcely any firepower remained.

Morale was equally low. The surviving soldiers were battered and shaken, and the hastily assembled Home Guard existed primarily on paper, of little to no use in actual combat.

Diplomacy might prevail where military strength could not, but, despite their weakened position, London continued resisting. The fate of England wavered on the edge of oblivion, a candle in the wind.

Yet an unorthodox defensive strategy came into play. People borrowed the power of inhuman things, attempting to curse their treacherous foes. This tactic was hardly unprecedented, as there had been similar attempts made throughout the nation's history. When Napoleon,

Emperor of France, had planned to make landfall on England's coast, Pitt the Younger's government had employed the services of mages, witches, and alchemists to cast spells on their enemies, chanting, "Corsican Fiend, thou shalt never see Dover."

History repeats itself. England, desperate once more, risked committing taboo in the name of magical defense...

"Air Raid Warning! Large German Squadron approaching quickly from SSW. Launch all interceptors. Repeat: Air Raid Warning! Launch fighter squadrons ASAP!"

Torn from my slumber by the roof's loudspeaker, I reflexively flew out the window.

As the ear-splitting sirens sounded, pilots in flight suits ran this way and that. A day ago, this had been a quiet country airfield. Now, tumult and unease swirled about.

RAF fighters stood in rows on the green grass, guards swarming around them. They yelled to one another: "We finished refueling this evening, but ammo is only half done! How are the engines?"

"We won't need to warm them in this heat, but the winds are less than ideal!"

"Better than getting bombed on the ground! Get these birds flying! Someone translate for the pilots!"

As there was nothing for an outsider to do, I was better off not getting in their way. I spied an easy chair made of pinewood, a large parasol perched behind it. I hastened toward it, knowing that was where he'd be.

"Pah! Even a glorious Pegasus like the Spitfire is a lame horse without proper crew and guards to attend her. If the mechanics at Supermarine heard this, they'd burst into tears."

I didn't need to hear the ranting in Japanese to know it was him. My master had been this unpleasant long before I'd ever begun serving him, but that didn't mean I was prepared to let this pass.

I perched on the back of his chair and said, "Then no point importing them. You said the Japanese Navy would buy some if they proved themselves in battle, but at this rate, you'll never convince the Ministry."

"Sergeant Kirishima, you fail to understand me. The Spitfires are magnificent machines. I merely point out that their current handling leaves much to be desired. Bringing them back with us will greatly inspire the Navy Aviation Bureau. Naturally, we'd need a mountain of parts for the liquid-cooled engines, making them difficult to use domestically. Well...perhaps not. If we use them entirely on aircraft carriers, maybe there is a way..."

As I'm sure you can tell, my master was intelligent and

sharp-tongued. Ordinarily I would tell you his name, but circumstances force me to withhold it.

They say the devil looks after his own, and he had in this case—my master is alive and well. To this day, he wields powerful influence in politics and business. Revealing his scandalous visit to England would create no end of trouble at home and abroad. The man himself seems to revel in the potential chaos of such a revelation, but I have no intention of getting swept up in his wake. Thus, in this piece, I shall merely describe him as Commander G. For the rest, I must rely on my reader's discretion.

While I'm at it, let me introduce myself. My name is Kirishima. I've called myself by that name for a few decades now. I'm borrowing the name from the volcano where I honed my body and mind, but I've grown fond of it. Commander G called me Sergeant, but that was merely a nickname. I'm not in the military, and the Japanese Navy doesn't have a rank called Sergeant anyway. When I was still in training, Commander G saw me lecturing some ill-mannered colleagues and told me I was like a drill sergeant. I'd begged him to stop calling me that, but Commander G isn't the sort of man to change his mind.

"We'll have to discuss a joint purchase with the army. They're still dreaming about mainland planes, so it can't hurt to take the lead on this. Of course, if England falls, all chances of a deal evaporate," the commander said.

I had to argue that point. "The British Empire won't end that easily. Look at these pilots. They're all riled up to defend their homes."

"Take another look, Sergeant. They aren't even English. They're Poles. The Germans occupy their homeland. They have nowhere else to go. This war is already over for them. They are but resting their wings here until they reach a place worth laying down their lives." Commander G paused, silently mocking me. "Humans can live without a country, but a country cannot survive without people. By simply surviving, these men contribute to Poland's restoration. There is no point in wasting their young lives here."

"They're patriotic. A quality you seem to lack."

"You forget, Sergeant. I was a mage long before I was a soldier. I have no more patriotism than the stars that light the night. If I got hung up on that nationalistic nonsense I'd never be able to appreciate the true beauty of the world."

"Then why stay in the military? Why not become a hermit somewhere?"

"Several reasons. First, I am at peace here. The military's closed society is the ideal hiding place for a non-human. Secondly—"

"Don't bother. It keeps you from getting bored, right? Like you always say."

"Quite. Life is but a constant battle with boredom. I grow tired of being an observing officer. While God maintains his indifferent silence, allow me to assist evolution and creation," he said.

Commander G rose to his feet and headed toward the line of sputtering Spitfires. When he rolled up his left sleeve, I knew what he was about to do.

He wore a bracelet disguised as a watch, which was giving off an unearthly glow. The Sanskrit carved into it was briefly exposed. An instant later, there was a flash of purple lightning as he began chanting at speeds that would astonish even NHK's radio announcers.

"Eyelids, be as lead. Sleep like a maiden, fall like a hero, lie on the earth like the dead. Thy duty to oppose the rising sun..."

To kindle this spell, Commander G had sacrificed a Polish pilot; a mere boy. As Commander G's spell finished, the lad lost consciousness and crumpled to the ground like a marionette whose strings had snapped. The RAF mechanics tried waking him, but he remained asleep.

"Looks like the pilot is out of commission! Very well! I shall fly," said the commander.

A Cockney-accented mechanic with a beard like a daruma doll tried stopping him.

"Wait right there, guvner. You're the observer from Tokyo, yeah? Ya join the battle, there'll be trouble on both sides."

"We can sort out the details once the battle is won. This base will be carpet-bombed in a matter of minutes. One less plane in the air increases the risk of such a scenario. Your countrymen's blood, sweat, and tears made this plane. It'd be a shame to see it destroyed on the ground."

"Don't see how a bloody Jap's gonna fly a Spitfire," the man snarled.

"I can fly anything. Even a broom!"

I was the only one present who knew this wasn't a joke. While I waffled between anxiety and resignation, Commander G quickly changed into a flight suit and climbed into the narrow cockpit.

"Ready for takeoff. Sergeant, you come, too. One must savor living on the edge of death or lose sight of true country beauty."

"I'm more of a city boy. And the Spitfire's a single-seater! How am I to join you?" I asked.

"My knees await!"

"Something tells me it might be a bit too snug..."

"Then fly alongside me! I won't mind."

"Don't be ridiculous. You know my top speed's only around seventy kilometers per hour."

Depending on the type, a Spitfire could reach speeds of 586 kilometers per hour. I had no possible way of keeping up with one. I gave up arguing, fluttered my brown and white wings, and hopped into the space below the open canopy. The daruma-beard mechanic looked surprised.

"Guvna, ya gonna bring ya pet owl to the battlefield?"

Unruffled, Commander G replied, "This is no ordinary owl! And he's not my pet. He's my familiar."

The Rolls-Royce Merlin II engine roared like a wild thing, and the plane started down the runaway. The machine had a dry weight of two tons, yet as it accelerated, the wheels easily left the ground. My body grew strangely weightless. It felt very different from flying on my own wings.

Handling the stick like an expert, Commander G cried, "What a responsive machine! No complaints on lift or speed. Wings are thin but sturdy. Should be quite easy to maneuver close to the ground. A skilled pilot could really show his strength in a dogfight."

He spoke like a seasoned pilot. This was a brand-new model they'd rolled out ahead of schedule, its official name being Spitfire Mk IB. In time, this machine would be hailed as the empire's savior, but during the Battle of

Britain, many doubted its effectiveness. Then, as now, my opinion on planes was hardly that of an expert. But Commander G was like a child, delighting in his new toy.

I trusted he was right. He was the leader of the Naval Aviation's elite acrobat team, the G Circus, so if he gushed about something, that thing was worth gushing about.

"This is the oil temperature gauge, and this is the boost gauge. There are notes stuck to some of them, but they're all in Polish! Brings a tear to the eye, doesn't it?" he said.

Watching Commander G fiddle with the instrument panel out of the corner of my eye, I swiveled my head the full 270 degrees, watching our surroundings. My neck had more than twice the number of bones as a human's, allowing for such tricks.

I had found them. I could see far greater distances than a human could, and I had glimpsed the black specs on the horizon.

"Planes at eleven o'clock! Based on the direction, I assume it's the Luftwaffe flying in from France."

"Almost certainly. Our allies are headed for them."

The other Spitfires accelerated through the air to engage the enemy. Our plane lagged behind.

"What? I thought you wanted to fight the Germans?" I cried.

"Oh, owl, lord of the forest, when did you become so

bloodthirsty? I pick the foes worthy of my blade, that's all. Those pilots who manage to break through the Free Poland Air Force's formation will become fitting prey. We shall wait in the air above the runway, killing time."

This was arrogant even for him, but he did have the skills to back up his bravado. Commander G was a real whizz with machines, and a cunning mage. Rarely a day passed that I didn't regret becoming his familiar, but he *was* one of the top five pilots in the world.

Though the times favored aviation, Commander G was probably the first mage to abandon an eagle's wings and embrace those newfangled flying machines. Astonishingly enough, he'd never once relied on magic to help him. Commander G had acquired his piloting skills through practice alone.

As something of an experienced flier myself, I often issued him warnings and found fault with his methods. I argued that bending the laws of the natural world with magic was a small price to pay for a better chance of survival. If we died, there'd be nothing to regret.

But Commander G insisted it was wrong to use magic in combat, stubbornly rejecting my arguments to the contrary. I told him his stubbornness would ensure an early death, but he wouldn't listen.

Then, I heard a rumble like distant thunder.

"The smell's turned sour. Looks like the fighting's begun," I called.

"You've got quite the nose, Sergeant. I can smell it myself: burning flesh and the scent of blood. The smell of death and destruction."

"Who do you think will win?"

"If we trust the London bookies, I'd bet on England. They've the home-field advantage. They may get bombed to hell, but, if the pilots survive, they can soon join another squad. Same isn't true for the away team though. The Germans have to get back to base in France or Belgium. The RAF may have thrown pride to the wind, and they're scraping the bottom of the barrel in terms of crew, but that hard work will lead to victory in the—"

Before he finished his speech, I spotted a shift in the battlefield and yelled, "Incoming! One o'clock, in the clouds! German! Altitude: 2,500. Distance: 8,000 and closing!"

That was definitely a Messerschmitt Bf 109. Small for a fighter plane, it was the Luftwaffe's main firepower and the Spitfire's eternal rival.

Its speed and firepower made it adept at hit and away tactics, and the technical specs far surpassed the majority of England's planes. Only the Spitfire, with its superior maneuverability, could really stand a chance against it.

Even then the Luftwaffe pilots were frighteningly skilled and victories hard fought.

I watched the enemy plane with caution and awe, but it behaved quite oddly. There was no one on its tail, but it turned and zigzagged, eventually even doing a somersault.

"Strange. Is he taunting us?" I murmured.

"I doubt that. The pilot's panicking."

Commander G slid his plane sideways, maintaining speed while lowering his altitude to easily get behind the enemy plane. All he had to do was pull the trigger, and his bullets would tear the other plane apart.

But Commander G's finger didn't move. I realized why soon enough.

There was something on the Messerschmitt's wings!

It couldn't be human. It was clearly a neighbor and looked much like a rabbit. It was all black and brown, maybe fifty centimeters tall. Two pointy horns sprouted from its brow. A pair of tinted goggles hid its eyes, but the face was definitely fearsome.

It used its sharpened front teeth to chew through the Messerschmitt's wing, opening a huge hole in the plane's body. It yanked out some wires, slurped them up like spaghetti, and gave the pilot a diabolical grin.

The sight of something so unnatural, even in the

chaotic midst of a battlefield, had driven the enemy pilot to panic. The Messerschmitt's nose turned a bit too far off course, and gravity dragged it into a downward spiral.

"Sergeant, this might get a little rough." Commander G cranked the throttle all the way open, rocketing us to full speed. We closed the distance to the falling plane in no time, and our Spitfire nearly rubbed wings with it.

"Question for the gremlin! Who do you contract with? What reckless fool is using magic in a war between nations?!"

I was sure the gremlin heard the commander's question, but it didn't reply. It realized we weren't its allies though and waved its sausage-like index and middle fingers in front of its face, lips twisting. Then it bent its knees and jumped.

A moment later, wings sprouted from its head. Ah, so they hadn't been horns after all. The wings were several times longer than the gremlin's body and swiftly carried it away to the west. Meanwhile, the Messerschmitt regained control and flew toward the south.

The sounds of battle had died down. The gunfire stopped and the dogfight had ended as abruptly as it began. Victory and defeat had lost all meaning, and only Commander G's tirade echoed in my ears.

"Someone stupid enough to commit taboo here?

Who has the nerve to bring magic into a war between nations?"

Hoping to calm him, I asked, "Do you think it's an English mage?"

"What? Don't be ridiculous. A mage with my level of training can turn stone into metal, give wings to fish, and rot grain in the fields. Naturally, I could make a gremlin do my bidding before breakfast. But we would never do that! We know there are forbidden acts! One of the worst things you could do is show up where people are killing each other and start flinging magic around. English mages should know that perfectly well. This is some shameless witch or perhaps a desperate alchemist. And I have an idea who it might be..."

He thought for a full five seconds, then gave me his order.

"Sergeant Kirishima. Fly to the Isle of Man."

It was an island stationed in the sea between Ireland and England. Commander G had planned on visiting the place.

"You're going to Castletown Harbor, to the south. You'll find an old, protected cruiser moored there. You'll have to talk to the lieutenant. Using magic in war leads directly to the nation's ruin. I'll be right behind you, so you smooth the way."

Without allowing any questions, he opened the windscreen and shoved me out.

"Wait a minute! I'm a *Tyto alba*, the sage of the forest, positioned at the pinnacle of the food chain, and the most charming animal alive! You would use me as a mere errand boy?"

"Yes, I would. You asked to be bound to me, remember? It was hard work sending your wife and daughter to a better place. You could stand to do as I say sometimes."

How could I possibly refuse him now? Reflecting on the choice I'd made back on Kirishima Mountain, when I'd first met Commander G, I flew away from the Spitfire...

2

K IEL, LOCATED on the Jutland Peninsula, was the largest port the Kriegsmarine had.

Some strange objects floated in one corner of the Deutsche Werke shipbuilding company there. At a glance, they looked something like submarines, but were definitely not U-Boats.

First, they were entirely the wrong size. They were nineteen meters long, and four and a half meters across—tiny in comparison to a U-Boat. They had no means of propulsion and couldn't move on their own. These were more or less just floating cylinders.

There were four in all. Known as Wieges, these were intended for unmanned operations, but the first tube alone was fitted with a control room, allowing for a small crew.

KptLt Günther Prien stepped into this control room. Prien was Kriegsmarine's most famous U-Boat commander and was currently hard at work arguing with a mysterious figure.

"It's not that I don't trust you. I was able to enter the naval base at Scapa Flow and sink the *Royal Oak* because of the navigation course your auguries plotted. I don't profess to know the difference between magic, alchemy, and oracles, but all I need to know is that my U-47 returned triumphant. Your strange arts have earned my respect, but this next mission is too much. You won't explain your reasons to me, yet you expect me to take you to the middle of the Irish Sea?"

The middle-aged, special oberleutnant to whom Prien was speaking settled his tiny frame in the cramped seat. He replied, "Großadmiral Raedar has approved this plan, and so has the Führer himself."

The man's name was Henrich Hörbiger. He was a special technical oberleutnant placed with the Kriegsmarine.

He'd lived much of his life in England, and thus spoke with a thick English accent.

"And the success of this mission depends on the judgment and actions of the U-Boat commander. KptLt Prien, without your cooperation the entire operation will collapse, in which case the occupation of England is impossible, and Germany's future is bleak."

"I never said you wouldn't have my cooperation. I'm saying if you want it, tell me what I need to know. What is this tube I'm standing in? You want U-47 towing four of these, but why should I haul something when I don't even know what it is?"

Hörbiger thought Prien's viewpoint was entirely justified but couldn't risk telling him more.

"As far as the Wieges are concerned, I've adopted an idea proposed by the flight engineers at Peenemünde. Originally, they were to transport rockets or missiles; they're simply containers a submarine can haul, an ultimate weapon that will allow us to bring any city within bombing range. We're still in the planning stages there, so I borrowed a piece of it," Hörbiger said.

"Forget the outside. The cargo's the problem. I've heard the Wehrmacht are developing flying weaponry, but they haven't completed anything yet. So what do you want to haul in these?"

"I can't persuade you to let me share the truth once we reach the Irish sea?"

"This is a counterintelligence measure? My lips are as tight as my fist," Prien said.

"No. I want to prevent a loss of morale. Knowing the truth will frighten the U-47 crew, and they may refuse to take part in the mission."

"You think that little of my men? They're brave warriors. They've got guts. They aren't afraid of anything. They've faced death countless times."

"But they've never faced anything that came walking *back* from death. Right?"

When Prien fell silent, Hörbiger continued.

"I'm sure you've heard the Luftwaffe are struggling with their raids on England. Are you aware of the reason why?"

"The Messerschmitts have shorter legs than the Japs. Can't even fight for more than fifteen minutes."

"Certainly a factor. But have you heard any stranger stories? The returning pilots have had some bizarre experiences, claiming they were attacked by strange monsters during bombing runs."

Prien's face twisted like that of a student with a failing grade.

"Mere fables. Embarrassed pilots concocting stories about gremlins to hide their own failures," he said.

"No. Gremlins are real. England has brought alchemists into the war."

"We're hardly in a position to criticize. Our command is up to the same thing. The Führer decides when raids happen based on what his fortune tellers prophesize. He's completely on board with your relative's World Ice Theory."

"We can gripe about my great-uncle on another occasion. Occult research isn't the issue; actually bringing it to the battlefield is. London may be at a disadvantage, but for them to actually turn this into a magical war..."

Hörbiger's countenance was grim, but his real feelings were quite different. He was barely suppressing a laugh.

Prien wasn't a fan of this entire conversation. "So we're retaliating, with our own self-described alchemist in charge?"

"Indeed. England violated the taboo first, so we need hold back no longer. That's why Berlin chose to activate Operation G. We were right to prepare for every eventuality. I am overwhelmed with admiration for the Führer's foresight and wit in giving us those orders."

After a long silence, Prien spoke as the U-Boat commander.

"We have no choice but to obey orders from the Seventh U-Boat Flotilla command. But if we must do this, let us do what we can to ensure victory. There is little chance of success when we cannot trust our own comrades. I alone should know the truth at least," he said.

At last Hörbiger said what he really felt. "I intended to do just that once we were at sea, but, if you insist, I will tell you all the details of Operation G now. What is it you wish to know?"

"The specific location of our mission."

"The Isle of Man."

"That's a dependency of the British Crown, correct?"

"Exactly. That island is very important to mages. Many alchemists gather there. London must have convinced those alchemists to join the war effort. Given the nature of the island, the mages will be in charge. It's likely the magic craft artificers will be doing their part as well."

"Wait. I heard these people work alone. They aren't the type to band together," Prien said.

"You are correct. The only reason they would unite is if they were aware of our ambition."

"So the G Program has been compromised?"

"No, the details are likely to remain a mystery. We still have a chance to strike first. Our best and only chance of landing a blow on England's alchemists is to hit directly where they gather on the Isle of Man. We especially need to turn Castletown to ash."

"Sounds like you've done your homework."

"No need. Before the war I lived there for fifteen years, studying as an alchemist. I was disguised as a merchant."

"Hold on one second. The Isle of Man isn't exactly a small island. It's at least as big as Bornholm in Denmark. How is *one* U-Boat going to level the place? If we're really trying to conquer the island, we'll need to bring many battleships and their guns."

"We will not win with firepower, only brute strength."

"You've lost me. You're planning a surprise attack from the air? Or do you expect my crew to suddenly play army?"

"No, we have infantry ready. These Wieges are underwater containers that will transport them."

They were both silent for several seconds, then Prien shrugged.

"No time for jokes in war. How many can you fit in these tiny tubes? At best, twenty? Four tubes, so that makes eighty men? Not even enough to scout the place."

Hörbiger's poker face never wavered.

"We will bring only fifteen soldiers, but every one is a special ops soldier who has overcome death. We shall also bring my darling children, only just born. I have waited years for this. My own flesh and blood. I guarantee they'll slaughter their objective: the true force controlling these gremlins. If we can but eliminate one woman—she who rejected me in every imaginable way—the threat will disappear. If we win the war of magic, England's occupation will be achievable, and my own desires will vanish with time..."

Oberleutnant Hörbiger fixed the other man with a steely gaze.

"KptLt Prien, science's ascendancy over magic is right around the corner. I wish to carve my name into history as the last alchemist before science becomes so advanced that the difference between it and magic is impossible to perceive."

3

MY ORDERS were to fly right to the Isle of Man, but it took a full seven hours to arrive, and I hadn't been dawdling. Rather, I'd endured a series of trials and tribulations, and had used all the wisdom, courage, and gumption I possessed to overcome them.

The distance from Southampton to the Isle of Man is 420 kilometers as the bird flies. But rather than flying directly across the Irish Sea, I decided I was better off flying up the west coast of England to St. Bees Head and making my crossing there. It added one hundred kilometers to the overall journey but proved to be worth it. One impasse after another filled my path.

In Birmingham, I was caught in an unexpected bombing raid. High-speed bombers—Heinkel He 111s—chased me, and I lost half the feathers on my left wing. In Manchester, I took shelter in a large cathedral to rest my wings, only to be shot at by anti-aircraft fire. I'd like to believe this was an error, but perhaps the enemy knew my true nature and deliberately tried to kill me. In times of war, people naturally want to eliminate those who fall between the category of friend and foe.

The worst was the Cambrian Mountains. Desperately hungry, I'd landed and was eating a wild rat when a gang of local magpies beat the hell out of me. Just as in the Kirishima Mountains, I discovered that outsiders were forever unwelcome.

At last, I fluttered free of my pursuers and began my flight across the Irish Sea. It was a fifty-kilometer journey before I could reach the Isle of Man, but, with my wing's injuries, that distance seemed foolhardy.

Was there a boat around? As the years passed, I'd grown twice as heavy as the average barn owl, so driftwood may well sink under me if I tried to float. I was much better off resting my wings on a passenger ship.

Prior experience suggested I would be welcomed. In

Japan, the word for "owl" ("fukurou") sounded exactly like words meaning "no hardship" or "bringer of good fortune." An owl on a ship was seen as good luck.

In Europe, some fools saw us as quite the opposite of luck, but there were also those who treated us as symbols of wisdom. Sailors tended to be particularly superstitious, so if a bird they regarded as auspicious landed aboard, they'd often feed that bird. Turning my eyes into saucers—rather, like radar dishes searching for an enemy fleet—I scanned the ocean and located a gray object on the horizon.

A long ship with four smokestacks, it was clearly no merchant vessel. A number of single-mounted guns stood on deck, and the White Ensign flew at the stern. From the mast hung a flag with three legs arranged like a shuriken, a symbolic image used on the Isle of Man since ancient times. I was relieved; my season of horrors was over. This must be the protected cruiser Commander G had ordered me to find.

England possessed a great number of colonies abroad, and protecting them required a great number of ships with substantial range. Trying to balance cost versus ease of use had resulted in these protected cruisers. However, their heyday had been forty years ago. The more modern light cruisers were in fashion these days, and most protected cruisers had been scrapped. This ship I'd found was clearly an exception.

As I descended toward it, I became certain this was the right ship. As a familiar, I had a heightened sense of smell, and, right now, my senses warned me that this ship possessed an unusual level of spiritual energy.

The scent of magic was overpowering, drawing me like a moth to a flame. Acutely conscious of my injured wing, I descended. Firmly gripping the rear mast with my talons, I took a long look below.

A magic circle drawn on the front deck instantly caught my eye. I had no idea what the effect of it might be, but an alchemist must have drawn it. Mages like Commander G preferred to disguise their true nature, hiding themselves in the human world, so it seemed unlikely a mage would leave a magic circle around to announce their presence.

Alchemists tended to hide from human eyes as well, but given the need to pass on their knowledge, they were more likely to demonstrate their skills. Based on the circle's sheer level of artistic detail, a highly trained alchemist must have created it.

I flew from the mast to the top of the bridge. Ships this size had open air lookout posts. I planned on speaking to the sailor on duty there.

As I descended, I saw someone running up the gangway. It was a naval officer wearing the pure white summer uniform.

I was surprised—I hadn't expected to see a woman on board a ship.

Her posture was impeccable, yet she didn't appear stiff. She looked directly at me. Her features were even, so it was likely she'd be considered beautiful, but she was also fairly advanced in years. The braided hair under her military hat was clearly white and fraying. I couldn't tell her exact age, but I doubted she would object to being called old.

"I apologize for the sudden intrusion. I believe this is the cruiser that protects the Isle of Man. I am here on behalf of Commander G from the Empire of Japan. They call me Kirishima. My business is urgent, so I would like to request an audience with the captain."

Though I was a familiar, my tongue was ill-shaped for human speech. I had acquired a skill that allowed me to communicate telepathically with others. Simply by focusing on them, my intent was expressed without the need for words.

Clearly understanding me, she replied, "No need. I am captain of the *Princess of Wales*, Lt. Rose Diana Gandly. I knew you would be coming."

Magic power radiated from her, wrapping around her head and limbs like silk thread and giving off the occasional burst of discharge. I could sense no spirits, ghosts, or demons in the vicinity, so, based on that, I concluded she was neither a witch nor a mage. Rose was an alchemist, and a very good one. I had to keep a cool head about me or I'd be swallowed up.

"I thought I had disguised my aura as a familiar, but to be detected by one of your skill is hardly embarrassing."

"No, I didn't detect your approach with magic. Commander G phoned me. He said a sergeant named Kirishima was on his way and that I should have some food ready. He was quite a rude, ill-mannered sort of mage."

Damn him. What phrasing! Like I was a child. "Allow me to apologize for my master's uncouth ways. That I am extremely hungry, however, is true. If you are willing to provide, I will happily partake."

Lt. Gandly held up her arm like a falcon trainer. Feathers hid my feet, but my talons were much longer and sharper than they looked. If I wasn't careful, I could hurt her badly. I landed as slowly as I could, doing my best to make it easy for her to catch me.

"No need to be so careful. I'm used to handling familiars. Like so," she said and snapped her fingers. A sinister shadow appeared, compressed itself to a single black dot, and the space around it warped and expanded. What emerged was an apparition that resembled a blackish-brown rabbit.

A gremlin sat on Gandly's other hand. No doubt about it, this was the same one we'd seen on the Messerschmitt. I prepared to chant a spell that would harden my beak into obsidian, but the gremlin seemed to bear me no ill will, making no move to attack.

Lt. Gandly whispered something to it in a Celtic language I didn't understand. The gremlin nodded, unfurled its long, wing-like ears, and flew away toward the sunset.

"I ordered it to search for a different visitor. It would just get in the way of our talk."

"I have some questions for that gremlin, too," I said.

"I'll answer those questions. I'm afraid it understands neither English nor Japanese."

She took me to the captain's cabin, where I was finally able to eat.

I said I was fine with a rat or a mouse, but Lt. Gandly gave me smoked herring. She called them "kippers"— apparently the Isle of Man was famous for them. I'd have preferred the fish raw, but preserved foods had their own appeal. I soon cleaned the plate, which met with her approval.

"You have the best appetite on the entire *Princess of Wales*," she said.

"I am an omnivore who will eat basically anything. My kind will even eat each other if it ensures our survival."

I knew how ominous this sounded, but if I didn't flash a little steel I was unlikely to get anything worthwhile out of her. Commander G hadn't given me any specific instructions; he'd left the negotiations to my discretion. If she gained the advantage over me, I was done for.

The lieutenant sipped her tea. "Humans are the lords of creation; owls the sages of the forest. We wouldn't dream of mocking you. Not only do we eat each other, we engage in vicious wars against our own kind. Survival requires healthy appetites and lusts. My subordinates all eat like birds. No offense."

"I eat more than most birds, to be certain. My lusts have not yet forsaken me either. Though they are no match for human men in either quantity or quality," I said.

The lieutenant gave me a mischievous smirk and said, "There's not a single man on this ship. The *Princess of Wales* does not allow men. All 318 souls on board are female."

A ship crewed entirely by women? Astonishing. I could imagine why that would be necessary, but this was hardly the proper time to dwell on that, nor was the lieutenant the proper company.

"England has grown desperate enough to put women on battleships? You have my sympathies. However, I am here regarding your operations against the Germans. Perhaps your contributions to the war effort…"

The lieutenant sipped her tea, taking this in stride.

"Sergeant Kirishima," she said. "If you stop beating around the bush, you may get more useful information out of me. First, how shall we address each other? I shall address you simply as 'Sarge,' so would you call me Rose?"

Her English was clipped enough that I could easily understand her, but there was clearly a trace of an accent. Cockney, I thought, much like the daruma-bearded mechanic I'd met in Southampton.

"I beg your pardon, but I value my life too much to call a ship captain and an elder by their first name."

"What do ages matter to us? You're over a hundred yourself," she said.

If she knew that, then I had no choice but to accept her harrowing request.

"Very well. Rose, I am here to confirm that you're the one sending gremlins into the war."

"I have no intention of denying it. I've sent him out seventeen times today alone."

"Why go so far? My master was quite irate. No war is worth bending the rules of the natural world."

"England is too desperate to obey the rules of engagement. The fall of nations is nothing new, but we must avoid losing the alchemical knowledge and techniques we have built up over the years. For that, we must leave no stone unturned."

"So the ends justify the means? Yet you fight to preserve your traditions rather than to save your country. I suppose an old alchemist has no more patriotism than mages and witches do," I grumbled.

"We simply place a little more emphasis on imparting the knowledge we have gained. And the ends don't justify *all* means. I've told the gremlin to only damage their planes, not kill them. That apparition hasn't killed a single German pilot."

"Killing the enemy isn't the priority in any battlefield. Injuring or disabling is always preferable. If they survive, they must be treated, and that reduces the enemy's ability to fight."

"Correct. We just want them to run away. We want them to return to base and rant about the monster that attacked them. That was the only approach I could think of that would keep magic and alchemy from becoming the military's plaything."

"That sounds inherently contradictory."

"How do you teach a stubborn child that fire is

dangerous? Have them put out a match with their fingertips. It will burn them, but they'll know better than to play with fire again."

"So in this analogy, the Germans are the stubborn child, and you're using the neighbors as your match?" I asked.

"What choice do I have? Berlin plans to put a neighbor far more powerful than a gremlin on the front lines. They've been working on it for years and have finally gotten to the point where they can transport it with their U-Boats."

A possibility crossed my mind, and I felt all my feathers stand on end. A neighbor more powerful than a gremlin? What could that be?

"Rose, I understand your predicament. Yet I remain concerned. Your side has now used the neighbors first. Is that not just giving the Germans an excuse to use theirs?"

This old woman must have been very beautiful when she was young, but now her expression twisted into something rather unattractive.

"That's my goal. The gremlins are nothing but bait. I'm going to draw them out, and once they've shown themselves, crush them completely. That's why I put the *Princess of Wales* back to work," she said.

This expression caught my attention. "This ship seems

to be nearly as old as the two of us. And with only women on board, how much use will it be in a fight?"

"You think I have no plan? Give me a little more credit. This is the one ship in the Royal Navy officially classified as Special Alchemy Craft."

She shook her head and continued. "There are plenty of skeptics on my side as well. The rest of the fleet calls this ship *The Flying Dutchman*."

My feathers ruffled at the name. The *Dutchman* was an infamous ghost ship that had sunk near the Cape of Good Hope, and rumor said it was doomed to wander the seas until Judgment Day. A Wagnerian opera had made it famous. "Flying Dutchman" certainly wasn't a good nickname.

"Unfortunate. Why 'Dutchman' when you're all English?"

"Have you heard of William, Prince of Orange? Perhaps you've heard of William III, who brought about the Glorious Revolution. He began as Stadtholder of Holland and was later crowned King of England. I am heir to a branch of his family," she said.

Nobody worth anything bragged about their ancestry. Yet she spoke not with pride but something closer to annoyance.

"Poor ship, everyone treats her like a ghost. She was

finished forty years ago. The official name has changed any number of times, but she's still got life in her. The equipment is new, and many of the crew are experienced alchemists, though the majority are still in training."

"A ship crewed by alchemists? I'm surprised the hardheads in command allowed it."

"It wasn't easy. They rejected the proposal from the Isle of Man council, but fortunately Churchill understood. He's often been accused of being a warmonger, but to ensure victory he alone considered the impossible."

"So the Prime Minister himself has signed off on this? It still sounds like you're playing with fire to me. If you provoke the Germans, they'll come at you with everything they have."

"And then we will defeat them. Dictators do not take kindly to failure, so a decisive defeat here will mean they never use magic and alchemy in war again. We're fighting here so we can keep our existence hidden," she explained.

"You sound very confident. You have information on your enemy?"

"Naturally. I know their secrets, and I even know the name and identity of the man behind their plans. Oh, is something wrong? You winced, Sarge. Never seen an owl do that before! Are you hungry again?" she asked.

"I am merely surprised. If you know the enemy's name,

then you've as good as won. If it is no secret, would you be prepared to share?"

There was a brief silence, then she said, "'enrich 'ör-biger. A mad devil."

That sounded clearly wrong. I assumed she was trying to say a male, German name, but I didn't recognize it. Perhaps he just had a very strange name, but I'd heard Cockney accents tended to drop the H. In which case, his actual name...

"Hmm. So this Henrich Hörbiger has a history with you? Oh, your brow has just furrowed, Rose. I believe you already have plenty of wrinkles, no need to add any more."

"I know why Commander G praised you so. He told me not to underestimate his forest sage."

"I appreciate the praise, but shouldn't you tell me about this Hörbiger now?"

"Yes. He had a mansion on the Isle of Man and lived there for quite some time, earning himself a reputation as an eccentric. Even more rude and ill-mannered than your master, he had an unusual aptitude for alchemy but lost his way and fell to ruin. To me, he was a sympathizer, a betrayer, and even a man I loved. But all of that is in the distant past. Now he is merely an enemy who must be defeated and will be attacking tonight..."

I'd lived many years and seen many overconfident

people. I knew full well that most of them met tragic ends.

"Rose, your plan sounds egotistical, as if the *Princess of Wales* sailed out solely to crush this man's ambitions."

"It has done exactly that. One must become evil to fight evil."

"In Japan, we have something called the Night Parade of One Hundred Demons. If apparitions appear visible to the eye, that means what you're doing is extreme and unjustified, no matter its purpose. Win or lose, the resulting grudges will stain the world for time to come."

I knew she was well aware of this, but I had no other argument to make. A wave of sadness passed over her face.

"I have one question for you," she said. "Commander G implied that you requested the familiar contract with him. Would you tell me why?"

Commander G could be a chatterbox. I wasn't sure how much he'd told her, but lying would get me nowhere, so I told the truth.

"Once, I had a wife and hatchling. My wife was barely older than a hatchling herself, and the child was the spitting image of her. They enriched my world with their mere presence, but my lack of magical ability resulted in them becoming trapped between worlds. I could neither restore them to life nor send them on their way to death. They forgot how to come home, lost their place in this world and the next, suffered in darkness without end...until Commander G released their spirits. That action alone made me deem him worth serving. Although, if you ask if I have ever regretted it, I am not sure what I would say."

"I see. Then you will never be anything more than a mere spectator. I know it was my idea, but can I ask that you not call me Rose again?"

"Very well. Lieutenant Gandly, I am prepared to see these events through as a spectator."

No sooner had the words left my mind that the phone rang shrilly. The lieutenant picked it up, and the voice on the other end spoke in rapid English.

"Lieutenant, the fishing vessel stationed at the designated dowsing point has spotted an apparent periscope. As per earlier orders, this ship is making its way there full speed ahead."

Lieutenant Rose D. Gandly rose to her feet, and, with a manner that would make even the Knights of Stuart obey, proclaimed, "The hunt is on!"

4

"KAPITÄN PRIEN. I am grateful for your help conveying the Wieges this far. It's time to set them free. Please cut the Nabelschnur."

In an iron cylinder adrift on the night sea, Special Technical Oberleutnant Henrich Hörbiger spoke into a headset.

"You sure? Without support from the U-47 you'll have no means of getting home." KptLt Günther Prien's reply was clearly audible. The control room on the first Wiege had a comm wire running directly to it. There was no noticeable static on the line nor any risk of being overheard.

"I never intended to return home. I am prepared to slaughter the enemy before us, make landfall on the Isle of Man, and occupy it."

The coldness in Hörbiger's voice rattled even Prien, a man rightly considered implacable. After a moment, he replied, "I respect your fighting spirit, but make sure that enthusiasm does not prove your downfall. We've a long war ahead. It would be a shame to lose a man of your talents here."

"I disagree. The war will end tonight. Once the world knows what my children can do, England will be forced to settle things peacefully. The battle tonight will end the war in Europe."

"That sounds like a boast, but, if you're a real alchemist, I imagine you are capable of just that," said Prien.

"Kapitän, you successfully navigated us through the Dover Strait, a feat akin to magic. Now it's my turn."

"A shame I can't personally see a real alchemist demonstrate their full power. This is the last contact we will have. We've spotted a ship off the east coast of the Isle of Man. A big one. Distance: 120,000. If you'd like, the U-47 could sink it with our torpedoes."

"Let's be more prudent. My bitter enemy is aboard that ship. A U-Boat could never hope to harm it."

"My U-47 has sunk battleships, yet it's not up to this task?" muttered Prien.

"It is not. That ship is the *Princess of Wales*, formerly known as the protected cruiser *Andromeda*."

"As I recall, all ships of that classification were scrapped."

"It's an old ship, commissioned in 1899, so it's forty-one years old now. Rare for a ship to ever get that old. 140.7 meters from prow to stern, standing dry weight of 11,000 tons, top speed of twenty and a quarter knots. Removed from the front lines in 1914, she underwent several name changes, and was used to train young sailors and as a torpedo school."

"You could learn all that reading *Jane's Fighting Ships*. No need to fear some fossil."

"But there is! That ship is no longer a protected cruiser. It's become a Special Alchemy Craft and is a grave threat indeed. The crew is entirely female, every one of them an alchemist or someone with similar powers. Odds are high they've already detected the U-47. KptLt Prien, leave the rest to me. Make your retreat."

"Wait. You can't just say the crew is all women and hang up! Who's the captain, some old witch?"

"Neither a witch nor a mage. Her name is Rose Diana Gandly, chief alchemist of the Isle of Man. She's certainly quite advanced in years, though she never told me her real age. Either way, she has clearly lived far too long. The time has come for my children and me to snuff her out."

"Sounds like this ship's captain is your primary target," Prien murmured.

"I admit it! I developed Project G primarily to send that woman to hell."

A moment after acknowledging this truth, the darkened control room's clock let out a soft warning alarm.

"KptLt Prien, it is time. I will carry out my plan. If you wish to remain alive, put some distance between yourself and the Wieges."

"Will you really be okay alone? I'd planned on observing and supporting from offshore."

"I am always alone. I will defeat the woman who sentenced me to such isolation and then die in peace. My life can have no greater meaning. Please, do not get in my way."

After that, Kapitän Prien gave up his attempts to convince the alchemist. He reverted to a professional tone, signing out with, "Roger. U-47 will retreat at full speed. May your mission be successful."

They spoke no more. The Nabelschnur—the towing cable that housed the comm line—had been severed, and the four Wieges were no longer connected to the U-47. The Wieges, with no comm capabilities, were now mere iron tubes floating in the ocean, yet Hörbiger felt no fear. Rather, a sinister sort of elation washed over him as he turned his attention to the instrument panel.

"G Series. All fifteen units steady at eighty-five percent awakening. No abnormalities detected."

He announced his check aloud, both to prevent careless oversights and to temper his excitement. Hörbiger viewed himself as but a component in the plan, a mechanical part that existed to perform this task. In the past he'd allowed his emotions to get the better of him, ruining everything, and this was the result. His opponent acted exclusively on her emotions. Becoming a machine was the only way to defeat her.

"Filling ballast tanks on tubes one through four. Monitoring angles, shifting to vertical positioning."

A dull pumping sound echoed through the cramped control room. He listened as the ballast tanks beneath his feet filled with water. In sixty seconds, the Wiege's tail was below him, leaving only the nose above water. To an observer, they appeared to be on the verge of sinking, but as these vessels had been designed for aquatic launches of explosive missiles, this was normal operational procedure.

"Pyrotechnic fasteners activated. Nose cones released," he said.

A muffled explosion sounded overhead. The sudden loss of pressure shook his eardrums, but Hörbiger ignored this, clutching the microphone.

"Earth, draw near. Fire, dance. Water, swell. Keter, Chochmah, Binah, Chesed, Gevurah, Tiferet, Netzach, Hod, Yesod, and Malchut; the ten sefirot with Da'at added, become emeth. I speak for the Shem HaMephorash, and as your father, I now release the seal upon thine eyes. Awake, Golems!"

Beneath lumps of earth, Hörbiger could hear the sound of pottery shattering...

5

"GOLEMS? *That's* the Germans' secret weapon?" Finding this hard to believe, my voice was louder than I'd intended. "The clay dolls that Jewish rabbi make? I heard those were useless for anything beyond household chores. Only women and children would be afraid of them!"

The assembled officers all shot me looks of disgust.

Naturally, they were all women. Most were quite young, around twenty, and some even looked to be still in their teens. My dismissal of women and children had definitely been a poor choice of words, but it would be useless trying to take it back now. But how had they all understood me? I thought I'd been directing my thoughts directly at the lieutenant.

The girls here were alchemists, or at least apprentices. Mages were in contact with my "side" of things at all times and so could easily perceive my nature and voice. But that wasn't true for alchemists. They would have had to undergo a great deal of preparation to hear my own "voice."

I suppose Lieutenant Rose Diana Gandly had gone to just those lengths to prepare. I looked closely at the floor and spied the answer: a small magic circle drawn on the bridge. Anyone within range would be able to hear me.

Before I managed to recover from this realization, the lieutenant turned toward my perch on the naval charts and explained calmly, "We fear golems because they deserve to be feared. Those who fail to fear them often die. I've lived long enough to know better."

I adjusted my posture and tone. "Preconceptions can certainly lead to defeat. In which case, please explain. Your mortal enemy created these golems we are about to encounter?"

"Indeed. 'enrich 'örbiger was obsessed with golem research when he lived in England. He immersed himself in Jewish mysticism, memorizing Sefer Yetzirah and Sefer Ha'Zohar in the original Hebrew, and talked about artificial life awake or asleep. He returned to Germany five years ago, mainly because the elder Magus Craftsmen and I refused to help him."

"Whatever the reason, England lost the foremost expert on golems to the enemy then. You could have imprisoned or killed him rather than allowing him to return home," I said.

The lieutenant shook her head sadly. "'enrich performed many experiments, several of them nearly successful. No matter how I objected, nothing got through to him. I told him golems could never contribute significantly to the war, that they'd never be worth the cost. And you know what he said? 'When the tab is settled, everything comes out a net loss. But as the numbers rise, that loss turns to profit. One day, I will lead a profitable band of golems.'"

"I have not met the man, but he clearly does not lack confidence or vision. Rational arguments make no headway with men like that. To battle them, you need an approach that defies reason..."

No sooner did those words leave my mind than realization dawned: The *Princess of Wales* was exactly that reason-defying approach. As I was about to be flung onto the front lines of this battle, my mind reeled, but I wasn't given time to recover. Something pounded furiously on the window.

The gremlin was perched outside. It stuck its face in a tiny gap, saying something to the lieutenant in words I couldn't understand. Its already sinister features twisted in a manner altogether uncanny.

Lt. Gandly nodded, frowning, then in a voice that belied her age, announced, "Ready the searchlights. Objects floating at three o'clock, distance of 9,000. Lookouts, confirm position and distance."

Using searchlights in an area where U-Boats might be lurking was a huge risk, but she would have known that. Gandly had decided that locating and eliminating the enemy must take priority over all safety considerations. The bridge instantly filled with a hum of activity. Beams of light shone onto the water's surface, the chief navigator spun the wheel, and the gunner shouted orders down speaking tubes.

The *Princess of Wales* became a single living organism that rocketed toward war.

"Word from the lookouts. Objects confirmed in designated area. Clearly man-made. Resemble periscopes but far larger!" one of the women said.

This report made up Lt. Gandly's mind.

"Don't let them get away! Increase speed to forty knots!"

I couldn't believe my ears. This ship could go that fast? Old protected cruisers could barely top twenty knots. From the smell of the smokestacks I knew this ship was burning coal, not oil. This would make rapid acceleration nigh impossible.

Despite that, the *Princess of Wales* moved along, as fast as a brand-new destroyer or torpedo boat.

"Lieutenant. Is this ship not burning ordinary coal?" I asked.

"You caught that, huh? This ship's chief engineer is an expert in phlogiston alchemy. The coal is mined in Birmingham, but it burns fifty times brighter than normal."

"Impossible! The boiler would explode!"

"Not ours. Strengthening spells have been cast on the boiler and turbine. Ours may be the most durable machinery in the entire Royal Navy."

"That's not the end, is it? To achieve acceleration like this you must be working against the rules of the natural world on any number of levels."

"That we are. We've dramatically increased lubrication on the ship's hull. Fluid friction with the sea water and the friction surrounding the screw are both greatly reduced, to the point where this ship treats the water's surface like an ice skating rink," she said.

Alchemy on this scale would require calling in favors from the world's greatest alchemists or at least gathering a large number of still fairly impressive ones. Even mid-tier alchemists and alchemists-in-training could do a great deal in sufficient numbers. Special Alchemy Craft truly was an apt name.

The lieutenant gave the order to attack. "Scattershot anti-submarine guns, prepare to fire. All charges at a distance of 300. Load fresh charges as soon as you're done!"

In less than thirty seconds the guns mounted on the bridge spat fire, and the night sky lit up. These were two mounted guns for mortar fire. Ordinary anti-sub depth charges would be released from the racks at the ship's stern, or fired from the ship's side, so being able to fire in the direction the ship was headed was a huge advantage.

Two years later—having gained the official name "Hedgehog"—this weapon would be officially unveiled, granting the British a great advantage in their battles against U-Boats, but the paths traced by this first launch were clearly not ordinary as they didn't follow standard launch arcs. Ignoring gravity and the laws of physics, they changed direction and freely rocketed toward their targets.

"Those shells—they're guided by alchemy?" I asked.

"Yes. Aren't my students talented? Mortar shells fly slow enough that they can easily correct the course. If the war had begun a year later, I'd have trained them to the point where they could redirect the main battery's fire. That travels faster than the speed of sound, but alas, it remains a mere theory."

As she finished, the fireworks went off. Not all the shells hit their targets, but several clearly did. The light of the explosions briefly turned day into night...and gave us our first look at the real threat.

It moved toward us, as though its feet literally walked upon the night.

Its head was like the Great Buddha in Nara; arms like the trunks of sacred trees; narrow, jointed waist like a hornet's; spindly legs like that of a newborn fawn.

Screams echoed across the bridge. I nearly screamed, myself. The creature's monstrous form loomed right over us, close enough to reach out and touch.

"Lieutenant...is that...a golem?" I whispered.

Even Lt. Gandly had turned pale. She managed to answer me though.

"I can't believe it... Even if you grow a golem for ages you might get them to be three meters; the largest are never taller than four. They're nothing but dolls made of dirt and sand and water. If you make them bigger they simply collapse under their own weight."

"How deep is the water here?"

"Lots of shallows on the south shore of the Isle of Man. Likely around eight meters."

"The thing's at least fifteen meters above the water. That makes it over twenty meters tall. Is this ship any match?"

Silencing me with a glare, she ordered, "Ready main cannons. Armor Piercing Rounds. Target the giant golem!"

The *Princess of Wales* had four 15.2 cm/45 naval guns. As the protected cruiser *Andromeda* it had had sixteen guns, but they'd removed the extras to make way for other equipment.

Whatever the caliber, there simply weren't enough weapons. This weak fire wasn't going to help. To bury this monster, you'd need the main battery on a battleship.

But my fear subsided mere seconds later. The guns fired at quick-fire speeds, trailing rainbows in their wake, and pierced the shambling golem. Only one bullet hit home, but it was clearly a fatal strike. That one blow demolished the monster's head, literally blowing it clean off.

"Accuracy seems pretty good. Are you sure you can't guide the main guns yet?" I asked.

"We can't, but we can make the bullets fly faster. We've

carved alchemic writing into the rifles' barrels. If we know our shots will fly straight, even an amateur can aim."

The ladies' faces lit up on the bridge, but it was too soon for joy. Even with its head gone, the golem remained upright, beginning to once again make great strides toward us.

Fear flickered through the room again, but Lt. Gandly had regained her composure.

"Hmph. I get it now. I've figured out the enemy's plan. He likely thinks it brilliant, but this level of cheap theatrics is all he's capable of. Did he learn nothing new back in Germany?" she muttered. Then she grabbed the mike. "The monster to our port side is not what it appears. It is simply standing on the shoulders of ordinary-size golems. Maintain distance and continue firing. Just in case, make preparations for direct engagement."

Ah ha. Columbus's egg: Stack golems like a human pyramid to make this one look gigantic.

"This German alchemist has been interested in mass production from the start. Keep moving and firing, and victory will be yours. However, lieutenant, it has no ranged weaponry. Would it not be better to use this ship's speed to maintain a safe distance?"

"That thing absolutely cannot reach the Isle of Man. We must eliminate any chance of it escaping. May I remind you that you are a spectator, Sarge?" she snapped.

Her harsh tone made me cringe, but the enemy's transformation quickly restored my nerve.

"This is not the time for spectating! Look at that!"

Something was happening to the golem. Though no bullets had hit it, its left side was melting. This wasn't the only change: The right side began expanding like a balloon. The right arm was now several times longer, and when the headless golem swung its monstrous limb through the air...

It snapped off. Centrifugal force won out, ripping the arm out at the root. The dark brown lump soared through the air, landing in the center of the *Princess of Wales*. A dull thud echoed through the ship, shaking the vessel so hard everyone fell over. I'd reflexively leapt off my perch, so I escaped through a window. That was the only way to evaluate the situation impartially. I soon found the source of the impact: Behind the bridge, a sinister figure was clinging to the side of the smokestack.

The figure was roughly four meters tall, with a tiny head and long arms that nearly reached its knees. The monster had striking reddish-brown skin. Its frame was spindly, but it clearly didn't lack for power. Gleaming eyes darted this way and that, and a moment later it vanished into the smokestack. I hastily flew back to the bridge.

"The golem's after your engine! It aims to stop you from within!"

I knew I was right but had no countermeasures to propose. I could already hear screams coming up the speaking tube from the engine room. The silence on the bridge was shattered by the sounds of slaughter.

"Captain. Communications with the engine room have been lost."

The ship came to a halt. The hideous giant golem, twisted as it was, strode inexorably toward us. The guns still fired, taking off more pieces of the damn thing, but even that did not slow its advance.

When it reached the *Princess of Wales*, the golem no longer looked human at all. On board, it split in four. Bodies like the one I'd seen on the smokestack dashed off across the deck, closing in on the bridge. They moved faster than seemed possible for their size.

"They're attacking the bridge!" I cried.

Flapping my wings, I flew higher just in the nick of time. The four golems raced each other across the deck, clambered up the sides, and launched themselves into the lookout station. A whirlwind emerged, flinging me away.

I heard a number of short screams. I turned my eyes toward the lookout station; the women posted there were gone.

The four golems, their fingers sharp as any blade made by Masamune, had sliced through the lookouts.

I stared at the golems in horror. They were unnatural but not in a craggy fashion. They had no brows, flat noses, and their mouths were but a thin line. Their hair was the oddest part. They sported bowl cuts like kokeshi dolls, turned red with the blood of their victims. That detail aside, there was something Eastern about their look, something that reminded me of young Japanese girls.

Lacking expressions, their actions grew puzzling. As one, they began climbing the long, thin mast. I thought at first they were trying to destroy the communications antennae, but no. They formed a group at the tip and stood still.

A moment later, Lt. Gandly's voice echoed in my mind.

"Sergeant Kirishima. They should be behaving quite oddly. Am I right?" she asked.

"As you say. It seems their master is having trouble giving orders."

"'enrich is close by. I would like your help finding and eliminating him."

"I thought I was an observer. Can't you use your gremlin?"

"He's always liked 'enrich. He might betray me. Grant my wish, and I'll accept any one order from you."

6

As the instigator of Project Golem, the creator of the Golem Squad, and the frontline commander of said squad, special technical Oberleutnant Henrich Hörbiger was well aware of his creation's weaknesses.

They were sluggish and unresponsive.

He'd carefully combined the four elements—fire, air, water, and earth—then added the liquid metal with which German scientists had become obsessed. This addition had greatly improved the golems' overall sluggishness, but he could do nothing about their feeble minds. Hörbiger intended to compensate for that.

The earthenware pottery was key to his planned golem operations. Like medicinal vials, he'd planted nine in each golem's head. The alchemist controlling them could shatter a specific vial with long distance brainwaves, exposing the rock slab within and activating the command spell burned into said slab. It was impossible for golems to adapt to any given situation on the fly, but if the alchemist activated appropriate orders with the correct timing, they could dominate the field of battle.

To track the situation in real time, he'd added a TV camera to their chests. Hörbiger had fifteen monitors in his control room and as such knew exactly what was happening aboard that ship. This wasn't advanced technology as Germany had already employed live broadcasts during the Berlin Olympics four years earlier and had recently begun experimenting with cameras on guided antiship bombs. Hörbiger had simply borrowed that tech.

He'd done everything he could, but the unexpected always occurred in actual combat. That's where the golems' stupidity was revealed.

The fifteen golems had left the Wieges, formed a pyramid, changed shape, and landed a solid first hit on the enemy vessel, all according to plan. One golem had gone down the smokestack and destroyed the engine room, stopping the *Princess of Wales* in her tracks, and Hörbiger had believed victory was in his grasp.

Enemy gunfire had destroyed ten golems. Only four additional golems reached the ship, but that was plenty. Hörbiger shattered the vials containing the ultimate order.

"Go to the highest place on the ship and kill the women there," he said.

He'd wanted to specify they should take over the bridge and rip Lieutenant Rose D. Gandly's head off, but that would be too complex a command. Considering how long it would take to teach them what a bridge was, it was better to simplify the order.

Unfortunately, the golems were quite literal. They swept right past the bridge, conquered the lookout post, then began climbing the mast. A mast was certainly the highest place on the ship but strategically useless to Hörbiger. The inability to reasonably deduce and infer was artificial life's fatal flaw.

The golem that had gone in the smokestack also stuck to its order to "find the hottest area at the bottom of the ship and destroy everything." It was now busy pointlessly pounding on the deserted machine room.

But he'd expected something like this. Without hesitating, Hörbiger broke the next vial which contained the following instructions:

"Enter the tower and kill the old woman you see."

The golems quickly took action. They leapt off the mast and onto the lookout post, clung to the walls like monkeys, kicked through the glass, and entered the bridge. Surprisingly, there was no one there. Through the rough imagery of his black and white monitors, he saw only a dimly lit, empty room.

Just like six years ago. She's already run for it.

No sooner had the thought crossed his mind than the images sent by the four golems grew much sharper. A light glowed on the floor.

"Oh, no! The seal of Camael!" he cried.

Camael was the archangel tasked with safeguarding happiness and Mars, the leader of 144,000 angels. A magic circle carved with his name brought cleansing, blessed fire.

Resignation was Hörbiger's only option. There was no time and no means to order a retreat. He hadn't placed any withdrawal orders in the golems' vials.

The trap on the bridge sang a song of death. The circle's heat and light pulverized everything around it. The *Princess of Wales*'s main tower exploded, along with the golems into which Hörbiger had poured all his effort.

His lips tightened, but the father of golems wasn't yet ready to despair. His fifteen children hadn't been entirely wiped out. The one rampaging through the machine room was still active. It was too soon to admit defeat.

"Climb to the deck. Find an old woman and kill her," he ordered, the simplest directive possible. Just as his brainwave shattered that vial, a pounding echoed through the Wiege's control room. There was no wall between the control room and the golem storage, just a flimsy sheet of plywood—and something was trying to break through it!

He glimpsed a fearsome beak, followed by a white face. A giant barn owl with a two-meter wingspan communicated telepathically with him.

"I'm the sage of the forest, and you're making me act like a woodpecker!" the owl cried.

7

USING MY SUPERIOR EYESIGHT, sense of smell, and perception, I located something floating on the ocean like a chikuwa fish cake, and plunged toward it.

It was a small submarine, one turned at a ninety degree angle. This must have gotten the golems close to the Isle of Man.

I flew to the end of it, tore a cheap board apart with my beak, and entered some sort of control room. Once there, I discovered an astonishingly small man. He couldn't have been more than 140 centimeters tall. His age appeared advanced, but he had a youthful gleam in his eyes. The intensity with which he glared back at me was shocking.

But I couldn't let him intimidate me. I chided him for forcing me to act like a woodpecker, then said, "You mad alchemist! You will pay for your sins! Come!"

I hooked my claws into his shoulders and dragged his body into the air. He weighed less than your average child, proving no impediment to my flight. Whether frightened or unable to bear the pain, he didn't struggle.

I hauled him out of the tube and over to the *Princess of Wales*, a distance of some fifty meters. Below me, I could see the protected cruiser was on fire. The bridge had exploded, and flames danced across the center of the ship. But, more than that, the magic circle on the front deck drew my eye. The circle glowed an uncanny blue, reminding me of the lights that guide planes in for landing. I saw Lt. Gandly standing inside the circle. I flew down just in front of it, dropping the little man onto the deck. Female sailors with small guns surrounded him, but the landing must have hurt his back. He didn't even try scrambling to his feet.

I landed on the anti-aircraft gun, watching Lt. Gandly carefully. She gave me a nod of approval, advanced to the edge of the circle, and spoke to him quietly.

"'enrich 'örbiger, why would you do something this stupid?"

The weight of their history obvious, he replied, "My name is *H*enrich *H*örbiger! You never once pronounced it right. Why did I come here? To make a stupid, selfish woman feel regret. Sadly, it appears that feeling will be short-lived. You saw the children on which I worked so hard, no?"

"When we lived together, you were a man of reason and good sense. No such man would call those monsters his children. Whose power did you borrow? No matter how much work you put in, you would never be able to make golems that move so well."

"I worked with a man whose power rivaled that of any alchemist I have ever known. He called himself the Wandering Jew."

I didn't miss the lieutenant's scowl.

"He helped in exchange for access to every painkiller that German medicine has ever developed. Apparently, he fears physical suffering. He vanished before the golem squad was complete. Has he shown up here?"

There was a long silence, then the lieutenant shook her head.

"If a being like Cartaphilus arrived in England, the witches and mages on this island wouldn't stand for it. You were ready to die with these 'children' of yours, weren't you? You've become a pathetic little fiend."

"So be it! I've learned that 'gomli,' meaning seed, is one of the root words of 'golem.' These earthen dolls were the perfect creatures to send after the woman who refused to bear my child."

"That was your fault for falling for an old woman."

"That's what you said fifty years ago! I should have realized it then. You only wanted me as an alchemist. You never wanted my love! A child would give that love form, so of course you never wanted one. Think about it! A child born to alchemists as skilled as we may well have turned out to be a sleigh beggy!"

"It couldn't. Not ever. Sleigh beggy are but a twist of fate. Love and alchemy combined wouldn't create such a being, and golems could never replace a sleigh beggy. That's why I killed them, blew up both them and the bridge."

"You can't kill a golem because they were never born."

An instant later, several gunshots echoed, followed by a series of ear-splitting screams. Behind us, something heavy began lumbering across the deck.

I could see it, that earthen figure with its terrifying visage. Its body was a boiled, reddish-bronze, but its expression remained as blank as ever. Its hair was stained red with the blood of its victims.

The sole remaining golem approached the magic circle and swung its blade-like arm toward the lieutenant, but a defensive wall of blue-white energy blocked its attack.

"What use is there in further destruction and death?" Gandly said.

Hörbiger gave her a sinister smile. "None," he said. "All that remains is to finish things. You there, owl! Will you serve as second to my final act?"

Well, that was unexpected. "You intend to end your life? I am unable to wield the katana required, nor do I own one," I said.

"You won't need it. Just remove the *e*. Turn *emeth* to *meth*. That will suffice."

Dragging himself across the ground to the golem's feet, Hörbiger spoke a spell. The word "emeth" appeared on the golem's head.

Realizing what he was about to do, Lt. Gandly shouted, "Don't! Death is the coward's way out!"

"Rose, as my final request, do not make me feel more pathetic than I already am."

He glanced at me and nodded. His were the eyes of a man who'd lost his child; I was sure mine must have looked the same when I first met Commander G.

I flew to the golem's head and scratched out the *e* with my talons, thus changing the word on its head from emeth to meth.

This was a spell for death. The golem ceased all movement, returning to the clay and water from which it was formed. An avalanche of mud rained down upon Hörbiger's head.

I looked away as his small frame was crushed. The golem's remains covered him completely. The whole lump then rolled across the deck and fell into the waters below.

Had this been victory or defeat? Even Lt. Gandly seemed unsure. Illuminated by the bridge fire, her profile suggested a woman who'd lost her family, most likely a son.

As someone who'd lost his wife and child, I felt a sense of connection, but the situation didn't allow me to consider it further.

"Fish!" someone screamed. Oh. A torpedo...

An instant later, the stern erupted in a pillar of fire. This final explosion finished off the aging *Princess of Wales*.

8

"SEEMS LIKE the U-47 fired that torpedo."

Three days later, Commander G at last showed himself. He appeared seemingly indifferent to the whole proceedings.

"The German papers proclaim the hero of Scapa Flow sank another English battleship. It was a Special Alchemy Craft, not a battleship!"

Commander G and I were looking down at the *Princess of Wales*'s remains, which had been towed to a pier in Castletown Harbor.

"If they knew only women died, would that cause a loss of morale?" I asked.

"Thirty-nine dead, sixty-one injured. Hard to say if that's a lot or surprisingly few, but it's unlikely Berlin will learn the truth until the war is over. Either way, well done.

You have expertly performed your duty as my familiar, Sergeant. Lt. Gandly sends her regards. Said she'd never seen an owl as gallant as you."

"That she survived the explosion without a scratch on her shows how powerful her magic circle was. Incidentally, I received a promise from her. In return for my assistance, I can give her a single order."

"Oh, I already gave that order," the commander said.

Never had I wanted to kill him more. "May disaster befall those who usurp their servant's privileges. What did you ask for? She's England's premiere alchemist. She must know secrets of which you can only dream. Did you ask for those?"

"No. I told her to defect to Japan."

I must have looked astonished.

"I verified this in London, but the British Government intends to eliminate all trace of alchemy from the Isle of Man."

The dots connected for me. "So they're striking all alchemists and magus craft artificers from their ranks?"

"Yes. Apparently they had no further use for them, what with the German alchemist dead. In times of war, you must eliminate any uncertain elements, anything you cannot place as friend or foe. The Isle of Man will be an island of mages once more. We are on the verge of extinction, and, like us, the poor alchemists have already lost many of their own to the war. Now they'll lose their jobs as well. They will be driven to death, and much knowledge and experience shall be lost with them."

"I see. Before the hands and feet are cut off, you'll pluck the head and take it home," I muttered.

"Sergeant! Your mind is like lightning this morning!"

"Owls are famous for their quick minds, especially when considering what one as resourceful as you might do. I figured you'd find some way to turn this to your advantage."

"Naturally. I must learn everything Lt. Gandly knows about golems. Perhaps we can even make some of our own back in Tokyo!" he said.

"Do you have the right?"

"I do. My initial is G, is it not? What better man to become Japan's golem master!"

"Will Lt. Gandly really help?"

"I am ready to persuade her. That's where the fun lies! At any rate, she said she's looking forward to her visit. Said any country that gives rise to familiars like you may one day give rise to a very special sleigh beggy."

Alchemists were hardly prophets, I knew that much. But Rose D. Gandly's words to Commander G rang true to me.

"What will happen to England? To the British Empire?"

"I wouldn't want a country with so many witches and mages and alchemists to fall. I'm sure it will be fine. The country that came to power through piracy, the industrial revolution, and cunning diplomacy will hardly fall to some upstart dictator. However, difficult times remain before them. But that is not a bad thing. To see the beauty of the world, one must step off the beaten path."

I saw a trace of melancholy on Commander G's face, and, once again, felt like I should follow him a little further.

Perhaps that was the fastest way to see the beauty of the world.

The End

Beneath the Stairs at Wald Abbey

SAKO AIZAWA

ONE LITTLE TIN TRUNK contained my entire life. I thought about that as I polished the marble floors. I'd never really thought about it before. I felt like someone had just whispered the notion in my ear, like this was an illusion that the grand old Wald Abbey had conjured up for me.

I gazed upon the rows of silent portraits and elegant furniture.

The head maid, Miranda, had called this room the Long Gallery. The London mansion where I'd previously worked didn't have any rooms half as big and impressive as these. I was on my knees before rows of gentlemen, all fixed in the same pose, hands on their hips, staring ahead in an empty fashion. Portraits of every Earl of Lowfield, the longtime rulers of this land, watched from the wall.

Shivering in the morning chill, I kept polishing the floor. The spate of bad weather had caused the grime and soot to build up worse than usual. Plunging my rag into cold water and wringing it out, I let my mind wander back to the strange thought Wald Abbey had whispered to me.

My life fit inside a tin trunk.

Since I was thirteen, I'd worked as a maid in a mid-sized London manor. When I started, my mother gave me the little trunk she'd used herself, but after years of neglect it had fallen into such disrepair that buying a used trunk seemed the cheaper alternative to mending the old one.

And so, my current trunk was even smaller than my mother's.

I'd filled this trunk with my work uniforms and a few personal possessions, dragging it behind me as I walked to Wald Abbey. The trunk's contents were nearly the same as when I was thirteen. The only difference was how much lighter my luggage felt. Five years of hard work had certainly built up my arm muscles. Up and down a narrow, spiral staircase I'd gone, carrying all manner of things.

"Katie, your hands aren't moving."

Her voice echoed through the Long Gallery.

I was still not used to being called Katie, so there was a moment before I responded.

"Sorry, Mrs. Banks."

I picked up my rag and began polishing the floor again. The elderly Mrs. Banks snorted, but she must have been in a good mood that morning, for she said nothing more. She turned and left the Long Gallery, the bundle of keys at her hip jangling. I breathed a sigh of relief until I realized she'd left footprints all over the newly polished floor and then hung my head.

❦

Naturally, there was a reason I'd left London and gone to work at Wald Abbey. I'd messed up badly at my last job. Another maid had accidentally broken an Eastern tea set that was a favorite of the lady of the house. The maid was just a kid, only thirteen, and I'd been responsible for looking after her. The lady was famous for her temper and would almost certainly have fired the girl.

"I'm finished, Cathy. I have nowhere else to go. They'll send me back to that prison of a poorhouse," the maid had cried.

I'd already lost my mother, so, like this crying child, Alice, I was an orphan. I couldn't bear to think of the awful future in store for her.

I put my arms around her shoulders and said, "Don't

THE ANCIENT MAGUS' BRIDE

worry. Leave this to me, Alice. We'll say I'm the one who broke it."

I believed we could trust the housekeeper, Mrs. Jones. I may get my wages docked to pay for it, but I foolishly believed I wouldn't be fired.

But neither the lady nor Mrs. Jones had any pity for a poor orphan like me. Without the means to pay for the set, I was immediately let go without a letter of recommendation.

Fired with no references!

Alice gave me an apologetic hug and I left, dragging my trunk behind me. Without references, it was hard to find employment. I went back to the busy corner of the East End where'd I'd grown up, living at an inn run by a friend of my mother's while I searched for a new job. But not many places were willing to hire a servant with no letters. One lead after another fell through, and right as things looked hopeless, I remembered my mother's words. If I ever lost my job and found myself in trouble, I should go to Wald Abbey, where she used to work.

I wrote a letter to the abbey. It was far away, in Greenfield. I realized the lady and the housekeeper who knew my mother might have passed on, but, as this was my last hope, I wrote to ask them for work. The answer surprised me: One of their servants had just come down with scarlet fever and moved back in with her parents, so they had a position available. This was a stroke of luck.

I put my entire life into that small, tin trunk and dragged it after me on my journey.

Greenfield, as implied by its name, had more verdant sights than I could have imagined. It was already getting late when I'd arrived, but, unlike London, the sky was bright and clear. An elderly gardener met me as I got off the train in the small station at Wald. He was balding under his faded cap, but when he helped me onto the wagon, his bony hands displayed greater strength than his diminutive frame would have suggested. He gave his name as Lloyd. He smiled for the briefest of moments, but that was enough for me to warm up to him.

Wald was a small place, and the wagon only traveled a few minutes before the surrounding homes grew scarce. The coach road ran between fields as if parting the sea, up and down low rolling hills. In the distance I saw a ridge shaped like the curve of a horse's back and beyond that a deep green forest that stretched as far as the eye could see. Hill after hill after hill, and so many trees. Lloyd's cap and the sky aside, everything in Greenfield was the color green.

At last, the wagon went through a beech grove and under an old stone gate.

"Is this where His Lordship's land begins?" I asked, clinging to my seat.

Lloyd's shoulders shook. Was he laughing?

"Don't be daft. Everything since we left town is his land. All of it belongs to the master you serve."

Eyes wide, I looked back the way we'd come. This vast territory must have been hundreds of acres. I stifled a mix of anxiety and anticipation as I looked down the road. Several hills ahead, I caught sight of it.

Like an old painting, Wald Abbey loomed over the desolate grassland.

It looked like an old fortress from the cover of a romance novel. Asymmetrical, misshapen walls were set with countless, beautiful, latticed windows. A large bay window loomed over the entrance, and the pillars supporting it were carved like the statues in a museum. Since it was called an Abbey, perhaps this had once been a monastery or convent, but it had clearly been extensively remodeled. The garden surrounding this country house was enormous, and behind it stood a dense, green forest, like...

"Seems like the sort of place faeries live," I said.

The wagon wheels clattered loudly, but Lloyd heard me anyway. He glanced back my way and laughed.

"That they do! It's an old place. They're in the house, too."

"They are?" I cried.

The house certainly was hundreds of years old. I could almost believe it had a faerie or two, but I was sure Lloyd was just humoring a young girl's imagination.

That day, the first time I set foot in Greenfield, I thought no further on the matter of faeries.

❦

After cleaning up Mrs. Banks's footprints, I completed the rest of my morning work. Wald Abbey had had many guests the last few days and that much more work to do as a result.

I changed into my afternoon clothes and ate downstairs in the servants' quarters. Normally, lunch was partaken in silence under the stern glare of the butler, Mr. Lawrence. But the last few days, that schedule had been upended, as Wald Abbey's guests had always brought their own servants and maids. When dining with visiting servants, we were allowed to make small talk.

"This place really is like something out of a faerie tale. Is it true you have real faeries here?" asked a young maid in the employ of Mrs. Maven. I thought she was more or less the same age as me, but had no accent, and, while plain, her clothes were quite high quality. If they hadn't been a decade out of fashion, she may have passed for a nobleman's daughter.

A footman named Arthur answered Miss Maven (whom we addressed by her employer's name to minimize confusion.)

"Aye, they do. There's a faerie on your ankle right now!" he laughed.

Miss Maven shrieked and jumped to her feet.

"They help with our work sometimes," Anna said. She was a laundry maid and a notorious chatterbox. "There's lots of them around these parts. Awd Goggie and the like."

"Awd..."

"They live in the forest and eat bad children."

Miss Maven turned pale, swallowing every word of this.

"Hardly a problem if you don't get lost in the woods," Arthur snorted. "But Diana is the most interesting faerie."

Arthur had told me this exact same story, with the same evident delight, when I had first come to Wald Abbey. According to him, a faerie named Diana had lived in this house since ancient times.

"Our good neighbor spends her time among us, pretending to be a servant. When she's in a good mood she helps with our work, but even those of us who meet her don't know her name or her face."

"What does that mean?" Miss Maven asked.

"We forget. She helps with the work, but we can't remember her after. We find we can't remember the name she's given, nor can we recall her face. We can't even remember if she was a man or a woman."

"How curious."

"Someone eating with us right now may actually be a faerie. Anyone here you don't remember seeing before?" he asked.

"Arthur!" Mr. Lawrence cut him off with a fearsome scowl.

Stories of Diana had been around since long before any of us had come here. It was possible such tales dated from hundreds of years before, when this place was still an active abbey.

It wasn't just the servants either; members of Lord Lowfield's family also believed the legends to be true. They always referred to faeries as "good neighbors." In this age of science, I was surprised to find people still believed such things, but, then again, all sorts of people had become obsessed with séances in London. Perhaps ghosts and faeries were the same sort of thing. It seemed the earl's family, Mrs. Banks, Mr. Lawrence, and the house's longtime servants all believed in Diana with something akin to religious faith.

"Thank you for suggesting the subject, Miss Maven. Diana is a good neighbor who watches after us all. She's nothing to be afraid of," Mr. Lawrence said quietly. "Now, let us resume our meal. We have much to do this afternoon."

This signaled an end to small talk.

Our afternoon workloads cast a pall over the meal, like a faerie's spell.

❧

Feeling like a well-wrung rag, I flopped down on my bed. My roommate, Ainsel, had already returned and was seated at her desk, reading by candlelight.

"You look exhausted, Cathy."

She was the only one who called me by my proper nickname.

"I am, Ainsel!"

Too exhausted to stand up again, I began undressing where I lay. Ainsel glanced up from her book, laughing at the sight.

She was a parlor maid and the first friend I'd made after coming here. She was just past twenty and had gorgeous blonde curls that framed her face.

The day I'd first come here, after completing my

assigned tasks (without even a moment to recover from my journey), she'd welcomed me with her Scottish brogue, and we'd talked late into the night. Ainsel had warned me that Mrs. Banks patrolled the halls at night like a prison guard, so whenever we heard Mrs. Banks's footsteps, we fell silent, staring at each other in the darkness, grinning like mischievous children. There was a knock, then Mrs. Banks came in, lamp in hand, to check that we were already asleep. Satisfied, Mrs. Banks shut the door and walked away, keys jangling. I enjoyed this so much I couldn't hold in the giggles. My laughter proved contagious, and Ainsel soon joined in

"We really should sleep. You came all the way from London, and you must be exhausted," she'd said.

Sandwiched between the hard bed and the thin blanket, I'd been bone-weary, but unable to fall asleep. At last even the moonlight had faded, and Ainsel had stopped replying. A wave of loneliness swept over me. This was all so different, like I was in a foreign land. My parents' graves and the church I'd attended were so far away. Surrounded by forest, this place was isolated, and all the memories contained in the stones of Wald Abbey made it a gloomy place. I was seized by the sudden notion that I would die alone here in this quiet manor. I'd never considered anything like that. Before I knew it, the tears were flowing. I desperately choked back my sobs, trying not to wake Ainsel with my sniffling.

I soaked my flat pillow with tears the first night I ever used it.

"Don't worry."

Warm fingers brushed against my cheek. Surprised, I'd turned my face to find Ainsel on her knees, smiling gently down at me.

"Don't worry. You'll grow to love it here soon enough."

Those words had comforted me, like I was praying in church.

"Thank you, Ainsel," I'd whispered and drifted off, sleeping like a baby.

I'd never had a coworker speak like that to me. I was sure our similar ages partly emboldened her. We both loved to read, which helped. I only read *Sweethearts* and other romance novels, books that made the mistress and housekeepers wrinkle their noses, but Ainsel was a real bookworm: Shakespeare, Browning, Dickens, and all sorts of books I'd never even heard of.

Tonight she was dressed for bed, and her hair was already down. While I struggled to get undressed, she said, "Cathy, your hands aren't moving," sounding just like Mrs. Banks. Then, laughing, she helped me loosen my corset. Ainsel was very good at imitations.

"They really worked you today, huh?" she said, undoing the knots. "You're extra worn out."

"The rain left mud everywhere. I've got to show Miss Maven where everything is, too. I'm exhausted!"

"There's a fox hunt tomorrow, so at least there won't be any bells ringing in the middle of the day," she said.

"Oh, good." Letting my hair down, I gave a sigh of relief. "But what of the ladies that don't join in?"

"They're going to wander the garden and then eat on the rotunda. Nobody told you?"

"Miranda may have said something." It was always the same: When Wald Abbey had visitors, so many instructions floated around downstairs that it became impossible to keep track of them all. "But the rotunda? You mean the thing that looks like an old shrine, with the round roof? There's a cave nearby—old places like that might really have a faerie living there."

I realized Ainsel was sitting on her bed, laughing at me.

"What's so funny?" I asked.

"That's a fake," Ainsel said. "A folly. The second earl built the thing to make the manor seem more impressive. The rotunda and that cave—the grotto—are both fakes designed to make this place seem like the ruins of an ancient abbey. I'm sure it has no faeries."

This was a shocking piece of information. All those

structures were fake? How much money and time had he sunk into making these vanity projects?

"Then there're no faeries anywhere."

"Disappointed?"

"Not like I believe in them anyway," I said, staring up at the gray ceiling. "But this manor has a strange air about it. Like I'm always being watched by something... And I find myself having unusual thoughts. People hereabouts say that's the faeries whispering to you, don't they?"

"They do. Bad thoughts, ill tidings, even an artist's stroke of keen inspiration. People around here attribute all manner of things to the faeries."

Ainsel seemed to be done reading for the night. She turned back to her desk and closed her book. Actually, it looked more like a magazine, and she didn't often read those. I thought I saw the word *Strand* on the cover, but it was too dark to tell for sure. She blew out her candle, and the room grew darker.

Only a pale glimmer of moonlight shone through the window's grime.

Hearing her sheets rustle, I drew my blanket up to my neck and whispered, "I wonder if faeries actually exist."

"Just because you can't see them, doesn't mean they don't," she replied.

"If it's just a matter of not seeing, then why can't we?"

"Hmm." She thought for a moment. "Perhaps because our hearts are so removed."

Pressing my cheek into my pillow, I searched for her face in the darkness.

"This is just my theory," Ainsel said. "I'm sure a long time ago, humans and faeries interacted frequently. But as the times changed, human beliefs changed, too. We no longer needed the faeries, and they certainly had no use for humans and their fickle minds either. So our hearts drifted apart, we no longer needed each other, and we could no longer be together. These days, only mages still need the both of us."

"Mages?" I giggled. "Like in Shakespeare?"

As I got used to the darkness, I could make out the blue of her eyes looking fondly back. Ainsel's cheek pressed into her pillow as she watched over me—a thought that made my heart dance. I was sure that last remark about mages had just been her little joke.

"So then that explains the stories about Diana," I said, trying to show I'd been paying attention. "We can't remember her face and name because we no longer need each other, and our hearts have drifted apart? Because she doesn't really matter, our memories of her fade away."

Ainsel dropped her gaze. In the darkness, I thought she looked faintly sad.

"Perhaps that's true. She lives according to different rules. It was always impossible for us to live together."

"If that's true, then that's very sad."

Ainsel closed her eyes, undoubtedly to sleep.

I rolled over, staring at the ceiling and thinking about Diana, the faerie who'd lived here for so many centuries. In my mind, she was a woman. She wore a maid's uniform, wandering like a ghost through the gloomy interior of Wald Abbey. She must be lonely.

Perhaps Diana was searching the Abbey for someone who could see her, I thought. Searching for a way to prove she was actually here. Just as I was, deep down...

❧

The next afternoon was cloudy and chilly but fortunately not rainy. As a result, Lord Lowfield's family took their guests fox hunting. I'd hoped that would ease our workloads, but Mrs. Banks ordered Miranda and the rest of us to clean.

I was near the mansion's entrance, wiping the windows of the Long Gallery from the outside, when Mary—another maid, still only thirteen—made a surprised noise nearby.

"What?" I asked.

"Look at this! They're falling around here again." Mary spoke with a strong local accent. Her family were farmers near Wald village.

"What's falling?"

Since she was so much younger, I kept thinking Mary was a new maid. But she'd worked here since she was eight, so she'd been in service as long as I had.

Mary put down the supply box she was holding and pointed to something on the ground. A number of acorns lay on one side of the Long Gallery windows.

"What are those?" I said, dropping my rag in the bucket and moving closer. I knelt down; they were clearly just acorns—but where had they come from?

"They're from the oak trees, I think," Mary said.

I agreed, but there were no oak trees anywhere near here. No one would ever ruin the view from Wald Abbey by planting trees next to the entrance, yet there were a ton of acorns about.

"You said *again*. Have you found them before?" I asked.

Mary nodded. Her baby face sported a ton of freckles.

"Last week. Same place, about the same number. Every three days, once a week. Sometimes it changes, but it's been like this around here for about a month now."

Well, that was very strange. If there were no trees nearby, then someone was bringing the acorns here. I glanced up at the forest on the nearby hill; they were all hunting foxes out there. This morning I'd been able to hear the dogs howling and chasing the foxes around, but now the place had gone eerily silent. It would be easy enough to collect acorns in that forest. But what use was it bringing them here?

"Maybe they're a gift from the faeries," I joked.

But Mary had had the same idea. "Yes, that's what Mrs. Banks said."

"She did?"

"She said if they're a gift from the faeries, we mustn't throw them out or tell anyone, or they'll never bring them again." At this, Mary clapped her hand over her mouth, her eyes going wide. "Oh! Does this count as telling someone?"

"Don't worry, I'll keep it secret," I said, giving her a reassuring smile. "But what should we do with them?"

"Bring them to Mrs. Banks. She'll keep them safe in the housekeeper's room. She keeps a treasure chest full of them."

Mrs. Banks, the housekeeper, had been working at this mansion longer than anyone. She'd been born in the area. Very superstitious, she believed in the faerie legends with as much fervor as the earl's own family.

"Come to think of it," I said, suddenly remembering,

"I found something strange lying around a few days ago."

"Strange how?" Mary asked.

"I think it was a can. A little empty one."

"A can?"

"It was on the ground near here. I thought someone must've tossed it out a window."

It had clearly been rubbish, so I'd thrown it out. As I spoke, I looked up at the walls and windows above us.

Right above, a woman's face looked down at me through an open window. Startled, I almost screamed.

"What is it?" she asked.

The woman in the window was a beautiful young lady, watching us maids with her sleepy, blue eyes. Looking closely, I realized she was the earl's eldest daughter, Lady Lavinia. Feeling like my heart had almost stopped, I forced my brain to begin thinking. Someone upstairs could see us cleaning!

It was one thing for the higher ranked servants to be visible, but maids like us were supposed to be as silent as the shadows, quietly curtsey, then remove ourselves from sight. But Lady Lavinia had spoken to us. I'd never had a noblewoman speak to me before, and I was beginning to panic.

"Oh, there were some acorns lying here, my lady," Mary said, before I could recover. She raised her voice to be heard, not at all rattled. "Do you know where they may have come from?"

Lady Lavinia shook her head.

"My lady, are you not feeling well? I thought you'd be joining the fox hunt."

The lady didn't seem put out by Mary's question at all.

"I wasn't feeling up to it," she said. "Riding is one thing, but I just feel sorry for the poor animals."

Speaking from the second story window, her voice sounded a little far away, yet I believe she was raising her voice a little for our benefit.

"I'm going back to sleep," she said and closed the window.

I put my hand over my beating heart and looked at Mary.

"Golly," I said. "You're amazing, Mary. You can just talk to the mistress like that!"

"That only goes for Lady Lavinia." Mary laughed. "You see, I was only eight when I came here, and back then Lady Lavinia and her little sister Lady Alicia used to come downstairs all the time and play pranks on us. But, since I was so little, they often used to stop and talk to me."

"Oh." I'd certainly heard many stories about children from upstairs playing tricks on servants. "Is Lady Lavinia good with horses?"

Fox hunts required chasing the hounds on horseback. It was a good chance to show off your skill with a horse, and it was quite common for ladies to ride out with the gentlemen.

"She is. She might be the best in His Lordship's family."

"Really? Even better than Master James?" James was the eldest son.

"Ever since she was little she's been riding with Mr. Gerald. Mr. Gerald's an expert horseman, so she learned from him."

"Mr. Gerald?"

"The vicar's second son. You know, the doctor."

"Oh, Mr. Gerald Neville."

If you went through the beech grove, you could just make out the tiny vicarage. I remembered seeing it before.

"The Nevilles haven't been invited round lately," Mary said.

They used to visit Wald Abbey all the time, but I hadn't heard their names in a while and only saw the vicar at church.

"About that," Mary said, stepping closer to me. Gossip among servants was always delivered in a whisper. "It sounds like the master and Mr. Neville had some fearsome row."

Mary confessed she'd only heard about it secondhand.

As if to put a stop to our gossiping, Miranda, our direct superior, appeared.

"Why are you just standing there? Are you finished?" she demanded.

We brought ourselves to attention and threw ourselves back dutifully into our work.

❦

The incident occurred a few days later.

We assembled in the servants' hall for the morning meeting. Mrs. Banks appeared to be in quite a state. She was always standing bolt upright, no matter the hour, but this morning she was slumped in a chair and muttering to herself.

"Oh, dearie me. How can this have happened?" she whispered.

We all glanced at one another, bewildered. Come to think of it, late last night Mrs. Banks had entered my bedroom, taken one look at my face, turned pale, and left. It had been so odd I'd assumed I was dreaming.

Mr. Lawrence was holding Mrs. Banks's hand with great concern. The cook, Mrs. Oliver, snorted, and took the kitchen maids with her to start their work for the day. Clearly, they were much too busy to fuss over Mrs.

Banks's condition. But the earl and his wife were absent, visiting another manor, so the kitchen workload should have decreased significantly...

"What on earth happened?" Miranda asked.

Mrs. Banks took several sips of laudanum before she was restored enough to answer.

"Diana... Diana is gone! She's left the mansion!"

We all exchanged glances again.

The gist of Mrs. Banks's tale was as follows: The other day, she'd been straightening up her room when she came across the uniform her late daughter had worn in her daughter's serving days. It was old, but if washed and repaired could certainly still be used, or so Mrs. Banks had thought. Despite the lavishness of Wald Abbey, Mrs. Banks herself was quite frugal-minded.

She considered asking the laundry staff to take care of it, but the day's laundry was already done. Never one to dither around, Mrs. Banks resolved to wash the uniform herself. The weather that day was temperamental, and the wind quite strong. Hoping to let it dry before the rains fell, she hung the black servant's dress not in the usual place for laundry, but in the central garden, out in plain sight where she could quickly retrieve it if it began raining.

But when she finished her next task and looked out at the garden, the uniform had vanished. She assumed the wind had snatched it away and went to look but found no trace of it. She had far too much work to do and was forced to abandon her search...until that evening.

When it came time for curfew, Mrs. Banks and Mr. Lawrence made the rounds to check the locks. Mr. Lawrence was responsible for the main doors, and Mrs. Banks handled the unused rooms and servant quarters. Afterward, they patrolled the servants' rooms, making sure we were all abed. Mr. Lawrence retired for the night after that, but Mrs. Banks still had work to do and retired to her room next to the servants' hall. She normally handled her work there, leaving the door wide open. Any servants trying to sneak out at night would have to pass her, and if one of the bells in the hall rang she could quickly answer it.

She'd been working on the ledgers for a while when a bell rang. She hastily stood and checked which bell was ringing. Someone of Mrs. Banks's experience could tell which room was calling based on the sound of the bell alone, but lately she'd felt both her vision and hearing were in decline. She held the lamp high, checking the row of bells near the ceiling. To her surprise, the call came from a guest room on the second floor, one that wasn't generally used and that she had personally locked earlier that same evening. It was very strange, seeing as Mrs. Banks had the only key that could open that room.

This was clearly some mistake, yet the bell kept ringing. Mrs. Banks took a bundle of keys from its hook on the wall, the same bundle that normally jangled ominously at her hip. There were two such bundles, with one for rooms in the servants' quarters, and one for rooms in the main house.

Lamp in hand, Mrs. Banks climbed the servants' stairs, heading for the second story guest room. By this time, the bell had stopped ringing. She used her key to open the door and checked the interior thoroughly by lamplight. Of course, no one was there. Even the windows were locked. There must be something wrong with the bell, she thought. Or perhaps this was a trick of the faeries. Something similar had happened a number of years ago.

Mrs. Banks locked the guest room, returned to the housekeeper's room, and resumed her work. But even she wasn't immune to the sandman's call and found herself nodding off. The sound of footsteps woke her, and she quickly turned toward the hall and saw someone pass by the door. It was a young maid holding a lamp. Mrs. Banks was so shocked her heart nearly stopped.

She didn't recognize the young maid.

There were thirty female servants working at Wald Abbey, but Mrs. Banks knew every name and face, even the kitchen staff not under her direct command. If she saw their face, she could recollect their name. However, she had absolutely no memory of the girl who'd just passed by.

Could she have been a faerie?

A thought struck her, and Mrs. Banks hastily ran after the woman. The hall through the servants' quarters was pitch black, and there was no sign of the maid. Assuming the stranger must have gone out the back entrance, Mrs. Banks tried to open the door, but she had locked it herself; it wouldn't budge. The woman had vanished without a trace. Mrs. Banks was sure there was only one explanation for this and became very upset. Trying to prove herself wrong, she ran to the servants' quarters and went room to room, knocking and checking the faces of every female servant. This caused a bit of a commotion. After checking every room, every female servant was accounted for. The woman she'd seen was definitely not anyone she knew.

Which meant it must have been Diana.

Her utter faith in the faerie legends, and her devotion to Lord Lowfield's family and Wald Abbey, left her despondent. It was her fault Diana had left the manor. You see, part of the faerie legend went as follows:

Never give clothing to a faerie that helps with the housework.

If the faerie puts that clothing on, whether angered or delighted, they will leave the house and never return.

In other words, Diana had found clothing hung out to dry in an unusual place and considered it a gift for her. And then she had left the manor.

❦

"I see. If the legends are true, then Diana is a faerie who guarantees the manor's prosperity," Miranda said, once the story was done. She spoke without expression. "If the master hears of this, he may well become upset."

"Yes, it's quite awful," Mr. Lawrence said, dabbing the sweat from his brow. "If Diana's leave leads to a dip in the family's fortune—" He hastily broke off.

"We're done for. I... If only it was just me. But if Wald Abbey passed into the hands of another...or if this brings harm to anyone... We have to let the lady know at once!" Mrs. Banks cried.

She staggered to her feet, ready to head to town and send a telegram.

"For now, please handle your duties as always. Do not breathe a word of this to anyone," Mr. Lawrence said.

Then he lent Mrs. Banks an arm and led her from the hall.

I followed Miranda upstairs to perform my usual duties. Miranda was as unperturbed by this commotion as the housekeeper was undone.

"What does it all mean?" I asked.

But Miranda just shrugged, despite the heavy burden in her hands.

"Who knows? Perhaps Diana really left, or perhaps Mrs. Banks is just seeing things."

For a while, I thought about all this as I worked.

Was it possible that Mrs. Banks mistook another servant for Diana? She'd chased Diana to the back door, but the door had been locked from the inside and locked by Mrs. Banks herself. A normal servant wouldn't have been able to unlock the door; they would use a window to slip out at night. This would be difficult on the second floor but easy enough for anyone on the ground floor. For a servant in the basement quarters, the side entrance to the kitchen might be the best bet, but Mrs. Oliver controlled the kitchen and rigorously locked up at night. Even if they went up the servants' stairs to the main house, Mrs. Banks had locked the doors on all unused rooms, and Mr. Lawrence had locked the main entrance. The first floor hallway had no windows through which a person could fit. You could fit through the windows on the second floor, but not without considerable risk. Because of that, no one in Wald Abbey, not even the master of the house, could get out at night.

After she'd made sure the back door was locked, she'd gone quickly back to the servants' quarters and checked us all, one by one. It was the middle of the night and she'd been flustered, but Mrs. Banks said we were all sleeping in our rooms. If she'd mistaken a female servant for Diana, then it didn't make sense for us all to be in our rooms. One of us would have been missing.

And if the back door was locked, the person she mistook would have been unable to get out, and Mrs. Banks would have caught up with them. Unless they could somehow walk through doors...

"Maybe it really was a faerie..." I whispered over tea.

Arthur and the other footmen shrugged it off, but Mary and Anna leaned across the table, saying, "It was!"

We finally had an easier workload, so the servants' hall was packed. Even Sophie was here, a lady's maid in training who was normally always in the company of the Lowfield girls. At my previous job, we had all addressed the ladies' maids by their last names, but, perhaps because she was still in training, everyone just called her Sophie. She seemed to prefer this, so I called her Sophie, too.

"Sophie, what's going on with the ladies? Have they heard the story?" I asked.

"No," Sophie said. "I was surprised when Mrs. Banks showed up in the middle of the night, but I only just heard the details when I came downstairs a few minutes ago. Both the ladies are acting like they always do. Lady Lavinia doesn't seem to be feeling well today."

"Yes, I brought some tea up to her earlier, but she was quite pale." Miranda nodded. "Sophie, better keep this to yourself."

"Certainly. But if the master finds out—"

"He's visiting the marquess, so I can't see him cutting the visit short."

The faerie's disappearance was being treated like a real crisis. The master was a particularly strong believer, so no one was sure how he would react to the telegram.

A faerie, vanished into thin air...

If Mrs. Banks's account were true, a faerie seemed the only possible explanation.

Then I remembered the strange dreams I'd been having lately.

❦

Had I begun having these dreams after Ainsel and I talked about faeries?

When I finished work, I went back to my room. I was

allowed to bathe today, but, naturally, I had to wait my turn. Surprisingly, there was no sign of Ainsel. Was her work taking longer than usual? Or was she just resting somewhere?

I laid my head down on my chilly pillow, lost in thought. Then, I heard something.

I rubbed my eyes and moved closer to the window. From the second floor of the servants' quarters, all we could see was the drabbest side of the garden. But a faint light was moving through the back garden.

"Cathy!" the light called.

I hastily grabbed a candle and ran downstairs. I went down the corridor through the servants' quarters, into the half-underground section toward the servants' hall. Then I went up a staircase to the back door and at last emerged outside. This was the only way out, presumably to keep the servants from leaving without permission. Arthur had once grumbled that they'd built this place like a prison, and I didn't think he was referring to Wald Abbey's exterior.

"Katie, what's going on?"

As I stepped outside, one of the servants having a smoke break called to me. I just said I was taking a walk and headed for the back garden, shielding the sputtering candle flame with my hands.

It was already quite dark. There was no moon tonight. The candle wasn't much help. I couldn't see a thing.

But I found that light bobbing in the darkness.

"Cathy!"

I thought I heard it calling again.

I ran toward it. The candle guttered out, but I just kept moving toward the light.

I realized I'd entered the forest when I heard the leaves thrashing in the wind.

A moment later, there was light all around me.

Strange, unlike anything I'd ever seen, it was much like the colored light through a kaleidoscope.

"Cathy, you came," it said, passing over my shoulder.

It was definitely a faerie.

If I had to describe it, it was like a tiny human with wings. It had pale green skin, the same color as its clothes. The figure was feminine, but the shape of its face definitely wasn't human. I held my breath, staring back at her. Strangely, I wasn't at all scared.

"You're the one who called me?" I asked.

"Yes. There's somewhere you need to go."

"Where?"

"Somewhere that needs you."

The faerie fluttered around me, speaking as if it read my mind. "Your life fits inside that little tin trunk. Everyone always forgets you. But if you come with me, you won't need to worry about such silly things."

"Silly?"

"Yes. Our home is a paradise."

She fluttered about like she was dancing, leaving trails of brilliant light in her wake. Flummoxed, I ran her words over in my mind: My life fit in a tin trunk; nobody needed me; no one would even remember me... All of this was true, but why did it hurt so much?

I'd been a servant since I was a child, serving the people upstairs and devoting myself to them. But the people upstairs didn't need us. Lighting fires like faeries, cleaning rooms like faeries, disappearing like faeries—All of us were just like faeries.

We *were* faeries.

"If I go there, I won't have to be sad anymore?" I asked.

"That's right! It'll last forever! Your mom is there, too!"

Tears streamed down my cheeks.

There was a hole between the roots of an old oak tree. It was real and ancient, nothing like that phony "grotto." In its depths, I could see a giant tree root that glowed with a blinding light; a light that waited for me. The faerie darted off into the depths.

Come. This is Tír na nÓg, the land of youth, of eternal summer, of eternal light. No getting old, no dying, no fighting. You can hear the birds singing all the time, singing their delightful songs...

The voice beckoned to me, and I stepped toward the light...

"Cathy!"

Someone grabbed my arm.

I turned and saw her there, panting, clutching my wrist.

I was awake again.

I could hear water rushing. I was out of breath, my heart beating a mile a minute.

Warm water surrounded my naked body. I thrashed, grabbing the side of the tin bathtub. My wet hair clung to my back.

"Cathy, are you okay?"

That voice surprised me. Ainsel was in the tiny bathroom with me.

"I..."

Surprised and confused, I finally remembered.

I was so worn out I must have fallen asleep in the bath.

"You never came out, so I wanted to check on you." She was dressed like a parlor maid, with a lace-covered apron and cap over her black dress. "Thank heavens the tubs are so tiny! If it'd been one of the tubs upstairs, you'd have drowned."

True enough—there wasn't enough room for my head to slide under. I laughed weakly.

"But how did you get in here? Wasn't anyone waiting for their turn?" I asked.

"Yes. Three of them, sitting on chairs outside, their mouths wide open, sound asleep. So I cheated."

Ainsel undid her apron and began undressing.

"Er, you're coming in? Hang on, I'll get out!"

"Don't be in such a rush. I'll wipe myself down first. You take your time."

"But it's already lukewarm..."

Ignoring my protests, Ainsel happily hummed to herself. She undid her spotless cuffs and tossed her frilly cap and black wool dress aside. Long, beautiful, stocking-covered legs peeped out from underneath her petticoats. Faced with those beautiful curves, like something out of a painting, I found myself holding my breath.

"What?" Ainsel said, giving me a puzzled glance. She began wiping herself down with a wet towel. "You stare at me too much, I'll get all embarrassed."

"S-sorry."

Then I saw a little blemish on her beautiful calf. She noticed my gaze.

"Oh, that? That's a burn. When I was a kid, I was playing with some boys when a spark jumped out of the fireplace."

"Oh." I didn't know what else to say. I looked away.

"Don't worry about it. Thank you for suggesting the subject, Cathy," she said, imitating the butler. Then she laughed.

She sounded so exactly like him I couldn't help but laugh myself. She was quite good at imitations.

"You were dreaming, right?" she said.

"Yes," I replied, the question bringing it all back to me. "Not a good dream. Probably because of all the gossip today."

"What gossip?"

"Master James's new venture failed, and that's affecting the whole family."

I'd heard Mrs. Banks talking to someone about it when I walked past the housekeeping room earlier that day.

"They said it might be difficult to keep Wald Abbey going now. That means they might have to sell some land...or let some servants go. Right?"

"True. I suppose they might not be able to afford the luxury of this large a staff forever."

"And if that happens..."

I would be the first one let go, I thought. I'd no special experience or skills, and was a new hire still not used to the ways of Wald Abbey. No reason to keep me on; and I was probably not the only one who'd be sent packing.

"Everyone's counting on Lady Lavinia's marriage to stop that from happening. She often stays at Sir Hume's, right?" I asked.

"Viscount Thomas Hume. Eldest son of the Earl of Lansbury."

"Right. The viscount is quite devoted to Lady Lavinia apparently. When he inherits his father's title, Lady Lavinia will be the new Countess Lansbury. That will take care of the finances, or so everyone says."

"Come to think of it, Lady Lavinia hasn't been feeling well for a while now," Ainsel said.

I nodded.

"She refused to go to London for the season last year."

"Yes." Ainsel nodded. "Lady Alicia was making her debut, but Lady Lavinia stayed holed up in here."

"I've heard people have made proposals to Lady Alicia as well, but the family hasn't married her off because they can't have her marrying before the eldest."

"Also because the offer came from Mr. Lowell, who had land but no title. Perhaps the master has a plan in mind."

Perhaps I was trying to avoid talking about my dream by plunging us into typical servant gossip.

I hung my head.

Then I felt a wet hand caressing my hair.

"Scary dreams should be soon forgotten. Like gifts from faeries."

Ainsel smiled gently right next to me.

I turned red and looked away.

"Thank you, Ainsel."

I added, "I...really value your friendship. Even if we end up separated, I hope we'll stay friends."

Hesitantly, I glanced at her expression.

She said nothing; just gently nodded.

❣

I had dreams like the one in the bathtub from time to time.

Building up the fire in the hearth one morning, my eyes wandered to the window. There, I saw a circle of people dressed in green dancing on the round hill in the garden. Once, on the way to church, I was passing through the beech grove and a voice called my name from above. I looked up and saw a beautiful woman in a white dress sitting on a branch, smiling back at me. Each time I saw such things I thought, uh-oh, better do what Arthur told me and close my eyes, pretend I didn't notice—else they might *take* my eye. But no sooner would the thought strike me than I'd wake from the dream. I may be mending a uniform, or perched on the bumpy wagon ride to town, or resting on my elbow in the servants' hall...

Each was a strange experience, like a dream yet not like a dream. When I discussed them with Ainsel, she laughed and suggested the faeries liked me. Mary and Anna were both surprisingly curious about them, and any time they caught me drifting off they begged me to tell them what dreams I'd had.

This gave me an idea. On my way to pray at church, I stopped by the general store in Wald and bought a pen, ink, and paper. Of course, I had no one to write a letter to, but I began recording my dreams on paper before the memories faded so I could remember them clearly for Mary and Anna.

On my breaks, I'd sit at a desk in the servants' hall, running my pen across the paper.

At my last job, I'd often seen colleagues writing to their homes or lovers. With both my parents gone, I'd never had anyone to write.

So even though these letters weren't for anyone in particular, writing them made my heart dance.

In time, I began embellishing the events of the dreams, whether influenced by the rumors around us, or wanting to add new elements to the folklore. I made my dreams even stranger and more intriguing, all so the girls would delight in the telling of them. This wasn't as easy as it seemed in the romance novels I often read.

"Writing a letter?" Miranda asked.

Hesitantly, I answered, "No. More of a story."

"Oh? You want to be a writer?" Miranda said, not batting an eye.

The idea had never even occurred to me.

I laughed it off.

I'd been born a servant and would be one till I married.

❦

Three days had passed since Diana went missing.

Our daily duties were as packed as ever. Mrs. Banks and Mr. Lawrence remained rather agitated, but we continued our battle against ash and dust. We were strictly forbidden from discussing Diana, and we obeyed; I hadn't even spoken to Ainsel about it. The servants were divided into two camps: those who genuinely believed the faerie had left us and those convinced Mrs. Banks had dreamed the whole thing. When Lord Lowfield received her telegram, he must have assumed the latter. He and his family remained guests of the marquess and were not due home for quite some time.

One night, I was at my work lighting fires in the bedrooms.

Before people turned in, we had to warm the entire building by lighting fires in as many unused rooms as possible. Wald Abbey would freeze this time of year otherwise. Naturally, once it was bedtime, the maids had to go around and put all the fires out. Fire and soot were a constant part of our work.

I was carrying coal from the basement to feed the fire when I felt someone looking at me.

Surprised, I put the bucket down and slowly turned... *It* was watching me from around the corner.

It was a tiny little creature, about the size of a human child, but furry and had a pointy nose and ears. It was hiding around the corner but stared intently at me. It seemed to want something.

My voice shook as I asked, "Are you Diana?"

The creature's furry features shifted, possibly into a smile.

"That's not my name," it said.

"Are you a Brownie?"

"A Brownie? Then you're a maid. Are you a maid? Do you like being addressed as 'Maid'?"

"No, I'm Catherine. Sorry. Do you have a name?"

"I do. But that's not important now, Catherine."

"Is there something you want to tell me?" I whispered.

"There is. The one you call Diana is still here, so stop fussing. We prefer things as they've always been."

"Why tell me?"

"Because you're special. Only you can hear and see us," it said.

"Why am I the only one?"

"Because you need us, just as we are."

I needed them?

What did *that* mean?

I blinked, and in that instant—

Nothing was there. I ran around the corner and looked, but found no trace of him. Because he no longer needed me? Because he'd said what he had to say?

I stood in the hall until Miranda came along and poked me.

❧

When I'd finished my chores, I returned to the hall to find Mr. Lawrence clutching his head. The elderly butler was famous for carrying out his duties without so much as a raised eyebrow, but all trace of that stoicism had vanished.

"What's wrong?" I asked.

He glanced at me but must have decided it was no use talking to a little girl. He just sighed.

"Our master seems to have run out of patience," said Arthur, his breath already smelling of liquor. With no visitors to wait upon, the footmen had finished work already. Sipping a beer, he smiled at me. "The master cut his stay short and will return on the noon train tomorrow."

"So?" I asked, not really understanding.

Arthur laughed again. Mr. Lawrence groaned aloud, forgetting to scold Arthur.

"An invitation from the marquess!" Arthur said. "They were to stay ten days, yet he suddenly packs up his bags and leaves? Why, because the house faerie ran away? I've no idea if the master told them that or not, but that marquess is famous for bearing grudges till his deathbed for the slightest provocation. Do you know what happens when those with power and wealth have it in for you?"

Only then did Mr. Lawrence finally bring himself to weakly scold Arthur for this uncouth gossip.

In other words, this could cause a rift between the marquess and Lord Lowfield. I wasn't well-versed in high society, but I was sure connections between nobility were of the utmost importance. Power and wealth... A marquess would have no shortage of either. A close bond between households could very well help the earl's family in their current financial crisis. But if this incident led to the destruction of that bond...

I now felt I understood the little neighbor's message. I didn't think the faeries really paid us that much attention. Perhaps I was reading too much into it.

"They're coming back on the noon train tomorrow?" I asked.

"That's what they said."

"Then we'll simply have to prove Diana hasn't left."

"Prove?" Mr. Lawrence said, looking up.

"If we can prove that by morning, we can send them a telegram. Reassured, they can relax and enjoy the rest of their stay."

"But how? This woman vanished right before Mrs. Banks's eyes! It could have only been Diana!"

"Well..."

I hung my head.

Diana was still in the manor.

The little neighbor had told me so.

If I believed his words, then the Diana Mrs. Banks had seen wasn't the real Diana.

That wasn't a neighbor, but a human.

But who, what for, and how?

How could we solve this strange mystery?

An idea struck me, and I ran off to find the wisest and most knowledgeable person I knew.

❧

Ainsel was reading a book by the faint light of a candle, as always. Parlor maids must have had lighter workloads than the rest of us, because she was nearly always in our room before me. She'd already changed into her night-clothes and let her hair down.

"I see. That *is* a mystery. Like Diana actually left us," she said, quietly nodding. She leaned sideways against the back of her chair, facing me.

"But she didn't leave. Diana is apparently still here! A faerie told me—"

"Cathy, why don't you sit down?"

Right. I put a hand on my beating heart and collapsed onto my hard bed. Ainsel put a finger to her lips.

"The only way out was locked, and Mrs. Banks didn't pass anyone by on her way... Fascinating."

"Fascinating?"

I blinked. This wasn't the expected response.

"I mean, it's just like *Rue Morgue or The Speckled Band.* I wonder if there's a word for those types of stories, where someone escapes from a place with no exits."

I didn't know what Ainsel meant, so I just blinked at her.

"This woman appeared before Mrs. Banks and was headed directly for the only exit. But that exit was locked tight, meaning she couldn't possibly have left through it. Yet she vanished into thin air, like magic."

"So there's no way a human could have done it," I said.

"A stage magician could have. Perhaps an alchemist. Or maybe a mage..."

Ainsel thought for a while. She closed her eyes and put her hands together like she was praying. I'd never seen anyone pray quite like this.

"Or maybe a faerie?" I said.

Ainsel opened her eyes and gave me a mischievous grin.

"No, that woman was no faerie. She was human."

❧

I stared at Ainsel for a while, my mouth wide open.

"'The more bizarre a thing is, the less mysterious it proves to be. It is your commonplace, featureless crimes which are really puzzling, just as a commonplace face is the most difficult to identify.'"

She sounded like she was speaking on stage.

"Are you imitating some actor, or..." I said, at last.

Ainsel looked hurt. "It's the talk of London! Haven't you read it?"

"I have no idea what you're talking about," I murmured.

"Fine. Point is, this case doesn't even have a crime. It's just people being people."

"You've figured it out?"

"Two hints: the acorns and the can you threw out, and the bell that rang in the guest room at night."

"Er..." I hadn't expected the acorns and can to show up here. "Oh, just tell me already!"

"Well, what's the simplest explanation? The culprit walked past Mrs. Banks's room and then used the key they were holding to unlock the back door. Once outside, they used the same key to lock the door behind them."

"Huh."

"Mrs. Banks chased after the culprit, but she checked the lock *after* the person had already turned the key from the outside. A door like that, you can't tell if it's been locked from the inside or the outside just by looking at it."

"But how did the culprit get the key? Mrs. Banks always has them on her," I said.

"Something strange occurred just before this, remember?"

"Strange? You mean the broken bell?"

"Yes. Mrs. Banks heard a bell ringing, so she left the room carrying the bundle of keys that unlocks the main house. While she was gone, the keys to unlock the servants' quarters were left hanging on the wall, including the key that unlocks the back door."

"They stole the key while Mrs. Banks was away, and they rang the bell as a distraction? But how? The bell was ringing from a locked guest room. There was no one in that room, so how could anyone have rung the bell?"

"That's easy, Cathy." Ainsel grinned at me. "If Mrs. Banks had to lock that room, then anyone could have gone in and out of it before she did."

"Maybe..."

"It's a simple trick. First, you tie a long string to the lever that rings the bell. You run that string under the door, leaving just the tip poking into the corridor. Maybe you stick the string to the wall with a little wax. Then, at night, you yank, and the bell rings. The string will break, and you pull out the rest of it."

"Wait, but wouldn't Mrs. Banks have noticed something like that when she came to lock up?"

"This room wasn't in use. There may have been a fire in the hearth earlier, but, before bed, you and the other maids go around dousing fires in rooms we aren't using."

"That's true."

"So there was no fire nor any other light. The room would have been dark. There's no risk of Mrs. Banks noticing a piece of string by lamplight, especially since her eyesight isn't what it once was."

Ainsel was convincing.

"Now, after the bell trick, the culprit hid in the shadows of the corridor. When Mrs. Banks reached the second floor, our phantom went downstairs, took the back door key off the bundle in the housekeeper's room, then returned upstairs and hid in the corridor again. When Mrs. Banks got back, she wouldn't have noticed the missing key right away. Later, the culprit changed into a maid uniform and went downstairs. Obviously, it would have been better if Mrs. Banks had gone to sleep, but unfortunately she was still dozing over her ledgers in the housekeeper's room. The culprit was forced to walk past that door and through the corridor to get to the back. They used the key to open the door and locked it so Mrs. Banks wouldn't follow them."

"Wait," I said. A question had come to me. "Why should they wait before they went out? Why not just go directly out after luring Mrs. Banks to the second floor and stealing the key? If they'd done that, there would've been no risk of them being seen at all."

"Clever, Cathy," Ainsel said. "Likely because they still hadn't received the signal. It wasn't time for them to go out yet. Late at night in this cold, you'd freeze to death waiting around outside. But if they waited for their signal before ringing the bell, Mrs. Banks may have fallen asleep and never noticed. In which case, the housekeeper's room would be locked and there'd be no way to steal the key."

"Wait, Ainsel. You've lost me. *Signal?* Who is this culprit? For this to work, they'd have to be from upstairs. In which case, the Diana Mrs. Banks saw wasn't a servant, but..."

"Exactly. I've deduced that the person Mrs. Banks mistook for Diana was actually Lady Lavinia."

Deduced.

Not a word you heard every day.

Lady Lavinia was Diana?

"What on earth—"

"And the signal was those acorns you saw. Someone threw acorns up at Lady Lavinia's window. She heard the noise and poked her head out, then the two of them plotted in secret."

"In secret? But if someone outside wanted to talk to someone on the second floor, they'd have to speak quite loudly. Someone would notice."

"But remember, there is a way to whisper sweet nothings without being overheard. It involves using another long piece of string."

"A lover's telephone," I murmured.

Another name for a tin-can telephone. These often showed up in romance novels, and children in London played with them all the time. Everyone knew about them.

"Oh, then the can I found..."

"I'm assuming when Lady Lavinia was pulling it up, it hit a wall or a window frame and the string came out, leaving just the can lying on the ground. The person on the other end could have picked it up, but it was so dark they may not have been able to find it," she explained.

"Right, so what's it all mean? Who is this person coming from the outside?"

"I'm assuming the vicar's son, Gerald Neville."

The lover's telephone. I could see them in my mind's eye, like an illustration from a romance novel.

Lady Lavinia leaning out her window, her hair loose like Rapunzel's while she lowered a string to her prince. The prince whispering down the line to his princess...

"Lady Lavinia and Gerald must be in love. He's been teaching her to ride since she was little. Not at all strange that feelings should arise between them. But she's the eldest daughter of an earl, and he the second son to a vicar. They live in different worlds, and the gap between them is far too great."

And the earl wanted Lady Lavinia to accept Viscount Hume's hand in marriage.

"That's why she didn't go to London for the season and refused other opportunities for gentlemen to see her. The master must have figured out what's between them, which is why the vicar's family are no longer welcome at Wald Abbey."

The earl had fallen out with the vicar to separate his daughter from a man beneath her station.

"But the two of them continued talking in secret. Using the telephone, Gerald visited at night to profess his love for Lady Lavinia. He must've been looking up at her as she leaned out her window in the moonlight, like something from a play. They continued their secret rendezvous, and this time, they met in person."

"So Diana..."

"My lady would have needed help from Sophie and so must have told her the plan. Lady Lavinia used the trick I've already explained to get the key to the back door, and, once we were all asleep, she waited for Gerald's signal."

"Then she changed into servant's clothing."

"On the off chance that she did pass someone, or was spotted, they'd think she was the faerie Diana. It worked perfectly. No one would ever imagine the beautiful lady would dress as a maid. The idea is so impossible that Mrs.

Banks, with failing eyesight, never recognized her."

"You said she must have had Sophie's help," I said.

"When she came back, she had to return the key to the bundle or Mrs. Banks would have noticed. But if Mrs. Banks had gone to sleep, the housekeeper's room would be locked up. That's where Sophie came in. She's a lady's maid, so she can go in and out of the housekeeper's room without suspicion. The next morning, Sophie distracted Mrs. Banks and secretly returned the key to the bundle. And poof, the magic is complete."

Magic.

A mystery so strange that everyone believed a faeric must have done it, and Ainsel had figured it out in just a few minutes.

I stared in astonishment at her mischievous grin.

❧

We had very little time. Early the next morning, I spoke to Miranda and Mrs. Banks and bought myself some time. I explained Ainsel's magic trick to Sophie and asked her to arrange an opportunity to speak to Lady Lavinia. Sophie looked rather pale but agreed.

And so I found myself standing alongside Sophie in Lady Lavinia's room.

She sat on the couch opposite me as I explained Ainsel's deductions.

I couldn't very well tell Mrs. Banks the truth, but I was equally sure we couldn't allow her to believe Diana had gone and frighten the master's family into spurning the marquess's hospitality. This problem was far too great for a little servant girl, so I placed the final decision in Lady Lavinia's hands, even if that required speaking above my station.

"Yes," Lady Lavinia said with a pleasant smile once I was done. "Thank you. I'll speak to my father. Have a telegram sent at once saying the whole thing with Mrs. Banks was a misunderstanding."

"Will Mrs. Banks accept that without knowing the details?" Sophie asked, nervously.

Lady Lavinia shot her a look. "If you tell her I personally requested it, that will suffice."

"Understood, Miss."

Sophie left the room.

"Hopefully we're in time," Lady Lavinia said.

"Um, will you really tell him the truth?" I asked, a little surprised.

"Yes. I rather thought it was about time I did anyway. As a member of the earl's family, I have a duty to protect this mansion and our holdings."

I remembered what Ainsel had said: Humans and faeries lived according to different rules and so could never be together. Perhaps this situation was similar. We servants were commoners, and a vast gulf divided us from the upper classes. We each had different rules to follow.

"Even so..." I began.

Even so...what? If only this were a romance novel. In fiction, it was always possible for love between folks from different backgrounds to bloom.

"I've lived here for nineteen years," Lady Lavinia said, after a while. "I thought I'd live my whole life surrounded by this huge house and garden, but that was wrong. This house is my father's, and in time will be my brother's. I have to find a place of my own, under my own power. If I could find such a place with Gerald..."

"You can! I'm sure. I know you can!" I said, tears in my eyes, though I'd no evidence to back up my belief. "That's what happens in all the stories! Love wins out! Differences in status or ways of life are obstacles to be overcome! True love doesn't care about those things! You can conquer money, mansions, titles..."

Just ignore the rules.

How convincing could these words be, coming from a lower class girl who'd never known love?

But Lady Lavinia rose to her feet.

She took a few steps closer to me, removing her glove. "Thank you. I'm sure you're right."

Her pale, thin, unblemished fingers brushed the tears from my cheeks.

I'd never had anyone from upstairs touch me like this. I blinked several times, and she nodded.

"But you're amazing," she said. "I thought my plan was foolproof, but you saw right through it. You're very clever."

"No, um..." Embarrassed, I told the truth. "My friend figured it out. My roommate, a parlor maid."

"A parlor maid?" Lady Lavinia said, her eyes opening wide. "We have a parlor maid?"

"Huh?"

"And you're a new hire, aren't you? I could swear I overheard Mrs. Banks saying she was getting an unused room ready for the new girl, but you have a roommate?"

Feeling dazed, I blinked several times.

That's when the truth dawned.

A faerie no one could remember...

"Um, sorry. Please excuse me, my lady."

Shaking off the daze, I left the room. I broke into a run, almost tripping over the hem of my skirt as I raced downstairs. I ran through the underground, up the stairs in the servants' quarters, headed for the room at the very back.

My room.

Our room.

Where my friend and I lived.

I opened the door, and there she was.

Morning light flooded through the windows while she read at her desk, just like always.

She was dressed as a parlor maid, in a lacy apron and cap.

"Welcome back, Cathy," she said, closing her book and smiling at me.

Breathing heavily, I spoke to Ainsel.

"So you're... You're actually..."

Ainsel turned herself around in her chair to face me, a little smile playing at the edges of her lips. She nodded.

"That's right. I'm Diana."

❦

Thinking back, there'd been a number of clues.

For one thing, houses tended to employ parlor maids when they couldn't afford sufficient footmen. Such places hired women since they could pay them less. Wald Abbey was big on formality and had plenty of footmen, and as such had no need to hire a parlor maid.

Besides, I'd never once seen Ainsel doing any work.

Certainly, we wouldn't have worked in the same areas, so it wasn't strange that I never ran into her. But why was it I never even saw her downstairs? Maybe I'd assumed the higher-ranking maids took their meals elsewhere, but it was basically unthinkable that I'd never once passed her in the servants' hall.

And that night, Mrs. Banks had gone mad about seeing Diana and checked every servant's room. She'd looked at my face and gone immediately back into the hall. If she was actually checking all of us, it made no sense she wouldn't even look at the bed next to mine.

"You're Diana."

Reeling, I staggered across the room and sat down heavily on my bed. I stared at Ainsel for a while.

"Diana is just a name the humans gave me. I hate it," she said, with a shrug. "I'd much rather be called Ainsel."

"Why?" I said, lost. I pressed my fingers to my temples. "I mean, you're the faerie everyone forgets. So how is it I can remember you? Can always see you?"

Part of me still hoped this was a bad joke, but Ainsel was totally serious. One look in her eyes convinced me this was real.

"Well...I think both our hearts were lonely," she said.

She looked down at her hands. I felt like her long, golden lashes were trying to hide the sadness in her eyes.

"If we both need each other, then when we're alone together, we can connect. You weren't used to this new place, had no idea what the future held in store for you, and felt isolated as a result. While I..."

Ainsel trailed off. I remembered how I'd pictured Diana, wandering the halls of this manor over the centuries, unable to find anyone who remembered her.

The pain of that isolation gripped my heart.

"I enjoy pretending to be human," Ainsel said, embarrassed, rather like someone admitting to a silly hobby. "Observing humans, imitating them, surprising them... I think that's just my nature. I love watching humans, reading the books they've written. I've been doing this for a very long time, by your standards. I wandered from place to place before deciding I liked it here. From time to time someone who needs me appears, and I give them a little surprise. It makes me feel like there's a reason to be alive. But humans these days can live without us. It's been a very long time since anyone needed me. Hundreds of years."

"I..." I put my hand on my heart, leaning forward. "I need you. I'm sure that's why I remembered you. I'm here with you, Ainsel."

"Someday you won't need me anymore."

"That won't happen!"

I couldn't bear to see Ainsel weakly clasp her apron, so

I took her hands in mine. They were frail, pale, cold little hands. I held them tight, as if to prove she were really here. The shape of her nails and the texture of her skin burned into my memories...but...

"We can't be together forever," she said. "Right now, we could be. But, in time, you'll fall in love, marry, and leave this mansion behind. You'll live happily in some peaceful village, or in the bustling corner of a city. Your memories of me will fade away until you can't remember my name, my face, my voice, the warmth of my hands, the feel of my nails against your palms, or anything else. Right now, we find ourselves in the same place. But should you leave this mansion, I'm sure you'll forget me, as I'm sure I'll forget you as the years roll by."

"No! How could I forget you? We're friends!"

I tightened my grip on her hand, so as to not let her pull away, and peered into her face.

But when she evaded my gaze, I knew.

Friends. I'd been the only one who had used that word.

I'd just assumed that we were.

"Listen, Cathy. We aren't like you. Our differences will bring misfortune eventually. Just as the cracks in a mirror destroy all they reflect, our world will crumble."

In time, we would no longer seek each other out.

We were different beings.

That was the fact of it.

"It's our fate. The time of parting always arrives, and that parting draws nearer as humans expand their world, as they no longer need magic. In another hundred years, maybe two, we'll no longer encounter humans at all."

Neither side would search for the other. The industrial revolution had changed how the human mind worked. We no longer needed faeries, and the faeries had lost interest in humans as a result. We were different beings. Just as the people upstairs and downstairs had little contact, as we humans made progress we forgot more and more about faeries. Much like how the people upstairs forgot about those of us downstairs. Much like how, after my death, no one would ever know I'd existed...

If one failed to live on in memories, it was like they'd vanished altogether.

Was that really true?

If so, how could one ever break the isolation?

"That's just awful. I won't ever let that happen," I said, beginning to sob. "I won't forget you. Not ever."

Ainsel looked like she was soothing a stubborn child. *But Ainsel, listen to me. Ainsel!*

I don't care what the rules say. What does it matter that we're different beings?

She and I felt the same. Strong feeling burned bright

in the hearth of my heart, much like blankets of ash when stirred by a poker. The heat rose and rose within me.

"Ainsel, we may be different, but *everyone* is different. The people upstairs, the people downstairs; every one of us is a unique being. Noble or not, we all have different values, and we all live in different worlds, but we still manage to get along, don't we? We have things in common. As long as we remember those things..."

My emotions burned so overwhelmingly that I could only say half of what I meant.

Like when Lady Lavinia had brushed my cheek with her fingers...

Someday, that fence dividing us would come down.

I couldn't say when, but I knew one day we would recognize our differences, and still connect.

I wanted to believe that.

So I looked up at her.

Her blue eyes shone with tears. I stared into those eyes.

"I'll write a story," I said.

The words came out of nowhere.

She looked startled.

"A...story?" she said.

"A story. I won't rest; I'll simply pour myself into writing this story. It will read like a dream, all about a chance encounter with the faeries and the strange events in this manor. I'll learn more about you, come to know more about you, and then I'll write stories. So many stories. That way... That way, even if we're apart, I won't forget."

I said it like a wish. Like a prayer.

Tears rolled down my cheeks.

Then I heard her giggle.

Ainsel was laughing.

"Yes. That's right. Stories are written. I supposed that's obvious, isn't it? Humans can write," she said.

"That's right! We can. And books can be read again and again. I'll write book after book! So I'll never forget you, no matter how far apart we are."

"What will the binding be like?" she asked.

"Huh?"

"You'd better make the binding beautiful. I want the book you write to leap off the shelf. What if it were embroidered with gold and silver thread? I love those colors."

"Er, um, yeah. I'll do that," I said, accepting her request.

Perhaps this was folly, a groundless promise. I was just a little girl, and a maid. I had no writing skills; maybe I'd never be able to convey what I wanted or finish anything.

But I could leave a record of what existed in this world.

If I could put my memories of you in prose...

"Cathy," Ainsel said, leaning closer to me with a little smile.

Tears formed in the corners of her eyes.

"Thank you. My friend, who saved me from my loneliness, thank you for seeing me."

She placed her forehead against mine. Perhaps she hoped her feelings came across to me.

Come, Ainsel. Listen.

Even if I travel far from this manor, I'll write stories. Stories about you, and about the other faeries, about beings from another world. I'll write so many stories, they can never fit inside that little tin trunk. And I hope the stories about you will preserve the bonds between us.

So that, in the future, even a hundred years from now, stories about people—and about those that are not people—continue to be told.

The End

Love is a Troublesome Tail
YOSHINOBU AKITA

I T'S SUMMER NOW, but let's begin with winter.

Every story is rooted in fate. Fate links the seasons together in an unending chain. To know what summer means you have to know winter, which requires an understanding of spring, and so on.

As far as winter goes, some cats loathe it so much they would prefer not to mention it.

Yet it's not so bad. As vexing as the heavy rains and cold can be, the season is not without its small charms. The blanket that warms Miss Margot's lap while she waits at the bus stop is thick and comfortable. When she's not using it, that blanket hangs on the wall, above the shelf with the potpourri. Gold Osmanthus and apple and... Oddly enough, I love the scents I can't identify more than those I can. They serve as a reminder that there is much I do not yet know about the world.

I began entertaining such thoughts during my second life.

The longer one lives, the more complicated one's perceptions become. You quickly learn there is more to the world than nuzzling at your mother's soft fur.

Yes, the world is so complex that one must consider each of the seasons.

In spring, people ecstatically welcome the sun's return. But as the showers fade and the mist thins, the sun outstays its welcome.

In time the winds change, summer arrives, and none speak of those frosty spring days.

Eventually, the sun grows so strong that humans worry about its ultraviolet light. Humans are the only ones concerned with such things. Serves them right for standing on their hind legs and walking around with their heads so high. To make up for this evolutionary mistake, they invented hats. I'm sure that's why their ears are so small and situated so oddly. Poor things. Why are other creatures so different from cats? I genuinely pity them.

The world was clearly made for us.

Cats live and reign throughout the known universe.

Ulthar is one such place, a human village where cats have lived in harmony for a very long time.

That day, I was asleep at my usual spot on the wall.

Every day I would rise with the sun to leave my bed and patrol my territory. By the time I reached the wall, it would have slipped into the shade of a nearby tree. I always passed my mornings there, enjoying the pleasant breeze.

When Margot walked by, she stretched out her aching back and rubbed my head. I didn't want to hear the popping of her joints or the accompanying grunt of pain, so when I heard her approach I jumped down off the wall. That way she could remain hunched over.

There was nothing to trouble me here. Even the ghastly sight of Mackowick, who had recently taken up jogging, could be easily avoided by shutting one's eyes. Sadly, evading the odor of his boozy sweat was far more difficult.

The wall was the perfect spot. I could doze off and savor that perfection.

What is the one consistent truth of this and every other universe?

All cats know the answer: There is nothing better than being a cat.

"Wait," I hear you cry. "Cats know about the universe?"

Naturally. We live with humans, so we know what humans know. As long as cats exist, everything belongs to us.

In return, I suppose, for complete ownership of

everything, cats are perfectly willing to share their bounty. Well, unless something is tasty; then it's wholly ours. We also lay claim to soft beds, animals' twitching tails, and a few other things. Well, several dozens of things. But we're not greedy. Cats are capable of great generosity.

People should know they are not like cats. They should be mindful of their imperfections, always an advantageous point of view. It's a state of mind that benefits not only humans but all non-cat creatures as well.

After all, there is nothing better than being a cat, nothing more right than being a cat, and nothing more perfect than cats.

Fools who cannot understand this will roast in the flames of hell. Not that any such fools exist...

"I hate cats! They're grumpy, creepy, and useless. Dogs are way better."

...I could have sworn I heard something, but the statement simply made no sense. How could one comprehend the ravings of a simpleton?

So I didn't heed it. My ears twitched, but not because those words bothered me. They didn't. I simply felt someone looking at me and looked back. A human boy and girl stood near my sleeping wall by the fork in the road.

I'd seen the girl before; she was one of the village

children. I didn't know her name, but she came from Tika's house.

Humans all had so little fur that it was difficult to tell them apart, but I still identified this child as Tika's girl. After all, she held Tika in her arms.

This girl was likely signaling her special position, a human permitted to live with a refined feline like Tika. But the boy was unimpressed by such elevated status and continued his delusional ramblings.

"You can't tell what cats are thinking! I mean, look at that cat over there! It's ugly, doesn't make any noise, and it's been glaring at us this whole time! Even though it can't possibly know what we're saying," he muttered.

Drop dead.

This thought came to me unbidden, completely out of the blue. An aimless whim, if you will. Naturally, cats paid no heed to the words of mere humans. The difficulty I had in retracting my claws was totally unrelated to the boy's words.

I didn't care at all.

I went back to sleep. This was the most comfortable time of day, and I wasn't about to allow crazy talk to ruin it. I licked my paws a few times, and my claws retracted.

I slept until the wind died down but noticed the faint, odd scent that lingered in my nostrils.

That boy...

His scent wasn't human.

"Hi, Palul. Haven't seen you at the Cat Place in a while."

Before we continue, I must explain two pieces of essential, cat-only information.

You may not believe this, but the Cat Place...was a place for cats.

Cats gathered there. It was a protected zone, where cats came together, exchanged information, peered into the depths of the world, and occasionally performed songs and poetry.

There was no set time to meet and often not even a set place. But all cats knew where the Cat Place was. No invitation required, no call sent out; if one wished to attend, one would find it. Such was the law of the universe; simply a fundamental fact of being a cat.

And the other, perhaps more pertinent bit of information is that my name is Palul.

"Hi, Cole," I said, returning the greeting. Cole was on his fifth life and like a brother to me. We'd been together since I could remember, and had lived our second lives together. I'd reached my third life first, but Cole had entered his fourth before me. And his fifth. I wondered which of us would reach our sixth first. It wasn't like we arranged these things, but for some reason neither of us had ever left the other far behind.

Cole had been in charge of this Cat Place for some time. There were no strict rules regarding management; he'd just fallen into the role. He was a natural advertiser, perhaps because his flat face resembled a billboard. A fat housecat with dark gray fur that blended into the night, he may have looked sluggish, but he could strike an enemy faster than anyone. Cole was the go-to cat for any important matters.

"Came across something that bothered me," I told him.

"When?"

"This afternoon."

Night had fallen. I'd finished my nap, patrolled my territory again, and come straight here.

Cole thoughtfully licked his paw.

"Then we've got just the cat to help you out," he said, pointing at the heart of the Cat Place. "Tonight is Tika's stage."

"Before I go over there, what do you think of her?" I asked.

Cole folded his ears and lay down.

"I think I'm too old for her nonsense."

"I'm looking for an evaluation, not a knee-jerk reaction."

"Same thing."

Cole was being very dismissive of Tika, a young cat in the prime of her second life. Certainly, seeing her ensconced in the center of the room, lapping up everyone's attention, I could understand how Cole felt. I, too, would rather be at home, asleep, my tail tucked cozily around me. However, this afternoon had put me on edge.

"My nose sensed trouble," I explained.

Cole raised a single ear.

"Well, then that *is* trouble. Careful, Palul. If you make a fuss, you could start a panic."

"I met a child today who didn't smell human," I said.

He flattened his ears again, snorted once, and muttered, "Not worth the fuss. I know better."

"You know what?"

"Human scents are unreliable. Even their breath and sweat can lie. They're born to be deceitful."

Simple, and very like Cole.

I headed toward the center of the Cat Place.

Cats had gathered in a circle and were getting all worked up rather quickly. Only the younger cats had come here tonight. Ordinarily, cats of good sense dominated the Cat Place, but today, Tika appeared to have thrown rationality out the window.

As I approached the circle, no cats turned to look. I listened in silence.

"He appeared again! The human devil! The devil child!" Tika shrieked, her white fur standing on end, her tail raised. Her eyes were wide and her whiskers quivered as she threw her entire body into the speech. "Take care! If we leave him be, he'll become a devil! He'll start killing cats! He's the devil's child!"

"Devil! Devil!"

"And to think, after such a creature had finally been vanquished! The king got rid of it!"

"You can try and cast it out, but the devil will never truly be gone!"

The other cats yowled similar things, their ears up, fur on end.

"We'll be killed! Killed again!" one of them cried.

"More blight! The blight!" said another.

"Blight! The king got rid of it, but it will return!"

Their lashing tails narrowly missed my nose.

The cats screamed so loud it rattled me. I couldn't quite figure out how to interject. Second-life cats weren't terribly sophisticated creatures. They tended to cry often, satisfied as long as their voices were loud and heard. At least they were a sight better than the first-lifers, who often forgot what they were even crying about.

"Tika," I said, but her performance continued unabated.

"I'm sure of it! I saw him! Right up close!" she cried.

"Tika, come talk to me."

"That child hates cats! The devil exists! My poor Emma went home crying, poor thing!"

"Tika, I'd like to ask about him."

"A cat-hater walks in Ulthar! The outsider! The interloper!" they all shouted.

"If we don't stop him, we'll be killed! Whoever kills him will be the next king!" she shrieked.

"Tika!" I roared, leaping into the center of the crowd.

After dragging two or three of them to the ground, the young cats let out a series of screams and fled into the darkness. Fur of all colors scattered. I picked out Tika's back and chased after. Pouncing on her from behind, I pinned her to the ground.

Tika tried to escape, but I put my teeth on her throat. She froze, giving in.

The commotion transformed into silence. Tika shook like a leaf. My teeth still at her throat, I said, "I'm going to let you go. If you run again, I will rip you apart."

"Okay."

Slowly, I let her go.

I spat her fur from my mouth and circled Tika. The young cat, thoroughly cowed, didn't move.

"Palul," she said, recognizing me at last.

"I want to ask about the boy," I said.

"I was just talking about him! Just—"

Maybe she meant that as an excuse. Her breathing grew ragged as fear flooded her.

I couldn't tell if she was afraid of me or recalling how afraid she'd been of the devil child.

"You smelled him?" I asked.

"I did."

"What did he smell like to you?"

"Nothing. He smelled just like a child."

"Okay."

Disappointed, I shook my head and walked away.

I was done here. But before I left, Cole called after me, sounding just as sleepy as before.

"Like I said, you're overthinking it," he muttered.

"Can't be too cautious."

"Really? After seeing *them*?" He flicked an ear at Tika.

He had a point, but I didn't want to admit it.

"I said cautious, not panic-stricken."

Apparently, Tika decided I'd moved far enough away. She stood up and began giving the same speech again, but her audience had cooled down considerably. The others kept their distance, cleaning their fur or sharpening their nails to alleviate the tension.

Honestly, I wanted to go home, but I'd stopped in to

talk. If I went home now, I'd feel as if I'd done nothing to remove the prick from my paw.

"When the king's away, it's hard to rein in the chaos," Cole muttered.

"It is," I agreed. "With the help of those visitors, the blight is finally gone. Ulthar is free from danger, but our mission is gone, too. The king quells these sorts of disturbances."

As I spoke, I realized the king's absence explained the young cats' skittish behavior tonight.

"Where *is* the king anyway?" I asked.

The king had left Ulthar a few days ago, but I still wasn't sure why.

Cole yawned.

"Humans took her to the next town over."

"Why?"

"I dunno. Maybe there's a good vet. Something involving her urethra? She'll be back next week."

"What about Jasper and Barney? Didn't she leave anyone in charge?"

"The humans suddenly threw her in a basket and put her in a car. Didn't have time to make arrangements."

"And she couldn't get word out from the vet?"

I sighed.

"Palul, you're a wise cat," Cole said. "Clever, even by our standards. Much more so than I."

"You think so?"

"But don't go freaking out over a human child. Don't go diving for prey that may not even be there, like a rat in a well."

"You're plenty clever yourself," I said. And with that, I left the Cat Place behind.

It could have ended there.

I could have forgotten my fears and returned to my routine, relaxed but prepared in case something happened. If... If that child *did* bring the blight back, I would hardly be the first he killed. Humans like that don't distinguish between cats. They always start with the ones closest to them.

Tika would be first then.

As dawn broke, I could taste her throat in my mouth again. Well, bits of her fur stuck in my teeth made me sneeze at least. For all her show of strength, Tika was still very weak. I remembered how she'd trembled.

Reluctantly, I left my usual patrol to look for the child.

Ulthar was the perfect-sized town, neither too large nor small. I found him quite easily.

Passing through the hedge behind Tika's house, I jumped over the drainage ditch and into a field. A grasshopper crossed my path along the way, but I wasn't distracted. After a scant twenty seconds, I stopped playing with it and made my way forward.

Mackowick was out for a jog, dragging his feet so badly I was able to pass him walking at a normal pace. The longer we walked in tandem, the longer I had to smell him. His breath was ripe with the alcohol stuff that humans drank, and Mackowick drank even more than most. I often caught him staggering home from the pub in the middle of the night. He made better progress then, jogging and mostly sober, than he did now.

Finally branching off from Mackowick's path, I breathed deeply and settled myself. Nearly there. I ran up a crumbling wall around the old bakery.

There, I heard a voice.

"Argh."

Well, more of a sigh. One that was intended to be heard.

It was the kid from Tika's house. I jumped onto the bakery roof to listen and crept along until I had a good view above a bay window.

"I'm never going to get a break. Mum said I could go buy this week's scone. One scone broken into six pieces to last me a week," she said.

"That's not much."

"Mum's rule, so how can I argue? I get dessert on Sunday, so that's No Scone Day."

The girl continued talking while I hid on the roof, watching the two children outside the bakery.

The girl and that boy.

Tika had said the girl went home crying. I guess either she got over it or her mother had scolded her for getting upset over nothing. Either way, she and the boy were together again.

I'd collected stories about the boy. He'd only just arrived in Ulthar the day before, which was why I hadn't recognized him. He was a distant relative of Tika's people, and he and his mother were staying with them.

They planned on renting one of the nearby houses. As the grown-ups were busy cleaning out the place, the girl had been ordered to show him around.

The boy was solidly confused by this scone situation.

"So just buy one," he said to the girl.

At last she got to the root of the problem.

"But if I go without *this* week, I can upgrade to a chocolate scone next week."

"Have you ever tried a chocolate scone?"

"No. But I've had dreams about them!"

The girl folded her arms and frowned, facing the toughest decision of her life, one that revolved around sweets and the coins in her pocket.

I could see how that was a difficult issue. No matter

how much you wanted something, the amount you received might never increase. Much like how I wished for the world to be overrun with infinite mice.

But the boy just stared up at the sky, clearly not at all interested. Then he suddenly tensed.

"What?" The girl asked.

He looked around. "There's a cat about," he said.

I pulled my ears out of sight before he could look my way.

Surprising... I hadn't expected him to notice me.

He was different than the local children. Ulthar humans wouldn't mind if there was a cat about, there were cats everywhere. This boy was unusual. Wherever he'd come from, it was a place that clearly lacked cats.

When she saw how rattled the boy was, the girl laughed.

"So it's not that you hate cats, it's that you're scared of them?" she said.

"I'm not scared! Cats can't do anything to me. They're useless!" he protested. Then he muttered, "Don't need anything useless in the family. Nothing that can't help and won't understand."

Then he pointed.

"See! There!"

He was pointing at the alley, not me.

A cat sat there, acting oblivious to the boy's yell. The boy's expression darkened.

"Black cats are bad luck," he said.

"It isn't black. It's gray," the girl said.

"But it's creepy."

Obviously, I knew the cat they were arguing about: Jasper, a seventh-life cat, and one of the Ulthar old guard. Not the oldest cat around but one of the most respected—aside from the king.

His dark gray fur was always shiny and immaculate. He was as nimble and hard to catch as a shadow. I need not even mention how clever he was.

I hadn't expected to run into Jasper here, so this took me by surprise. Ignoring the boy's cries, Jasper approached. I gulped. If that child really was a devil...

If so, he wouldn't show his true colors that easily. Jasper moved lightly past the boy's feet, perhaps playing on the superstition about bad luck.

As the child snarled, Jasper passed between the two kids and dove into the brush. Out of sight, he—

"Palul."

I nearly jumped out of my skin. Controlling myself, I found Jasper standing behind me. It had been a mere instant since he'd vanished into the brush on the other side of the road; he was frighteningly fast.

"Jasper," I said, trying to calm my beating heart.

Jasper lay down next to me, rubbing his head. As he washed his face, he said, "Didn't expect this sort of behavior from you."

"Has there been gossip?"

"Cole was concerned enough to come see me. Said you weren't behaving like yourself."

"I felt sorry for her," I said.

This wasn't an excuse, but it certainly came out like one.

Jasper paused licking his foreleg, confused.

"For who?"

The fact he had to ask just proved I really wasn't acting like myself.

I hung my head, flattening my tail on the roof.

"For Tika," I whispered. "She's a weak fool, but I didn't want to see her killed."

Jasper chuckled.

"You're beginning to feel protective? You're getting old."

"I don't know any devils."

"Mmm?"

I'd lost him again. This really wasn't like me.

I thought for a moment, trying not to repeat the error. Be like a cat, precise, and ever nimble.

"No cats do. We all know the blight, but none of us actually saw the one who became that blight."

"Hmm."

"So we can't recognize the signs. I can't just laugh it off as the young cats overreacting. Ulthar's history is older than any of us."

"That makes sense. What is it you noticed?"

"A smell. I was far away, so I couldn't be certain, but..."

"Your nose doesn't lie," Jasper said.

"I'm not so sure. Now he just smells like an ordinary child."

Today, the boy had seemed perfectly normal.

Jasper pondered this a while.

"Right," he said at last and sprawled out on the roof.

We were side by side. I watched the boy, and Jasper sunbathed.

Was he disappointed in me? Softly, I muttered, "Am I being a fool?"

"I don't think so."

"But Cole said I was looking for trouble, and I thought he had a point."

"Well, if Cole's right, he's right. What's the use in talking about it?" Jasper purred. He opened his eyes and beckoned to me.

Hesitantly, I pressed my paw to Jasper's fur, then licked it. Jasper rubbed his face against my ear.

"I don't know a thing about the boy, but I can say a few words about that nose of yours," Jasper said.

I perked up my ears. "Oh?"

"The boy didn't change. You did. You're about ready to start differentiating."

"Differentiating what?" I asked.

What a cryptic comment.

Jasper explained, "Your sixth life draws near. Pretty soon you'll be able to sniff out the nature of human hearts."

I went still.

"Then what I smelled..." The boy's heart?

"There's something on that boy you don't often smell on the village children."

"I can't sense it now."

I slowly lifted my head, looking down at the boy.

The kids had switched topics. The girl was exclusively interested in talking about muffins, so the boy looked extremely bored. His expression alone told me everything. He wondered if muffins were the most interesting topic to be had in this boring place.

Nothing more, nothing less. Boredom did not a devil make.

Jasper rubbed up against me, mussing my fur. "My nose senses nothing off about the boy either," he said.

"His heart. Human hearts."

I believed humans had hearts. Even during my first life I'd been vaguely aware of the idea. Humans gave you food if you begged and would help groom your fur. If you cried in front of the door they'd open it. True, even a dumb, automated device could feed you and groom you and open doors, but humans had moods and free will. Sometimes they'd help, and sometimes they'd refuse. They also lied, so they must have had hearts.

Still, that was all conjecture. Believing in such a weird notion was like the faith humans placed in their God.

"What lies within the human heart?" I asked.

Jasper stood up and said, "You may find this surprising, but the human heart is mostly love."

"Love?"

My tail twitched. I groaned.

"They have no tails, but they know love?"

"Yes. They have no tails, but they know love."

"But...they have no *tails*," I said.

Love is a troublesome tail.

Every cat knew the meaning of those words.

A first-life cat's closest friend was their tail. Your tail was always with you, following wherever you went.

In your second life, you noticed the truth. What appeared to be an entertaining friend prone to unexpected movements was actually just part of your own body. If you bit it, you'd hurt yourself.

When a cat made this discovery, they often asked the big question: Are we alone in the universe?

Even poor non-cat creatures felt lonely when faced with this question.

Being alone wasn't isolation. Being the only one who knew what isolation felt like, now *that* was isolation. Playing with your tail did not help. Even if one acquired good friends, a mate, and adorable kittens worth fussing over, all those loved ones were no different from tails.

All cats knew love was a troublesome tail.

"If you can smell his heart, why do you say you don't know the boy?" Jasper asked.

I couldn't understand the question. It wasn't that I thought Jasper was wrong, but...

Jasper smiled. "Blights are always born of love," he said.

His smile faded, but the feel of it remained.

"People's hearts may grow corrupted. Most humans never discover the worst within themselves, but some fall apart and destroy their own lives in the process."

"Is this because humans lack tails?"

I wasn't sure if I was joking or not, but Jasper definitely didn't think it was funny.

"Maybe," he said, nodding gravely. "With no tails,

humans never realize the extent of their isolation. Perhaps that's the devil's origin story. But that's also exactly why humans seek out love. The power to seek becomes the power to know. Knowledge changes them. Even monstrous, inhuman creatures may take a bride and change. Is that love? Corruption? Are these things as different from each other as the ground and the sky?"

"But we, who already know—" I began.

"Most likely never change," Jasper said, quietly.

I couldn't tell if he was speaking out of pride or talking to himself.

A thought seemed to occur to him. He added, "Come to think of it, the king calls the humans she possesses her 'owners.'"

"I've heard as much. It seems a strange way of thinking to me."

"I actually asked her about it. The king said it means we cats don't need to change. That to be unchanging was all we could do."

He left me with one last thought: "This roof is hot! Hmm, 'cat on a hot roof' sounds like the title of a third-rate play. I'm gonna find some shade."

He vanished as abruptly as he'd appeared.

I poked my head over the edge of the roof again. While we'd been talking, the children had both disappeared.

I was alone on the hot roof. My troublesome tail twitched on its own, flitting around the edges of my vision.

I no longer had a reason to follow the boy.

Worrying about the danger he posed was meaningless. Jasper and Cole had both said as much, and I knew that perfectly well myself.

Yet the next day and the day after that, I left my patrol to search for the boy.

I no longer bothered to hide, instead choosing to lie in plain sight where the boy could see me. The boy always moaned when he noticed me. When he saw other cats, he let out a cry. After two days, he was walking around town on his own. A cat-hating human was all wrong for Ulthar, and humans tended to isolate what they felt was wrong.

I'd never really understood the problem with being left alone. What was so bad about isolation? We were all alone in the universe, but were humans *that* unhappy unless they formed little groups?

Cats formed groups as well, of course. We congregated to protect one another, to patrol, to help deliver and raise kittens, to serve our king... But no one was ever as close to us as our own tails.

Love?

Love was a curse humans clung to in place of their tails. Perhaps I just wanted to talk to mine.

No one criticized me for it. Cats never critiqued strange behavior. They either ignored it or joined in.

In time, cats began bringing me rumors of the odd child.

"Apparently, he came here fleeing a curse," one of them whispered. I watched the boy standing by the creek, doing nothing in particular.

"A curse?"

"They were unable to annul a contract with evil blood."

Hook-tailed Giovanni wasn't the type to tease other cats.

"If they're fleeing a curse," I said, "is this child the sacrifice? The one offered?"

"Maybe so. He seems rather frail. Doubt he could even catch a mouse."

"That's true of most humans. No matter how many catches you bring them, they all just scream."

If human nature was so changeable, you'd think they would learn more easily. Well, that was beside the point.

"You planning to keep up this surveillance?" Giovanni asked.

I neither confirmed nor denied. All I said was, "Well, we see a world that's invisible to humans. Perhaps they, too, have a world we can't see."

Giovanni snorted, a standard cat reaction.

"Humans are simple creatures. They can't hide anything from cats," he said.

A yell interrupted him.

"I-I'm sorry!" the boy said.

Mackowick was lying on the ground, breathing heavily. He waved his sweaty arms around and swore.

"You little brat! Where are you even from?!" he snarled.

Apparently, Mackowick had bumped into the boy while jogging. Unsurprising, as the boy seemed pretty out of it.

"I'm sorry, really!" the boy said.

He backed up, looking ready to cry. He seemed nothing like the sullen kid with a grudge against cats.

Looking at him, Giovanni muttered, "Wrong way to handle this."

"Yep," I said. Even if you were to blame, you should never apologize to Mackowick. He'd feel free to get even angrier.

"Man's been alive fifty years without ever running once," Giovanni said. "Drunk himself half to death and now he's jogging out of desperation. You know why he suddenly took up running last week?"

"No."

"He scoffed at fate. Now he's paying the price." Giovanni wrapped his hooked tail around himself, wearing a spiteful grin. "A long time ago, he had his eye on a single mother. The kid was in the way, so he conspired to send the boy off to military school. It worked out well for him, and he married the woman. Ten years later, that boy's a big man who's been trained to kill, and he's coming home next week."

I could see why Mackowick would be desperate. His rage was dangerous. Normally he'd yell a bit and be satisfied, but now he'd grabbed the boy and was screaming.

"You're one creepy little kid! Can't tell what you're thinking! I said, where do you live? Can't you even answer a simple question?" the man shouted.

Maybe we should step in?

Giovanni and I glanced at each other, then a new voice chimed in.

"What are you *doing*?"

It was Mrs. Mackowick.

She had Tika's girl with her. They must have heard the yelling.

Mackowick didn't seem to notice the girl, but when he saw his wife he leapt like...well, like a startled cat.

"What? Why are you—" he started.

"Why *wouldn't* I be? You're yelling so loud the whole village can hear you!"

"B-but this little brat... I'm trying really hard here, and he mocked me for it!"

"Mocked you for what? Embarrassing yourself in front of the whole village? Everyone's laughing about the crying barrel that rolls through town!"

"Erp..."

This deflated him.

"Fine then! I'll never run again! To think I married you hoping for comfort in times of struggle! I quit!"

"Thank God! If you got all healthy and outlived me, how would you ever fend for yourself? Don't make me worry about what'll happen to you when I'm gone!"

Her husband collapsed in a flood of tears. She dragged him away.

I watched them go and whispered, "Love, huh?"

"What?" Giovanni said, puzzled.

I just shook my head.

It didn't matter what humans did.

Mackowick and his yelling wife had vanished, but the boy continued sobbing. The girl hesitantly put her arm on his shoulders.

He just sobbed loudly. He didn't even thank the girl, who'd clearly gone to fetch help. But I didn't think he was being rude on purpose. He was so shaken he couldn't even speak.

"Is it usual to cry that much?" Giovanni asked.

I had no way of answering, but I swore I caught that particular scent from the boy again.

It took a while for the boy to stop crying. Giovanni yawned five times and left as the sun began setting. The breeze chilled rapidly.

The boy had recovered to the point where he could talk to the girl again.

"Mrs. Mackowick said sorry for everything and gave me a little money for both of us. Now I don't have to worry. I can buy all the chocolate scones I want and even more plain ones. Oh, it's so hard to choose. I can't decide!" she cried out.

She stared down at the rectangular piece of paper in her hand, looking gloomier by the second.

"I guess there's no such thing as no worries," she sighed.

"Thank you for staying. I'm fine now," the boy grumbled.

They walked away together. I didn't follow them.

Instead, I went back to my usual resting place and slept. The next day, I returned to my patrol. Giovanni and Cole found me sleeping on the wall and asked if I'd gotten bored. I didn't answer.

"For sure, that crybaby could never be a devil," Giovanni said.

"Crying isn't the same as weakness," I argued.

"You know something you're not sharing with us?" Cole asked.

"No. But I don't think there's any need to watch him."

The king came home the next day. The cats' fears subsided, and Ulthar was peaceful once more.

The rest of the summer passed without event. The sunlight dimmed, and it became fall. As the season turned, our thoughts switched to winter once again.

I saw the boy around from time to time, generally once a day. He still didn't like cats, but apparently the girl and her friends had become used to this. The other children accepted his strangeness, possibly thanks to Mackowick. Crying after an encounter with that old man counted as a rite of passage among them.

Mackowick's stepson had come to town, but not only had he failed to kill his stepfather, he hadn't even hurt the man. His behavior toward his family was perfect, and after a brief stay he went back to the city. I suppose his future was promising, and Ulthar was all in the past.

Mackowick kept his word and never went jogging again. He'd also begun drinking less.

That was all of Ulthar's worthwhile news. I could discuss how Tika's girl used up the extra money inside of a week and got a scolding from her parents, but it's not terribly interesting.

Then, as the nights grew longer, the unsettling *thing* I'd been waiting for arrived.

It was no devil, but something every bit as horrifying came racing into Ulthar.

That particular evening, I was in the boy's house.

Well, in a tree behind the house. I'd heard a violent racket, like a landside, from some distance away. Approaching, I saw light slicing through the darkness.

It was a car, driving at speeds rarely seen in Ulthar.

The stone-paved streets clearly didn't make for the smoothest of rides. The house's back door opened, and the boy came running out. He didn't appear surprised by the racket; he actually seemed to be expecting this. I'd heard him answer the phone a few days before, while his mother was out. The boy had spoken to a man on the other end of the line, discussing a time to meet. This was that time.

The boy wore a sweater far too heavy for the season— likely these were travel clothes. If he'd anticipated their journey, he was probably pretty bright for a human.

Or maybe the man in the car had told him what to wear.

The car tore through the streets of Ulthar. Its flashy red color really drew the eye. The car had no roof, which made no sense to me. It looked nothing like any of the cars I was used to seeing in this town. Some people apparently owned cars designed for pleasure, not practicality. They were the types of cars only people with covered garages (a favorite cat hiding place) could have. The types of cars wealthy people owned.

But this car wasn't shiny, like most rich people's possessions. It was dented all over and rather dirty. Had the driver been careless and left it outside? Several large bags waited in the back seat, but I was most concerned by the man behind the wheel. Wealthy people never looked as desperate as he did.

This was the face of a man running from something, yet no one was chasing him. Or perhaps only *he* could see his pursuers. I thought the latter option seemed fairly likely.

The car stopped behind the house where the boy waited. The moment he saw the man in the car, he yelled, "Dad!"

The man didn't answer. He opened the passenger side door, beckoning to the boy.

The mother realized something was wrong; I could hear her calling the boy's name from inside, but she was too late. The boy got in the car, and the man drove off.

The car tore out of Ulthar. It roared along a winding mountain road, one that would take them far away.

When the car had stopped at the boy's house, I'd jumped down between the bags in the backseat. I'd landed upside down but had managed to quickly right myself. Fortunately, neither the man nor the boy had noticed.

"Dad! Dad! You came!" the boy said, excited.

The man nodded, pretty worked up. "Yeah! I came. I really did."

"I-I've been waiting. I knew! You aren't drinking! You can drive and everything!"

"That's right. Don't worry. I said it would be fine."

"I didn't tell Mum. I knew she'd never believe, but if this goes well we can go back and convince her!"

"You can't trust her!" the man said.

The car bucked, and not because of the bumpy road. The man punched the steering wheel.

"They... They're all out to get me! They locked me up! No way to treat a man... I'm not letting the same thing happen to you!"

"But Dad—"

"Shut up! This is for your own good!"

He backhanded the boy across the face.

In a car this loud, it was amazing how silent everything could become.

I could clearly smell that particular scent coming from the boy.

"Dad... You aren't better, are you? Did you run away from the hospital?"

The man didn't bother answering. The boy clutched his arm.

"Dad. Dad! You can't do that. Mum said you were going to get better!"

"Shut up," he growled, glaring at the boy.

I was watching this conversation in the car's mirror. That little surface couldn't reflect the whole of the man's face, but I could read his every expression.

"I told you not to trust that bitch!" the man barked.

"You shouldn't talk about Mum like that..."

"Why can't you understand?"

"I wanna go home! Can we go back?"

The kid twisted away, but the car was going very fast. He could jump out if he wanted, but he'd almost certainly die.

So the man didn't try to grab him. He snorted, hands shaking.

But then the boy said something that changed everything.

"If you run from everything bad, there'll be nowhere left to go."

The man gasped.

"So let's go back. Come on," the boy said.

At the boy's plea, the man let out a long sigh.

And then he muttered, "Are you really my kid? Are you?"

"Dad?"

"It's not some sort of trick? She lied to me a lot. Maybe you're a lie, too. Get better? There's nothing wrong with me. Everyone lies to me! That woman, you, the doctors, the cops—"

That particular smell surrounded this man, too.

There is one universal truth: Nothing is better than being a cat.

All cats believe that to be true.

Humans didn't think like that. They lived precarious lives, shielding their delicate hearts. Often, they grew too feeble to do even that.

I could smell this man's heart breaking.

In the back seat, I moved on top of the bags and waited for my moment.

I was probably going to die. I wasn't sure this was worth sacrificing my life. I wasn't the king. I had no way of knowing what a meaningful death was.

But I *was* a cat. I ruled over anything weaker than me. And in my domain, I wouldn't allow that intolerable odor of pain.

The road twisted like a snake. The car slowed. I waited for it to make a big turn to the right, then jumped from the back seat and landed on the man's head.

No matter how fast the man reacted, to my cat's instincts he was slow as an inchworm. I jabbed my claws in the man's eye. The car turned over onto its side, and I was thrown out.

I don't know what happened after that. My body hit something, or something hit my body. A deep, deep darkness enveloped me.

When winter came to Ulthar, I rolled over on Miss Margot's knees, spending my afternoon telling her where to pet me. She was moving about less than she had a year ago, but the blanket on her knees still smelled good, and she talked ad nauseum. Today she was telling me all about her great-grandchildren.

"Yes, just like that! The whole time, talking about things I couldn't follow in the slightest. But that's fine. Instead of buying toys I don't know, it's so much easier to give them money. It makes them so happy."

Miss Margot knew life was full of things one understood and things one did not. For a human, she wasn't a bad conversationalist.

Then Margot suddenly jumped, though not enough to knock me off her lap.

I looked down and saw a ball at her feet. One of the children playing in the vacant lot had missed a throw. Margot picked it up, and one of the children came over to get it.

"Sorry, ma'am."

"Be careful, now. Don't throw it in the road. The bus goes by here," she said.

"I know."

It was that boy.

The girl came running up behind him. She seemed more interested in petting me than in the ball. I allowed her to rub my belly.

As they went back to their friends, I heard them talking.

"That cat's all better now," the girl said.

"Looks like. Forgot all about his injuries, the lazy thing."

"You brought him back, Matthew?"

"I found him lying by the road after the accident," the boy said.

"I thought you hated cats."

The boy stopped and looked back at me.

He thought about it for a moment.

"I *do* hate cats. But cats are everywhere here. I can't run away from them all, and I don't want to."

I didn't really get it. Maybe that boy had grown a tail.

Come to think of it, I hadn't died. I still wasn't on my sixth.

My nose hadn't changed, so I wasn't sure if that heartache smell had really gone away.

Neither Ulthar nor the universe had changed.

But there was no hurry. No matter how fast you ran, your troublesome tail would follow.

That was good. So I napped in my familiar spot and enjoyed my time in Ulthar to the fullest.

The End

Agnella's Song

SUZUKI
OOTSUKI

OLD MEMORIES stir within me.

I remember the heat. Warmth. Joules. Life's pulse, fluttering beneath the bones and flesh and blood and skin that shaped it. But in time, that life would follow the second law of thermodynamics—everything breaks down—and grow cold and motionless. So I did what I could to prevent it. Calming, binding, embracing, hugging, wrapping, adoring, and when all else failed—dissolving. Occlusion. Unification. Mating. Melding. Mixing. Melting together. Forming one thing: heat.

Oh. How warm...

There are children in this world whose mothers sing them lullabies, whose fathers read them bedtime stories.

Children who know neither hunger nor thirst, who count sheep and fall fast asleep on a comfortable bed with no rusty springs. Children whose sheets are warm, and free of mold, and don't stink of the old man who used them last.

I grew up with none of that. To me, these sound like stories, like dreams, the stuff of imagination. Children sniffling, their backs hurting, their bellies empty; that was real to me. The furious creaking of misshapen box springs served as my childhood lullaby. In place of sheep, I counted the scabbed, itching wounds on my back as they healed. I owned nothing but my pain and the fact that I'd survived another day. My knees pulled up to my chest, I would curl into a ball on my side. This sleeping method was the first thing children learned in the orphanage.

I was eleven years old.

I was born on a stormy night, a few days before Christmas, in a poor farmer's rundown barn. The wind bled through the walls. Unlike another child born on Christmas, the three wise men didn't appear by my pillow. Indeed, I received no blessings at all; I was born and abandoned like a stray dog.

Normally, that's where my story would end. A newborn infant hardly has the stamina to survive England's harsh winter. If only my life had ended there, parentless, quickly growing cold. The light of my life would have been snuffed out before morning, and I would have slept until the trumpets called forth the rapture.

But it didn't end there. The farmer found me. This farmer—the man who later adopted me—told me this story at every opportunity. He'd seen a strange green light through the barn windows and realized something must be wrong. In his mind, the Lord guided him to me, appealing to the goodness in his own soul. But when they investigated later, they saw no signs of any light or fire— it was believed my mother or parents had gone about having me in the dark, intending to abandon me. In other words, the spirits he'd imbibed that day had made him see things, according to my adoptive mother's more rational analysis.

Either way, my adoptive parents took me in, and my life was spared.

Naturally, this decision hardly came from the goodness of their hearts. They had four children of their own and a grandmother who lived with them. My food didn't cost much, and the experienced old woman and the family's youngest daughter cared for me. If I grew up to be useful, that was good; if I became a jewel they could sell off, even better. If somehow my relatives emerged and offered a reward for my safe return, my adoptive parents would be both rich and renowned for their mercy. For poor people, orphans can be a worthwhile investment.

They named me Agnella—Purity.

They gave me the name of their fifth child, a victim of cot death some six months earlier, reusing it to avoid the trouble of thinking up a new one. Fortune has never truly smiled on me, but in that way I was lucky. Having baby wraps and diapers on hand probably factored into their decision to adopt me. Whatever its origins, I genuinely like the feel of my name. Agnella. Most people simply address me as "hey" or "you," my adoptive parents included, but this name is the one thing that's mine alone.

I lived with that family until I was nine. On good days I received two meals. I worked from the time the sun rose until it set. My bedroom was a drafty corner of the barn, otherwise occupied by a scrawny bull named Brown and a pair of garbage-eating mountain goats named Gray and White. This was the same barn where I'd been born. I had no reason to complain. I slept on the straw with the flies in summer and huddled up against Brown, Gray, or White for warmth in winter. I spent many moonlit nights singing myself to sleep, the animals my only audience. I worked as I was ordered, without thought or complaint. They beat me sometimes, but I didn't object to this treatment. I had no concept of right and wrong. I knew no other world. The barn, the fields, the forest and rivers, the little village we sometimes visited, the bull and goats, my adoptive parents and family—that was the only world I knew.

But two years ago, I abruptly lost that world. It began with Brown's death.

One winter morning I woke shivering in the cold. The moment I opened my eyes, the bull let out a long sigh and closed his. I shook him, calling his name. He looked at me one last time, then glanced toward the window and closed his eyes again.

I stayed by his side until his heart stopped for good, and all traces of his warmth vanished from the world.

The bull's loss was a fatal problem for my adoptive family: He'd towed their plow. For a while they unsuccessfully tried this and that to gain the funds needed to buy another bull. Then, one morning, they called me by name, a rare occurrence. They said I wouldn't need to work that day, that I should bathe in the river before noon and change into my cleanest clothes. I did as I was told. When I returned, they handed me over to a visitor I'd never seen before. There was no time to say goodbye.

My adoptive parents had simply sold what they owned, earning the return on their investment. Meanwhile, I was put into a car and driven east.

They'd sold me to a place named Arkham Home, a small orphanage near the town of Norwich in Norfolk.

❧

Arkham Home was an old convent repurposed as an orphanage, a gloomy prison whose sturdiness was its sole virtue. The building boasted high ceilings and imposing walls that shuttered the place in twilight at all times of day. At night, ominous shadows gave shape to the darkness. In summer, the air was moist; in winter, a merciless cold chilled us to our bones. The place was a fortress, and according to rumor it had been an internment camp at one point. The rumors were likely true; with a cliff behind the building and a surrounding ditch making it impregnable, escape and infiltration were both difficult.

A small well inside the compound provided more than enough water to sustain the place. That meant the orphanage had very little actual plumbing. Our lives were extremely dependent on the water we could pump up from that well. The well water was heavy, cold, and so hard that it made soap lather poorly. According to Sister Abigail Williams, the orphanage's manager and dorm mother, all of these things were "trials from God." Therefore, there could be no improvements or alterations of any kind.

Twice a day, at dawn and dusk, the younger children pumped the water we needed. The water was clear and freezing cold all year round. It destroyed the children's fingers. It split their puffy red skin, removed their finger-prints, stiffened their joints so that they refused to bend. Kids often went to bed moistening their fingers with lips and tongue, warming them, enduring the itching and pain. But they lacked the skills to do anything more than work the field and look after livestock, under the super-vision of the nuns and the older children. Those kids who had learned reading, writing, and math were given more complex tasks, sent to work "outside." It was their job to bring money into the orphanage beyond charitable dona-tions or financial aid.

My first year, I, too, was sent to pump water. Until we reached the quota for drinking, food prep, laundry, baths, and other uses, I would silently work the manual pump handle until the bucket was full. Then I would carry it, pour it out, pump it full, and carry it again. Once that was done, I had the rest of the day's work to look for-ward to. Working the fields with cold-ravaged fingers was brutal even for me, who'd grown up on a farm. The brief period of classes before bed was no trouble; that involved sitting in a chair, doing nothing but listening to the in-structor talk after all. I learned less out of interest and more from a desire to see how much I could retain. It took me only six months to master the basics of reading, writing, and arithmetic. As a reward, I was given work that required my newfound skills and freed from the terrors of the pump.

The children's literacy rate wasn't very high. The orphanage was structured so that the better you were at reading, writing, and math, the more opportunities you had to enter the outside world. Because of that, the number of properly educated children never went above a certain threshold. Naturally, an orphanage wasn't a place of permanent residence. Once we became too old, we were told we were "independent" and shipped out before they'd arranged proper homes for us. Talented and attractive kids would, of course, be adopted in the end, while those of us who were neither would be left to languish. Apparently, the orphanage had purchased me to maintain a certain head count to qualify for government funding.

Sister Abigail insisted that suffering wasn't a punishment, and the righteous path would bring us closer to God. This was the orphanage's primary creed. As an approach to life there are worse mantras, but it provided no comfort whatsoever for orphaned children. Sister Abigail seemed convinced that these trials polished our souls and would lead us to the gates of heaven. But these weren't trials from God; rather, they were trials she'd invented. We needed something akin to warmth, something that would help us to endure and overcome life's hardships.

Instead of warmth, we got Julian. Julian was a saint who had lived here in Norwich, fond of a whip commonly known as the cat o' nine tails. Sister Abigail called it a "tool of learning," but each of the nine leather straps ended in a hard nub that could easily break the skin when applied with enough rigor. For example, when eight-year-old Cathy spilled her milk at the breakfast table, she was given one whack. When six-year-old Georgie wet the bed, he was given one whack. Yolanda, thirteen, made a mistake at work and received a particularly strong whack. Use dirty words, one whack. Take the name of the Lord in vain, one whack. At night, unable to sleep from the cold and the pain on their backs, Georgie and Cathy crawled into my bed where I held them, their warmth reminding me of life in the barn. I sang softly to comfort them. We could find no blessings in Julian's trials.

Life in the orphanage was simple and hard, likely not all that different from the lives of the nuns who'd once lived here. We rose before five. The older children went to work in town, delivering newspapers and milk. The younger children fed and cleaned up after the livestock and pumped water, and we all gathered for breakfast at seven. After breakfast came prayers. Then we'd do laundry and care for the chickens and cows we kept while the older kids went to work in town. After lunch, we had the occasional lessons. At six, everyone returned home for the evening meal. Then came more prayers, lessons, and a very small amount of free time before bed at nine o'clock. At five the next morning, the same routine began anew, over and over and over again. Only the seasons provided any variety.

For example, spring. Norwich springs didn't last long. The weather was fickle and could change in an instant. A pleasant morning would give way to heavy clouds and rain in the afternoon. The rains were light, but often accompanied by strong winds, making coats and hoods necessary. By evening, the winds would have blown the rain clouds away, and the blue skies would return. The children waited for this, making the most of the sun and the dry air. April and May usually passed with a chill. Throughout the year, the rain fell two weeks out of every month. Living in this land meant living with the rains.

By early summer the days were longer, and by June the skies stayed bright until after our bedtimes. The children fell asleep a little later than usual, spending the extra time lying in bed, talking about their harmless little dreams and desires.

Each room had two bunk beds. The crybaby Georgie lived above my bunk. He always talked about how someday his parents would find him, pick him up, and take him away to live with them where he could eat all the good food he wanted. The lower bunk opposite mine belonged to the dreamer Cathy, who always talked about how God would send her a good man, make her a "lady," and she'd have lots of children and live happily ever after. Determined Yolanda slept on the top bunk and always talked about getting out of this prison, surviving in the world on her own skills, enjoying a life of freedom filled with nothing but what she wanted.

By mid-July it got properly warm, and the dark gray sky gave way to sunshine and balmy breezes. When the temperatures rose, the boys took their shirts off and spent the afternoons half-naked. Within the orphanage walls, the girls were permitted to bask in the sunlight wearing rather bulky chemises. This was a rare opportunity for extra vitamin D, the lack of which greatly increased the rate of illness, so the sister was reluctantly forced to turn a blind eye. To the children, these skimpier clothes were also a means of protection. Even Sister Abigail realized letting outsiders see Julian's marks may not be the best idea. This time of year, Julian rarely appeared, and far fewer children went to bed crying.

But it didn't stay that warm for long. Once September arrived, the temperature dropped, the clouds returned, and so did the rain and chill. October passed, and strong wind warnings frequently came on the radio. There's a poem in Mother Goose that goes, "The north wind comes with November/See how the leaves do flit/The snow storms come with December/Make sure the fires are lit." Once autumn was done, we entered the hardest season: winter.

But even then, I looked forward to one thing.

Not my birthday, of course, nor Christmas. Sure, we'd get a scrawny turkey for dinner and a roast of bitter Brussels sprouts, along with a Christmas pudding that wasn't nearly sweet or nutty enough—different from our usual fare but hardly worth celebrating. The Christmas presents were simple toys and stuffed animals gathered from donations or hand-me-down winter clothes. I never looked forward to New Year's Eve either. We got to stay up late and watch the fireworks near Big Ben and the live broadcast of Hogmanay in Edinburgh. While we looked forward to that, we weren't even given pretzels to snack on.

No, it was none of those things.

In winter, I looked forward to the funfair.

A normally deserted area on the fringes of town

became an enchanted landscape filled with sparkling lights, games, and stands. Crowds came to visit the day and night before the fair. Tons of massive trailers rolled in from God knows where. Engineers and craftsmen scurried this way and that, and somehow got everything set up in a single day. A small Ferris wheel appeared, making a brilliantly lit circle in the air, and a little double-decker bus honked its horn. Teenage boys boasting about their strength swung a hammer, trying to ring the bell atop a giant pillar. There was a balloon clown so large that kids could climb inside, though it terrified the younger children. The smells of buttered popcorn filled the streets of the town.

For the four days of the fair, the orphanage children were allowed to walk around in groups of five selling "Orphan Biscuits" (instead of Girl Guide Biscuits). Of course, the official name was Arkham Homemade Charity Biscuits, but we kids never called them that. Christmas was a good time to encourage benevolence and charity, so the board of health permitted us to set up a small stall at the fair. The mayor and councilmen would show up and sample a biscuit, buy a few boxes, and get their pictures taken for the paper, so the sister always put vast amounts of work into that booth. She would thoroughly check our clothes and hygiene to make certain we didn't look too shabby (which might attract attention from kindly grown-ups and child welfare officers). Then we were sent to the fair, where we wandered around selling biscuits until the evening, while another group of children stayed at home and made more biscuits all day long.

The mood and booze got to some people. Spiteful drunks sometimes came after us, and seeing people with their families, lovers, and friends forced us to compare our own circumstances, which could be brutally hard. But if you could get past all that, there was fun to be had.

On the last day of the fair, the city gave us each a single sheet with ten tokens on it, and the orphanage would give us about ten pounds spending money.

Tokens were tickets used for the attractions. Stuff like the trampoline or balloon clown cost a single token; most rides were two, and the main-event attractions like the roller coaster could go as high as four. In other words, you could carelessly burn through your ten tokens very fast. The money, as well, was only enough to buy two or three things at the stands, but this was our sole opportunity to spend as we liked. We had more freedom during the festival than the whole rest of the year.

I'd arrived at the orphanage the previous winter, and had used money for the first time in my life at the funfair.

In the beginning, I wasn't at all sure what to do with it. I'd wandered around aimlessly, watching people. Children happily munched popcorn. Children screamed on the roller coaster. Children ate frankfurters with the intensity of a philosophical conundrum. Children used real coins to try knocking over pins in an attempt to score a ten-pound note.

At last I found the paint booth and went inside.

While selling biscuits, I'd seen people walking around with their faces painted. Soccer balls or colorful fruit, Union Jacks, cute animals and angels covered their cheeks or shoulders. Some people wore full-face makeup like it was Halloween. Like the nail art and costume booths, the face paint got people into the festival mood. I felt like I should do something along those lines. I needed to get used to all this. With that in mind, I went up to the register. A girl with a long-horned goat painted on her cheek smiled at me and asked what I wanted.

Full or half-face paint cost a pretty penny and seemed like a bit much. It was all I could do to ask for the cheapest and smallest. She put a little foundation on my left cheek, the first makeup I'd ever worn. She added a bonus one on my right cheek, then a little blush. Her brush danced, quickly filling out the thing I'd asked for: Agnella, my name, with a brown bull lying on top of it.

When she showed me in the mirror, my heart beat wildly. The blood rushed to my face, and it felt like it was on fire. She laughed, saying most people just ask for cats or dogs. But, hey, she had a goat herself.

Then I went and used my first tokens. I remember looking at the ticket collector's hand and trembling, afraid he'd get suspicious and arrest me. I remember how beautiful the view looked from the—rather small—Ferris wheel. I remember the night sky, our orphanage tiny in the distance.

What should I do this year? Should I take Cathy and Georgie, and all go around together? As I wandered about selling biscuits, I considered.

The sun began setting on the last day of the fair.

I looked up at the Ferris wheel, bright against the darkening sky. I looked around at the target range, the balloon shop, the toffee apple shop, the coffee cup ride, the go-kart track—which the boys would certainly love. A merry-go-round stood in the center of the fair, and people of all ages were riding the horses. The music and lights were so intense that they seemed to force back the night. Families and groups of friends packed the fairgrounds. Smiles flashed all around, and the other orphans were already eager to join the fun.

It was almost time. Our squad leader, Kay—at sixteen,

the oldest girl in the orphanage—checked the sales with practiced ease and announced our return to the booth to cries of delight. Once Sister Abigail had checked our numbers, she would officially declare the "Annual Funfair Arkham Homemade Charity Biscuit Fundraising Drive" over. Then, finally, she'd begin handing out the token sheets and ten-pound notes that would allow us to experience two hours of absolute freedom. Our sales for the day hadn't been bad, and it seemed the other squads were in similar shape. If we'd done well, we'd finish with the sister in a good mood, and when we went back to our normal lives tomorrow there'd be peace for a while. Our feet were light as we headed back to the meeting spot.

But when we arrived at the orphanage's booth, the mood was ominous. The other groups looked tense and stood in silence, almost like they wanted to blend into the scenery. The children in my squad stopped in their tracks. I alone moved forward because I recognized the crying voice coming from the center.

Georgie knelt on the ground, bawling his eyes out. Sister Abigail and the other nuns stood before him. The group of children with bowed heads had to be his squad. I couldn't very well pretend this had nothing to do with me and stood nearby.

I saw a familiar face in the group and ran over to her.

"Yolanda!" I cried.

"Oh, Agnella."

Yolanda held Cathy, who was silently crying. She looked tense.

"What happened?"

"Agnella! Georgie, he..." Cathy said, looking up. She grabbed me and buried her head against my chest. Her little body was warm against mine.

Yolanda shrugged and shook her head. "Georgie tried swiping some of the sales money from the Orphan biscuits to buy some cotton candy."

"What? But..."

Theft was, of course, absolutely forbidden, and there was no way it was even possible. Each squad calculated their own profits competitively, and the units sold were tracked on a computer only the nuns could use. If we were even one penny under we'd be strictly scolded to the point where nobody wanted to be the one holding the cash.

"Yeah, of course he got caught. But he's a new boy and didn't know better, so he got stuck holding the change."

She jerked her head at the squad behind Georgie.

"The impulse got the better of him. He's in for three full swings of Julian for sure. Gonna be sleeping on his stomach for a while, and he's gonna be the only one with no tokens or money tonight."

"Oh no!"

Georgie was a crybaby. This was the first fair since he'd come to the home, and he'd been excited about it for days, barely able to contain himself. I never thought it would turn out like this.

"Really, if you're going to do it, make sure you don't get caught. Or just wait a little longer and buy it with your own money! They found him before he even took a bite of the cotton candy, and the whole thing ended up in the mud."

Yolanda was clearly very upset.

"And we're forbidden from buying anything for him. Unfortunately, some very important people noticed what was happening, and the sisters are all furious."

"If only you or I had been with him..."

"Yeah, but the sisters chose the squads."

"Poor Georgie," Cathy said, her voice choked up. "I promised him we'd eat some sweet Yorkshire pudding with loads of whipped cream together..."

Cathy was much younger than us, but she'd lived at the orphanage for three years, longer than anyone else. She knew exactly what life here meant.

Yolanda and I looked at each other. We both knew Georgie's parents had abandoned him when he was two. He believed he'd just gotten lost and that they were out there looking for him. Apparently, they'd abandoned him at a festival, and he'd gotten separated from them in line to buy some fluffy pink cotton candy. His parents had stuffed some coins in his hands and told him to buy some, and the money hadn't been enough.

"Agnella, you think it was the funfair?" Georgie had asked.

"Think what was?"

"The festival where my parents lost me. I don't remember. But if it was, then this isn't my first time!"

We knew exactly why little Georgie had been so excited and nervous the last few days.

"I'll tell the sisters."

"Agnella?" Cathy said.

"Tell them what?" Yolanda sighed. "Even if you do, this is still his fault. He brought it on himself."

"Yeah, but..."

I saw a flash of green light. Translucent emerald light, with something sticky and red melting inside of it. My head hurt.

What could it be?

My heart beat so fast my chest ached.

My body moved without thinking. I hated to let go of Cathy's warmth, but I peeled her off me. Cathy reached out, but Yolanda was faster. She threw her arms around me.

"Don't blame me for what happens," she said.

"Yeah. You two try to enjoy the fair."

"Agnella?!" Cathy yelled after me, but I turned on my heel.

My head throbbed. Something moved at the edge of my vision.

I turned my head to look; there was nothing there. My imagination? But then I thought I saw something moving in the other direction. I quickly turned to look again. The world wobbled. Cathy watched me anxiously, and Yolanda frowned. I saw nothing else. The attractions' bright lights left trails across my vision. Maybe that was what I'd seen.

I felt a little better. I turned and walked up between Georgie and the sisters. I felt like the more I moved my head, the less it hurt.

"Agnella?" Georgie said. My shaking head seemed to concern him.

"Sister," I said.

"What?" Sister Abigail said, glaring at me. "We haven't closed yet. Wait until then."

"No, that's not it. I want to ask you to forgive Georgie," I said.

She narrowed her eyes.

"He committed a sin. He must be punished for it."

"His punishment..." My head throbbed.

Brown, the bull. The goat on her cheek. The Ferris wheel. Tokens. The winter barn. Snow falling, frozen ground. Memories of being taken from my adoptive parents' house flooded over me, but I didn't care. The hint of fear in my adoptive parents' eyes. I didn't care about them or the children hiding behind them. I cared about the two goats, Gray and White. Had I said my proper goodbyes to them? And what had happened to Brown's body? Normally a Jersey male would be slaughtered for food shortly after he was born. Brown had likely died from old age and the cold. I'd felt the warmth leave his body as I stared up at the open roof hatch. And the green light there...

Green light? Why did I picture that? My head hurt so much, I shook it. I shook it a lot.

Georgie looked more concerned. My brain trembled. Sister appeared worried, too.

"The punishment, I'll... Put it all on me. Y-you can... All of it. I... B-Brown's..."

"Brown?" she said.

"Brown's grave... I."

I hadn't dug one.

"What are you saying? Who is Brown? Agnella. We're talking about Georgie's punishment."

"The sin... It's all m-mine."

My tongue wasn't moving right. It was so hard to get words out.

I could smell maple syrup from the pudding stall Cathy had mentioned.

And rot, also. The foul stench of a swamp.

"Gray and...White, too. That way..."

My thoughts splintered. I felt feverish. Fireworks exploded behind my eyelids. Headache. Shaking head.

I couldn't hold it back.

"I can't hold it back."

My thoughts came tumbling out of my mouth.

It was so cold.

"So cold."

I wanted...

"I want..."

Warmth.

"Agnella? You seem confused. Very well," Sister Abigail declared. "Whatever the reason, I understand you are willing to accept the punishment of your brethren. I accept this request. Very good. Julian of Norwich, the Saint of Sight, who beheld a vision of God's will in this very land once said, 'All shall be well.' Therefore, I shall forgive Georgie's sins. In exchange, I shall visit upon you three blows from Julian and revoke your rights to the tokens and special allowance. Until that time, you may rest over here."

Given her absolute faith in trials, she was, ironically, very much in favor of taking on other people's punishments. She viewed my strange behavior in a positive light.

At her word, two of the nuns stepped forward and grabbed my arms. Another nun opened the orphanage van's sliding door.

"No, you can't!" Georgie cried.

"Agnella!" Cathy sniffled, watching all of this from a distance.

"Idiot," Yolanda hissed.

I saw everything. I heard everything. But...

I was...

❧

Blood fell like rain. The heart was still beating.

The delightful squelching sound reached its crescendo, and the bones and flesh collapsed. The tendons and muscles and nerves and blood vessels came tumbling out of the body. Blood spread, darkening as it lost oxygen, cooling as its heat faded. The ground's moisture formed needle ice, which absorbed the pool of blood and turned it a brilliant red. Crimson ice needles. Ah. Such a waste. I closed the wound while he screamed in pain. This wasn't good. The sound might summon unexpected company. I reached both arms up and wrapped them around his neck, pulling his face close, sealing his lips with mine. I pushed inside to the back of his throat, all the way through the stomach and into the intestines. There, I savored the gurgling sound he made as he drowned and spent a pleasant time in his embrace.

I was...

❦

I woke up. The van door was still open. They hadn't yet shoved me inside.

Oddly, there was no one around. No customers, no one working the booths or attractions. Not even the nuns, or the other children, or Sister Abigail. Just rows of attractions and rides, music playing as if nothing were amiss. The lights brightened the night sky. I guess the funfair itself wasn't over yet.

"Georgie? Yolanda? Cathy?"

No one answered.

Just in case, I called for Sister Abigail and the other nuns, too. No response. Everyone had vanished. What was going on?

"Ow..."

My headache was totally gone. I felt like a mist had lifted, clearing my thoughts. But I also felt a dull, heavy pain below my waist. Still, I wouldn't get answers just standing around like this, so I started walking.

It was like walking through old photos of Coney Island, some foreign amusement park with more staff than customers. This was a desolate place; a very strange experience. I walked through the center of the fair, gazing up at the big, flashy merry-go-round. I passed the deserted chocolate banana stand and a punching machine. I ducked under a roof laden with magic 8-balls—presumably the winner's prize—and walked on down the empty main road.

"Another merry-go-round?" I muttered.

Before I knew it, I was at the very back of the fairgrounds, where I discovered a smaller merry-go-round. Warm, orange bulbs covered this one, and an organ played a friendly song. The ride chugged along softly like a locomotive as it slowly turned. Of course, there were no riders. Ponies made up more than half the animals on the slowly turning stage, but I also saw baby elephants, a Pegasus, giraffes, and dragons. They all looked as if they were having a great time. Antikythera, Becky, Charlotte, David, Elizabeth; each of them had a name tag, displayed in alphabetical order. All of them looked old. They'd clearly been running around this platform for a long time. Their creaky movements certainly weren't smooth, but they were well oiled, and their bodies appeared waxed and shiny. Someone had done a good job of maintaining them.

"Oh."

As I stared, flickering, hazy green lights appeared atop the animals. The lights held the reins and danced around on the carved wooden saddles.

Boys? No, girls.

They frolicked and played among the ponies.

Their hair fluttered gracefully. Their long limbs, if human sized, would undoubtedly appear very beautiful. But their legs turned into birds' feet at the knees, and colorfully-feathered wings sprouted from their shoulders. These wings were small however; it was hard to say how they'd ever get airborne. Their big, black eyes darted this way and that, teeming with curiosity. These girls were tiny, the largest of them barely a foot tall. They flitted and danced happily through the air.

What a rare sight, especially in town.

When had I first seen them? I'd first noticed them when I was very little and my adopted siblings took me into the forest. On the bank of a small pond, insects I'd never seen before swarmed through the air in spiral columns. But the other children ran right into the middle of that swarm, clearly unable to see them. That's when it all began. I thought I'd imagined it, but the eldest girl, who'd kept her head in the swarm the longest, came down with a nasty fever after we got home. After that, I was sure there were things in this world that only I could see.

Humanoid creatures like these girls weren't so bad.

Sometimes I'd see unfamiliar birds dart across the sky, or I'd glimpse an ungulate-like creature I could not identify. The easiest to see were swarms of insects, invisible except for their wings as they fluttered in the air. Or there were the black, mist-like patches that you couldn't focus on no matter how hard you stared.

Sometimes I'd encounter things I instinctively knew to avoid, certain that if our eyes met just once I wouldn't survive. I could smell the danger on them.

I mostly saw these creatures around old trees or hollows in the forest, near moss-covered rocks or springs, near faerie rings of mushrooms. So it wasn't all that difficult to act with caution and avoid them.

But honestly, I only knew they existed. I'd never communicated with them at all. They seemed wary of me, so if I ignored them, they wouldn't approach.

"What are they though?" I muttered aloud.

"Them? They're Gallopers."

That surprising answer came from a hoarse, alcohol-roughened voice.

"Who?!"

I jumped and turned around. In the merry-go-round's shadows, I saw a little hut. The word "Fortunes" was written in brilliant bulbs on the roof. People in a festive mood and ripe with a little booze would enter that hut hoping to speak with some magical thing—a god, Tarot, or a crystal ball. Such people wanted some guarantee of future happiness, a fortune teller's bread and butter.

I moved closer.

In the shadow of the entrance, an old woman sat behind an oddly-shaped, three-legged table. She wore Romani clothes, presenting the classic picture of a fortune teller, but I couldn't tell if she was a real Romani. I was only certain she was very old. An elaborately decorated Easter egg stood upright on the messy desk before her. The egg wobbled but somehow maintained its balance.

"Open those eyes of yours, and you'll soon understand. The wooden horses are all racing clockwise, yes? That's how you know it's a proper British Roundabout."

The woman seemed disinclined to identify herself. Well, she was right about this much; these horses definitely ran clockwise. The horses nearest me all faced left.

"An American Carousel will have them running counter. I'm sure you saw that one in the central clearing, all those Yankee horses that don't know what it is to be tired."

The old woman waved a hand dismissively.

"Their proper name is Gallopers. They're steam-powered, the old-fashioned way, slower than you could walk. Old-timers. They're verging on a hundred, you know."

She laughed. Honestly, at first I'd assumed "Gallopers" was a name for the tiny girls.

"So," she said, after a dramatic pause. "The little green ones flitting all about them? *Those* are good neighbors."

My jaw dropped, and I let out a strange little squeak.

"You can see them, right?" she said.

I wasn't sure what to say. While I gaped at her, she looked closely at my face. Her eyes were different colors and seemed to see right through me. From the way she moved, I could tell she was nearly blind.

"Hmm. I wondered why... That explains it," she muttered to herself.

"Wait, wh-what do you mean, 'good neighbors'?" I asked.

"Oh, you don't know?" she smiled. "Never heard of them in your bedtime stories?"

I shook my head.

"I...don't have any parents, so...no stories."

"Parents? Hmm. I see. Well, there you have it." She nodded, not at all sorry.

"Um..."

"Right. If you want to ask, sit yourself down."

She pointed to an empty chair. I sat down. Woven cane covered the seat and felt strange beneath me. It seemed light enough for easy transport, handy for Romani. It was oddly shaped but embraced my hips comfortably.

"So, about *them*."

I glanced back at the Roundabout, at the girls playing around the ride.

"Like I said. They're the true friends, the good folk, the Daoine Sídhe, the wee folk. They live in the forests and at the bottom of ponds, in the soil and mud, in the shadows of rocks, and sometimes in the hawthorn trees. We call them neighbors. You may know them better as faeries or spirits."

She reached into her pocket and pulled out a well-worn deck of Tarot cards. She shuffled and began laying them out on the table with unsteady hands.

"Specifically, those ones are Ariel. You might know them from Shakespeare's *The Tempest*."

I didn't, but I know what she was trying to tell me. They were the wind. They had wings and antennae, like insects.

"So they *are* faeries," I said. I'd wondered if they might

be, but I'd never told anyone I could see them and never met anyone else who could. That word had long stayed buried within me.

The old woman snorted. "The neighbors are all quite whimsical, the Ariel included. They often snatch away children or brides, tear up fields, and cause all sorts of damage. Don't ever call them by their true name—it's too dangerous. That's why we have so many other names for them."

"Oh."

"Everything started with a word: 'Let there be light.' A name grants one control over something, outside and in. Speaking of which, what's your name?"

"Oh. Agnella."

"Hope? Hmm, good name for a fatherless child. Let's see," she said and flipped one of the cards on the table.

The card displayed a beautiful, naked woman with a vase in each hand, pouring water onto the earth. Water from one vase formed a lake, while the other caused buds to rise from the ground. One giant star winked in the sky, and seven smaller stars clustered around it. It appeared to be early morning. On a branch in the background, a bird announced the dawn.

"Star," the old woman whispered. She reached out and turned another card—I wasn't sure if this was at random or following a specific sequence.

This time, the card showed an old, bearded man in a robe. He held a lantern in his right hand and a staff in his left. He appeared to be standing on some mountain precipice. He looked down upon a sea of clouds, nothing but empty space around him. There was something unworldly about his eyes as he gazed below.

"Hermit."

Her brows twitched when she turned the card. Was that not good? For too long I'd nervously watched people's faces, and now I picked up on the slightest changes in expression.

"Well, what next?"

She turned over another card.

"What?" I whispered the moment I saw the picture.

The words weren't English, so I couldn't read them, but the message was clear. Bad omens crowded the picture.

"The Tower," she said, her voice low.

Against a star-filled sky, a tower was being destroyed. Lightning struck the tower's summit and it collapsed, consumed by flames. In the air, I saw a golden crown, shooting flames, the lightning, stone fragments, and two men who screamed as they fell to the earth.

"Choose the last card yourself," the old woman said, looking up at me.

"But..."

"Doesn't matter which. These cards are older than me or that Roundabout, so treat them gently."

"S-sure."

I looked over the cards, around twenty in all. Three of them had already been turned face up.

They looked at me, and I looked at them. Which should I choose?

Then... Though it wasn't that unnatural for a winter's night, I felt a chill.

I reached out a hand, my fingers so numb I could scarcely move them.

The cold.

I knew this sensation; knew it well.

Inside my head, my guts, something was oozing. The core of me was somewhere warm, protected. My toes and fingers felt frozen, the cold slowly creeping up my arms and legs, leeching away my warmth.

"Oh." The old woman gasped.

I started, as if waking up from a trance.

Shaking my head, I looked down to find four cards face up.

"Did I turn that?" I asked.

"Yes." She nodded, her half-blind eyes staring at the card.

The card showed a man seated behind a three-legged table laden with cups, knives, and dice. A single leaf sprouted beneath his feet. His hair was curled and golden, and he wore a giant Bicorne hat twisted into the shape of the infinity symbol. He held a short stick in his left hand and a coin in his right. His brightly colored tunic was asymmetrical, and he wore pointy leather shoes over his tight leggings. He looked like...

"A clown?"

"No," the old woman said—I realized that her table exactly resembled the one in the card. "Although some would say there's little difference. He's the Magician, a card that shows the power you have."

"Power? You mean this weird—"

She shook her head.

"Nothing weird about it. Snakes see heat. Whales see sound. Wolves see scents. You see neighbors. Not everyone has a talent like yours. That's all."

"But—"

"Or perhaps anyone can see them under the right circumstances. The power itself is nothing special, just a power. A power any potential mage or alchemist has."

"A mage?"

I'd heard about them. There were few left, but real mages existed. Some were strong enough that the church couldn't just ignore them, but the authorities claimed the existence of mages helped proved that God was real.

THE ANCIENT MAGUS' BRIDE

"Agnella."

At my name, I startled. The old woman's eyes fixed directly on mine.

"I'm going to ask something strange, but can you answer?"

"Okay."

She hesitated, then said, "Are you happy now? Or the opposite?"

"Huh?"

Good question. Was I happy, or was I unhappy? When I'd lived with my adoptive parents I never would have even understood the question, but I may have a better idea now.

There was a story that went like this: A city mule met a country mule by the side of the road. The country mule carried a heavy burden on his back. His shoes were worn-out, so he walked very slowly. But the city mule's load was light, and he walked with a prance in every step.

The city mule said, "Oh, what a poor, unfortunate mule you are! Such a heavy load! You're doing such hard labor."

But the country mule just asked, "What's labor?"

I was now conscious of both fortune and misfortune, and I knew I wasn't fortunate. But at the same time, I'd never experienced good fortune. Did that make me unhappy? Or happy?

"Then what do you want, Agnella? We all said what *we* wanted." Yolanda had been lying on the top bunk opposite me, head propped up on her elbow.

We'd often chatted until we fell asleep. That day, I'd had nothing to say. Unlike the other three, I didn't have a dream.

"I don't know," I replied, gazing at the old woman.

"I see. If you could understand that, then...I wondered if maybe something like you could actually understand humans."

The old woman shook her head, gathering up the cards from the table.

"That's why you ate them? The dreams. Ate them whole. But you still didn't understand?"

Dreams. Like she'd read my mind.

"Huh?!"

What did she mean? What was she saying? Why was she saying that? Wasn't she just telling my fortune? My heart ached. A terrible pain started in my lower belly.

"Um, how much... I'm sorry, I don't have any money. So. Could you give me a good fortune?" But I had nothing with which to pay.

"There's nothing good or bad about it. I'm just here to check the milk that's been spilled," she said, sighing.

"Milk?"

"Like karma. Can't get ahead of it to stop it. Can only see the result. Spilled milk can't go back in the jug, but I always believe there may have been a better way for it to spill."

She sighed louder.

"Listen close, Agnella. You're a changeling."

"A...changeling?"

"Faeries snatch human children away sometimes. Sometimes they take and dote on the children, other times they work the children hard. Sometimes they eat the children, but sometimes they even fall in love. If they just snatched the children, then that would be the end of it. But sometimes they leave a faerie or troll child behind instead. Those are changelings."

"Then I'm..."

I remembered my adoptive father's oft-told story, about the green light in the barn hatch. Emerald. Something everyone could see under the right circumstances...

Everything wrong in my life suddenly made sense.

What irony was this? The real me had been abandoned by her parents the moment she was born. Yet they'd wanted her, and to cover for it they left me behind...

Oh. Head to toe, start to finish, I was...

"I'm not...human?"

"Far from it."

She put the last Tarot card back in the deck and moved to the desk in the corner. She picked up the Easter egg and gave it a little shake.

"For most changelings, this egg alone can start them over. But it seems you're a more troubling type."

"I don't understand."

"The goats. What happened to Gray and White? Did you say goodbye?" she asked.

"What?"

"The bull. What happened to Brown's body? Did you dig a grave for him?"

"Uhh... I..."

"Why did your adoptive mother and father fear you? Why would they spend all that time raising you to the point where you could finally work, yet sell you away to an orphanage for a pittance right after losing Brown?"

"I... I was... I... Gray...and White..."

"Like I said, the milk's already spilled."

She put her elbows on the table, steepling her fingers.

"When did it first spill? A long time ago, when Brown died and his body vanished. And shortly after that, when both goats disappeared. Perhaps when you ate Agnella and became her. You are the one who snatched her away and at the same time the one who was snatched away. And..."

"Ah," I whispered.

"You were never a faerie."

❧

Plop.

At last, Brown's head melted and fell off. Oh well. Outside, I held him in my arms; inside, I flowed through him, melting him. I carefully picked up the head and this time hugged all of it to me, piercing the skull, tearing through the membrane, melting into the soft, grayish brain. Maybe I melted too much. I temporarily increased my volume and came spilling out his eye sockets, mouth, nostrils, and ear holes.

His heart had stopped beating. Green light surrounded the faeries in the barn hatch, who watched me with interest.

At last all the warmth was gone, fragments of his body and the bloodstain all that remained. I wiped some of it up, thinking if I dug a hole I could maybe hide some more; but not all. There was no way to avoid questions entirely.

Oh well. At least I'd been able to savor all his warmth before his weakening heart had stopped.

Gray and White huddled together in the corner,

frightened and bleating. Oh, some day I would have to say goodbye to them as well. I'd lose their warmth, too. If that happened, what would I do?

❦

Oh. I was...something else entirely.

❦

When I woke up, I saw hell.

A sea of blood and guts lay before me. The Ferris wheel, the moon, the smell on the wind, and my own rotten scent blended in harmony, all combining to make this place look like the lid to hell had blown off.

Funfair customers sobbed, as did the orphanage children. Yolanda pulled Cathy away. Poor things. Poor, poor things. My heart ached. I thought it strange I had a heart that *could* ache.

"If you could understand that, then..." I muttered.

Perhaps these emotions were the answer that old woman had been after. In which case, perhaps I might have had a slightly different future. I wasn't sure. It was too late now. Forget milk; I'd spilled deep crimson that sprayed all around, filling my insides.

The air smelled of smoke and cold. A heavy fog covered us, like this was London.

I looked around. I saw half of Sister Abigail's face lying in the mud next to Julian. Her eyes, wide open, glared uselessly into the air. More pieces of her had been scattered far and wide, mauled beyond recognition. The other nuns had met the same fate, along with some of the children. The pieces were mixed together, all half-melted. Cold. But they didn't fill me. They couldn't fill me. They could never warm me.

"Georgie."

I tried whispering his name but wasn't sure I'd made a sound at all. I could feel precious warmth moving in me, as if in answer.

Crybaby Georgie no longer had the power to struggle. He'd melted in my belly, dreaming of his Mum and Dad.

Who was that old woman anyway? My thoughts connected my dream to reality. Had it really been a dream? Probably not. That may have been a real mage, so that "dream" was probably second sight. I was no saint—I wasn't even human—but I'd given those nuns a *great* revelation.

My throat rattled at the irony. Did I even *have* a throat anymore? Didn't matter anyway. What mattered was that I was here. I was here. Now we were both Agnella, and that was good. I shook my head and sighed. Sticky drops rained upon the earth with a squelching sound.

It was cold. I needed warmth. I needed Cathy and Yolanda. With them and Georgie, that would make three. I needed them to fill me, warm the inside of me, occlude, unify, mate, meld, mix. Melt together. Become one. Then I would understand a little better, a little more than now. About humans. About something. Mmm. I was sure.

Then I sang a little song, leaving a sticky trail behind me as I slithered toward them.

The End

Jack the Flash and the Rainbow Egg (Part 2)

YUU GODAI

7

"Now, then," I said, hands on my hips. "Tell us everything."

"About what?"

We were in my Brooklyn office. We'd snatched Jeffrey away from the gangsters and brought him here roughly twelve hours ago. Presumably, the crooks had recovered from the shock of meeting the theater's famous ghost skeleton by now—well, maybe it would take a bit more time for them to process everything. I'm sure Roderick had thoroughly enjoyed his moment in the limelight. Anyway, by now they must've been spread out across New York, searching for the man in the punk band T-shirt. But they didn't know that a jeans-clad woman—well, faerie— had snatched him.

Of course, there was no way a human could enter this office or even notice it. That was one reason I'd brought Jeffrey here. Nobody, not even an alchemist or another faerie could enter if I didn't let them in. The alchemist landlord who owned the place was a greedy son of a bitch, but, in return for brutally high rent, he *did* provide flawless security.

Larry was out buying himself a new jacket with what meager cash I'd managed to scrape together. With the loud-mouthed, sulky brat out of the picture, all I had to deal with was the *sullen,* sulky brat.

Jeffrey had been stunned silent while I'd hauled him around, but now, seated on a couch in my office, he quickly got his bearings.

He'd spent a while yowling about how he wanted to go back to Laura or freaking out about what his boss would do. After a series of empty threats, I made him go stiff and left him lying on the floor, unable to talk until he cooled off. Now he was sullenly sitting on the couch, knees bouncing nervously, glancing regularly at the leather pouch lying on the table between us.

"You oughta tell me who you are first," he said, trying his best to snarl but failing to hide the tremor in his voice. He tried grabbing the pouch off the table, but I was faster. "Hey!" he yelped.

The pouch floated high above his head. He tried to jump and grab it, but it wafted this way and that like a balloon in the wind.

"What the heck? Some sort of magic trick? Who the hell are you? What did you do to them? That skeleton—"

"Yeah, yeah, that's enough." The pouch flew to my hand. Even through the dampener I could feel the magic energy coming off the bag, beating like the heart of a bird. "Remember, I'm the one asking the questions. If it weren't for me, they'd have turned you into Swiss cheese. Only Swiss cheese don't bleed, and you sure would have."

That shut him up. He went red in the face and then pale. He looked from the pouch in my hand to me, and then sank into the sofa like his strings had snapped.

"I'm Jack. That's all I'm prepared to offer by way of introduction. The original owner of this...jewel...hired me. It's my job to recover it."

No reason to tell this human it was a dragon egg. Jeffrey was already plenty confused.

"That led me to Laura Winfrey, and you happened to be there, Jeffrey Chandler."

"How do you know my name?!"

I glanced at the table. A laptop appeared where the pouch had been. The screen opened, the computer turned itself on, and a number of files opened on the screen—the data the Baron had sent me.

When the laptop appeared, Jeffrey jumped like a bomb had gone off under his nose. But as the computer displayed one piece of data after another, he leaned closer until he was almost touching the screen.

"You're kidding," he said. "How do you have that photo? There was nobody there!"

"The walls have ears, and the shoji have eyes," I said, a Japanese expression I'd picked up from some anime. Jeffrey just blinked at me. "In other words, no matter how hard you try to hide them, secrets always get out. Just think of me as an investigator with really good eyes and ears."

I made a mental note to apologize to the Baron for claiming credit for his work. Didn't want him pulling another prank on me like the other day, when everything I'd typed had started line dancing across the screen.

"My information network caught you and your girlfriend, Jeffrey Chandler. Why is Richard Diefenbaker so obsessed with Laura? Keeping her prisoner, making her sing for him, and procuring jewels like this for her?"

I tossed the pouch lightly. Jeffrey twitched like it was about to sprout wings and fly away.

"Just to be clear, no one obtains this through any legitimate channels. This is a piece that would normally never reach the world at large. So how do *you* have something like that? A big shot like Richard Diefenbaker oughta be able to get something equally impressive from a legitimate source without ever dealing with someone like you."

Of course, that would be true for an ordinary jewel. No real jewel could ever compare to a dragon egg.

But to a human without magical knowledge, this egg would appear to be nothing more than an especially large, extremely high-quality opal. Most women would rather have diamonds, rubies, or emeralds. Of course, given just how much magic was concentrated in this thing, even an ordinary human would be drawn to it, unable to take their eyes off it. But buying an item of dubious origin on the black market didn't fit someone like Richard Diefenbaker at all.

"I mean, Diefenbaker must own any number of hotels or penthouses, much nicer places. Why isn't he keeping Laura in one of those? Wall Street kings don't usually lock girls up in the basement and make them sing. He can buy crazy expensive presents for her, so why isn't he treating her like a jewel? If her being on stage is such a big deal, then buy a local theater, staff and all, put a show together for her, and make Laura Winfrey an actual star— that'd be way easier. Why is she locked up in that decrepit, dirty room?"

I made another mental note to apologize to Roderick for that one. He'd helped me out, so it was low to go around insulting the theater he held dear.

"Instead, this guy hires a bunch of gangsters who drive any potential audience away. I dunno what Diefenbaker himself is after, but all that'll do is scare the girl. What the hell is he thinking?"

"Hell if I know!"

Jeffrey had calmed down somewhat while I was talking. The tension drained out of his shoulders. He looked much smaller; maybe exhaustion had taken hold. His arms hung limp at his sides, and he sank listlessly into the couch.

"I've known Laura since we were kids back in Kansas. Went to the same grade school, sat next to each other. She was always good at singing."

A dreamy look crossed his eyes, that rainbow glaze people get reflecting on the good times. My heart ached. I'd yet to have times like those.

"She always sang a solo at school concerts. Said she'd star in a musical one day, and I really thought she would. So when she went to New York after high school looking for work on Broadway, I was worried, but rooted for her. I thought she had what it took, you know? But..."

His laid-back Kansas accent slipped out from under the city-tough routine.

"I started hearing from her less. She never answered the phone. Then she stopped responding to emails. I couldn't bear it anymore, so I told my mom I was gonna look for a job here and came to New York. But she'd quit her waitress job and was holed up in her room somewhere, and I couldn't track her down."

The Baron's data had given me some of their back story.

Laura had started out waiting tables for room and board, and after she quit that she went from job to job, failing all her auditions. Occasionally she'd land a bit part, or an understudy, or get cast as a chorus member, but reality didn't work like the movies. Cinderella stories where the God-like producer spots the talented country girl didn't happen every day.

Meanwhile, Jeffrey had come after Laura—it could've been a movie title, *Chasing Laura*—and gotten lost in New York, both literally and spiritually. Local hoodlums kept him around as a handy errand boy, but he found no real work. After ditching the Kansas accent, he stole a few cars and picked a few pockets poorly, then got himself briefly sent to jail. The cops had a mountain of serious crimes and no time to deal with a small fry like him. Much as I hated to admit it, the Baron's chewing gum metaphor fit with how both the cops and the hoodlums had treated him.

"So how's a boy from Kansas get something like this?" I asked.

"I was at JFK, looking for a decent mark."

Jeffrey shifted uncomfortably, avoiding my eyes and twiddling his thumbs.

He'd planned on snatching bags from a passenger at JFK airport and was hanging out in the lobby with a few similarly minded companions. No one gave him much credit for his actual thieving skills, so he was acting as a lookout and a mark spotter when he noticed a commotion in customs.

When people are distracted by something, they often forget about the baggage in hand. Thinking this might be his chance, he stepped closer. He saw a nondescript man sidle up to a distracted woman and slip something in her shopping bag.

Hiding valuables in innocent tourists' luggage was a common means of smuggling items into a foreign country. Jeffrey decided it was worth the risk. He swiped the lady's shopping bag, took it to the bathroom, and checked the contents.

"It was just a bunch of cheap crap, like chocolate, scarves, and a snow globe of the Statue of Liberty. But buried in that pile of junk was a necklace with a fabulous jewel tucked in a blue velvet box."

Jeffrey closed his eyes, as if remembering the shock of that moment. I was starting to wonder if he might have a mild sensitivity to magic. The tinge of reverence that stole over his gaunt face didn't seem like the right reaction for your average small-time crook.

"I've never seen any really valuable jewels, but I could tell this was the real deal. I stuck it under my shirt, box and all, tightened my belt to hold it steady, and ditched the rest."

"You didn't mention it to your friends? Quite the prize."

"To those assholes?" Jeffrey scoffed. He seemed to surprise himself with the force of his reaction and shifted his gaze nervously. "Well, normally I would have. I guess. You're right. But my mind went blank; I couldn't think of anything besides the jewel. Before I knew it, I hopped on a bus and left the airport behind. I haven't seen any of those guys since. I changed pads, laid low a while..."

He went quiet again for a minute and then appeared to make up his mind.

"Truth is, I got sorta obsessed with this necklace. Just holding the box made my whole body feel warm, made me happier than anything. Not like a high or nothing. Like when Laura and I were little and having a picnic on Father Donny's farm, petting the foals and eating sandwiches and strawberry shortcake. Like I was riding on the clouds." Jeffrey looked up at me, his eyes pleading. "You know what I mean?"

I did. Totally. I wasn't a faerie for nothing.

He wasn't exactly an alchemist, but he definitely had some level of sensitivity to magic. Otherwise, he'd never have felt this way about the jewel—the dragon egg. A human with no talent for magic would have just treated it like any other jewel, no matter how beautiful.

And I had to be grateful that the man who'd obtained the egg just so happened to be sensitive enough to have some idea of its true value. If your average pickpocket had found the necklace, the egg would have vanished into the darkness of New York, washed up in the sewers of God knows where.

"So how does Richard Diefenbaker get involved?" I asked.

"Well, I ran outta money," Jeffrey said. He slipped his hands under himself, shifting uncomfortably. "I went uptown, hoping to earn a little something. Didn't wanna run into my old group, so I was wandering around Fifth Avenue when suddenly..." He broke off, looking at me.

"What?" I said, sternly.

He stared at his hands, muttering, "A crow landed in front of me and spoke to me with a human voice."

He looked at me like a child expecting to be scolded for lying. I didn't bat an eye, which seemed to give him courage.

"It said, 'I know what you have. I know someone who'll pay top dollar for it. There's no use in you holding on to it, but if you deal with me, you'll be rich and safe.'"

I nodded. So here's where the alchemist behind this whole mess came in. Casting spells on animals or dead things was par for the course with them.

"I freaked out a bit," Jeffrey said. "I turned right the hell around and went back to my room. But voices talked to me there, too. Crows, roaches and mice, my curtains, empty takeout boxes... It was like some insane Disney movie."

He licked his lips.

"At first I was so scared I didn't know what to do, but eventually, I decided that, if I was going insane anyway, I may as well answer the crow. I was getting desperate, needed the money. Eventually, I agreed to the deal."

"Is this the boss you mentioned?"

"I dunno if I can call him that. I don't even know his name." Jeffrey shook his head. "But he arranged a meeting, and the deal went down in a little fishing place near the Hudson. The place in the photo."

I looked at the picture again, a grainy security camera

still. Jeffrey was wearing his best suit and looked taller. Richard Diefenbaker's fat face was like a stone, his men clustered all around him as he examined the necklace.

"But," I said, adding just a touch of a growl to my voice, "that wasn't the real jewel, was it?"

"That's what the boss said to do!"

Jeffrey went white; he looked ready to collapse. I summoned a cup of water out of thin air and handed it to him. Jeffrey didn't seem perplexed by where it had come from and gulped it straight down before wiping the sweat from his brow.

"He prepared the fake, too," Jeffrey muttered, keeping his gaze firmly between his knees. "It looked exactly like the real one. Just at a casual glance, nobody would know it was fake. I put the phony in a box to give to the old guy and the real one in a special pouch prepared by the boss. In return, the boss gave me money. A lot of money." His lips trembled. "But...but then I saw the photo in his wallet!"

"Diefenbaker's?" I asked.

"Yes!" Jeffrey slammed the cup down on the table. "It was Laura! *My* Laura! Right there! All dolled up with crazy makeup, but you couldn't fool me! I knew it was her! That dried up old fart had her locked up!

"I was planning on giving the real jewel to the boss

and getting outta dodge, but the moment I saw Laura, it was like getting a glass of water thrown in my face. I remembered the reason I was even here. I'd come to New York to look for Laura! I figured this was my one chance to save her.

"So I called in some favors. Found out who the old man was and learned that he'd bought that theater and had locked Laura up in there.

I figured, if I've got this jewel, I can take Laura and get away. We can go anywhere we want. If I can get the money from the boss or keep the cash and sell off the necklace so no one's the wiser... I thought we'd make more doing that."

"That wasn't the only reason, was it? You didn't want to give the necklace up," I said, interrupting him.

He shut his mouth.

"Or, more importantly, the opal," I added.

If he had even a little magical sensitivity, there was no way he'd be willing to hand the opal—the dragon egg—to someone else so easily. This was a morally challenged, magic sensing lowlife with a rare treasure in his hands. This wasn't something he could give up easily, no matter how much money he stood to make.

The fake this mysterious alchemist had prepared was probably pretty valuable in itself, too. He'd likely used real gems and precious metals that would pass muster as a true piece of jewelry. But nothing compared to the value of a dragon egg.

A dragon egg was a mass of concentrated magic, and more valuable than anything else on earth. Feeding a girl-crazed billionaire a lesser copy while making off with the real one was exactly the sort of scheme a shifty alchemist might come up with.

Jeffrey's lips moved nervously.

"Take it from me, kid. You've stuck your neck in some business you really shouldn't have," I said. "The moment crows started talking to you, you should've dropped everything and run for it. But I am lucky you hung on to this. I'll be keeping it, so you can hide out here for a while. I'll talk things over with Diefenbaker and your boss and settle everything."

"What about Laura?" Jeffrey said, tears welling up in his eyes. "You left her there!"

"Oh, be quiet! Yeah, I'll take care of Laura too, okay? You behave yourself, kid. I do this sort of thing for a living. Once this gets back to its rightful owner, I'll help you out, you and Laura. I'm sure my employer will approve the expense."

"So I *do* have to give it back?" he asked.

"Of course!" I snapped. Jeffrey jumped and shrank

against the couch like a whipped puppy. Maybe that really *had* been a blow. I still had a bad habit of releasing magical energy when my emotions got the better of me; not a great idea in this line of work.

"I'll go talk to my employer," I said, avoiding the pitiable look in Jeffrey's eyes. "You watch the place, Jeffrey Chandler. Larry gets back, you fill him in, order some food, watch TV, play games, whatever. But don't even *think* about leaving here and going back to that theater, not unless you want both you and Laura turned into Swiss cheese."

That was enough for Jeffrey. He cringed and nodded. I didn't place a lot of stock in the man's moral code, but at least his feelings for Laura were real. If she was in danger, he'd stay here for now. Besides, normal people couldn't get out of my office any more easily than they could get in.

"I don't like it, Jack," Evan Dean said. We were in his filthy office, the ashtray piled high with cigarette butts. He leaned back in his chair, resting his well-worn shoes on the desk, looking less like a lawyer (his public persona) or an alchemist (his private one) than a stereotypical gumshoe detective. He nailed the part more than I ever would actually.

"You got the goods, that oughta be the end of it. Why you gotta keep meddling? Hand the thing over and you're done. With that special bonus, too."

He glanced sideways at his desk drawer. It took so much effort on my part not to follow his gaze. The drawer contained something I longed for—a booklet of dreams I'd drooled over at events and on Yahoo auctions nearly every night. In my fangirl fantasies the little limited edition book, signed by the voice actors and manga artist, danced ever nearer...

I coughed, making sure my voice carried.

"Can't do it that way, Dean."

"What?!" He'd been leaning over the desk, but now he shoved all the way back. I waved the pouch with the dragon egg.

"This has a strong magic dampener on it. I've heard Jeffrey Chandler's story, there's a powerful alchemist pulling strings behind this mess. Until I find him and catch him, the case ain't over."

"*We'll* think of a way to handle the alchemist ourselves," Dean groaned. "Alchemists deal with their own problems. No place for a changeling faerie to get involved."

"No matter what you say, I'm not handing this over to you, Dean. You may as well just report it to Lindel."

I traced a circle in the air with my finger. The circle

became a glittering gold thread that tied up the pouch. I hung it around my neck, tucking it into my bra to keep it out of the way.

"I get in quick, and I get out quick, but Jack the Flash never abandons a half-solved case. Round the whole thing up and finish it off, that's my policy."

"I don't give a damn about your policy," Dean said, spraying spit. "Gimme that thing!"

"Too bad!"

I turned and left the nicotine stench of his office. The door slammed behind me, but I wasn't sure which of us had done it. Maybe both of us had at once. I could feel Dean's glare boring into my back even through the door and the mountain of cigarette butts.

8

DEAN CERTAINLY had a point. Actually, I was pretty sure he had me dead to rights. I'd recovered the item, which should've been the end. Lindel would hardly be pleased with the delay and even less pleased that I was keeping the egg at all.

But I really didn't want to give it to Dean. I felt like placing something this beautiful in his nicotine-stained hands would be tantamount to blasphemy.

I may not be able to hand it directly to Lindel, but if I contacted him, he'd send someone to fetch it. Just as he'd explained the job in person, it only felt right to return the thing to him directly. Besides, I hadn't yet uncovered the alchemist behind all this. As long as I kept the egg, there was a good chance I'd flush out my quarry.

I know, I admit it. I just didn't want to let the egg go.

At the very least, I wanted to keep it a little longer. I'd accept any criticisms about unprofessional behavior. Any faerie that's ever been drawn to the sweet honey of a sleigh beggy would understand, I'm sure. This was instinct trumping reason. No faerie could easily resist the impulse to keep pure, powerful magic at their side. Those with no self-control would snatch it and try to run. Perhaps I couldn't blame Jeffrey for doing just that.

Feeling a little guilty, I told myself the delay was temporary. Just a few hours. I'd save Jeffrey and Laura, pop that dirty old man Richard Diefenbaker right in the kisser, then give the egg back. Let the alchemists handle the alchemist. They had some sort of council; no place for a faerie like me to butt in. If one of them had made a mockery of the ancient mage Echos and tried to swipe a powerful item for himself, the other alchemists would drag him down and punish him accordingly. The egg in my bra was beating like a second heart. I could tell my own heart was beating almost as fast.

"Sorry," I whispered. "I'll get you back to your family as soon as possible. Just hang on a little longer."

I considered going back to the office but decided this wasn't worth bringing Larry. He was probably still trying on different jackets, or maybe he'd swung by the game store and got caught up playing a demo. Considering Larry's priorities, I wouldn't be the least bit surprised if I got home to find him with a new game and no jacket.

Now, Richard Diefenbaker. I took out my phone and dialed a number. It rang a few times, then picked up.

"Here's looking at you, kid," said Humphrey Bogart's sexy voice. "Now, what sort of help does my Ilsa need?"

"No time to joke around, Baron," I said. "You know where Richard Diefenbaker is right now?"

"The Plaza Hotel," he said, without a second's hesitation. "He's been in a condo there for over a month. Spending what anyone else would consider a sizable fortune on a daily basis, but it's pocket lint compared to his overall worth. You gonna go at him direct?"

"More or less. Can you talk to your friends in the security system there and have them let me through? I'll handle the non-magical side myself, but I don't wanna trip any magical security they may have."

"Okay. Easily done, kid."

Baron gave a satisfied chuckle. An electronic spirit with no voice or body, when he needed to talk he used voice data sampled from movies and music. *Casablanca* was one of his favorites, so he'd pull out the Bogart act at the slightest opportunity.

"The security spirit there evolved from a copy of myself, so it'll be a cinch. Oh, look at that; we already worked it out. You can waltz in. Want me to slip a meeting with him onto his schedule? I'm sure his secretary will just assume she overlooked it."

"Thanks for the offer, but I'll pass. Don't wanna make problems for anyone if I don't have to."

At the Plaza Hotel, there'd be lots of magical types around. The building had quite a history, and history naturally attracts magic. The few alchemists rich enough to live here wouldn't appreciate trouble, and if they found out I was walking around with a dragon egg, all hell would break loose.

Hmm. Trouble... A distraction... "But if you could cause some sort of commotion right when I enter the building? Nothing major. Something that'll give me a few minutes with Diefenbaker alone."

"Your wish is my command. Is that all you require of your humble investigator?"

Crap, he'd definitely overheard that.

"That's all for now. And, uh...I'll make up for that other thing. I promise."

"Lookin' forward to it, sweetheart," he said, in a sexy whisper. He made a kissing noise and hung up. The Baron was somewhere on the network, hiding out in a logical construct I couldn't begin to imagine, eagerly awaiting the show I was about to provide.

There are loads of sci-fi films about AI evolving to the point where they rebel and destroy humanity. Total slander. Spirits like the Baron all love people. Or at least, they see humanity as a fascinating mass of chaos, one that produces a flood of delicious data. Just as humans don't kill chickens that lay eggs or cows that produce milk, creatures like the Baron would never destroy the humans that provide such good lunches and hearty dinners. I imagined Baron and the other electric loa with napkins spread on their laps, metaphorical knives and forks at the ready, licking their lips in anticipation of a four-course information meal.

I hoped that smorgasbord I'd given him wiped the slate clean on the whole investigator thing! Muttering as much, I walked north on Broadway and turned right near Central Park. The Plaza Hotel was on Fifth Avenue, not far from Dean's office.

Slipping between fast-walking New Yorkers and slow-moving tourists, I soon saw the Fifth Ave. fountain.

I passed the rows of horse-drawn carriages, went under the world flags hanging outside, and stepped into the massive lobby. My head spun from all the magical security cast on the hotel, not to mention the massive chandeliers and elegant flower arrangements. Of course, I'd seen my share of overwhelming sights in Tír na nÓg, but this hotel was...yeah. For someone like me, who straddled the line between human and faerie, this place was something special. Human and magic societies overlapped here in the realm of dreams. People came in pursuit of those dreams and left intoxicated by them. Historical incidents and the pitter-patter of human hearts piled up here, creating magic that would rival that of any great theater.

Work had brought me here any number of times, but I'd never actually gone past the lobby. I lifted my chin, made a bored New Yorker face, and fiddled with my phone. The Baron had sent a schematic of the hotel layout along with a list of current residents. Apparently, Diefenbaker was in an eye-poppingly expensive condominium on the twelfth floor overlooking Central Park.

There was a special entrance for condo owners, but one of the alchemists had cast a personal defensive spell, which meant I couldn't use it. Oh well. I'd figure it out once I was inside. I walked through the lobby like I owned the place, navigated the flow of guests into the Oak Bar, and headed for the elevators.

The uniformed bellboy didn't bat an eye. As soon as I'd stepped into the hotel I'd put my feet in the faerie realm, hiding myself from human eyes. Magical or unmagical, I was definitely a suspicious intruder, but at the very least no alarms went off. No security guards ran toward me. The Baron must have made arrangements.

I hopped into the elevator, following some guests dragging trunks behind them. The elevator itself was large but no bigger than your average New York apartment building. It stopped on the eighth floor. The other guests got off, so I did, too. This was the furthest the elevator went. To get higher, you needed to be either rich or famous enough to purchase a condo, your standard capitalism-based caste system.

I stopped and looked up at the ceiling. I peered through the soothing indirect lighting, white satin, and dark oak wainscoting, scoping out the floors above. I double-checked this against my phone and saw that Diefenbaker's condo was right above me. I put my phone away, took a deep breath, and stepped further into the faerie world. The hotel corridor around me wavered like it was underwater. I kicked the floor.

Sparkly stuff streamed past me. The forest of the faerie realm overlapped with the hotel interior. Out of the corners of my eyes, I could see the dark shadows of the alchemists' personal protection spells.

After a brief floating sensation, my feet sank into a thick plush carpet. My surroundings snapped back into focus.

I stood in the middle of a large living room decorated in dark blues and moss greens. The furniture looked imposing. Bookshelves crowded with leather bound books covered an entire wall. It didn't look like most of these books had been read. There was a mini bar stocked with every type of liquor, a glass of red wine on the table, classy light fixtures, and a giant window that opened onto blue skies and Central Park. A man in an expensive smoking jacket sat in a large wing chair near the window, perusing some documents with an irritated look.

There was a muffled explosion, and the sound of people screaming and running around. Guess the Baron had delivered on that distraction. At the noise, Richard Diefenbaker raised his head, saw me, and looked surprised. The documents slipped out of his hand.

"Sorry for the sudden visit, Mr. Diefenbaker," I said.

I reached behind me, felt the door, and made sure it was properly locked. Not just with a physical lock but electronic and magical locks as well. Good; it was. The Baron's friends were helpful.

"I'm here about the jewel you recently purchased. You're aware it wasn't acquired through legitimate means?"

I may have bought myself some time, but there was no telling when those gangsters would return. Diefenbaker was still frozen with shock, but I'd bet he had a few security buttons on him that he'd use once he recovered.

A guarded look swept over his pale blue eyes.

"Doesn't seem like you used legitimate means to get in here," he said arrogantly. He tried grabbing the black iPhone at his side. "Get out before I call the —"

The iPhone fell to the floor and slid across the carpet to me. It ran around my feet like a friendly puppy. I bent down and rubbed its head, and then picked it up and stuffed it in my pocket. Diefenbaker's hand was still frozen in the air, his eyes fixed on my pocket.

"I'll get to the point, Mister."

I used his shock to my advantage. I folded my arms, looking relaxed.

"I've been hired by the real owner to recover the jewels you illegally acquired. I'm aware you purchased them from a boy named Jeffrey Chandler for a girl named Laura Winfrey. And I know you have her imprisoned against her will."

Diefenbaker's mouth opened but only a weird squeak emerged.

"As I'm sure you've surmised, I am not involved with the police. I have no intention of doing anything to you. In fact, I already recovered the real jewels. I'm here to negotiate the release of Laura Winfrey and elicit a promise from you to do no harm to her boyfriend, Jeffrey Chandler."

"The real... The real jewels?" Diefenbaker's reaction was downright bizarre. His throat bobbed several times, and he said in a strangled voice, "But...but those were real! Top quality diamonds and platinum! A real opal! I'm sure of it! I had multiple appraisals done! It's still here! Laura hasn't even seen it yet! It's never left my hand!"

"What?" I said, not believing my ears. I touched my chest, making sure the dragon egg was still firmly lodged in my bra.

"I obtained it from dubious sources! You think I was fool enough to not have it appraised?"

Diefenbaker glanced at a small cabinet by the wall. I raised a finger, and the top drawer opened on its own. The blue velvet jewelry case rose from it as Diefenbaker's eyes nearly popped out of his head. The case landed in my hand. I opened it, checking the contents. It certainly was an opal necklace. Looked almost like the real thing—obviously, except for the magic—but it was fake. Even if the jewels were real, this had no power to it at all.

"You had this the whole time?" I asked, baffled. "Then why did you hire gangsters to run around looking for the real one and for Jeffrey?"

"Don't be ridiculous. Why would I do that? I acquired an item worth the price I paid. What more do I need?"

Diefenbaker seemed to have recovered himself a little. I caught his gaze wandering to something under the table, so I froze him to be safe. Good thing I had; his finger rested an inch from the emergency security button set under his armrest.

"What the—" he said, only able to move his mouth and eyes. "Are you... Who are you? Did you drug me?!"

"Nothing like that, don't worry. I just want to have a peaceful conversation." I cleared my throat. "So you believe you have the real jewel and never once suspected that someone pulled a switcheroo on you? So the armed men in black who have the theater on lockdown—"

"What?" Diefenbaker yelped, horrified. "I have nothing to do with anyone like that! Yes, getting the necklace was a risk, but I cut all ties once the deal was done. Keeping your nose clean is vital to modern business. If I were connected to anything fishy, my stocks would plummet! There's no shortage of people looking to pull me off my throne."

This was taking a weird turn.

I'd assumed Diefenbaker was those black-suited gangsters' "boss," but Diefenbaker didn't seem to know them. He'd thought the necklace was real. In a sense, he was right about that. To anyone unable to sense magic there was little difference between a big opal and a dragon's egg.

In which case, why were the men in black after Jeffrey? How did they know the real necklace was out there somewhere? Was another boss hiding in Diefenbaker's shadow and trying to make off with the dragon egg? Was this boss the alchemist? But the alchemist was using Jeffrey to get away with both the egg and much of Diefenbaker's money.

My head spun. Diefenbaker started fidgeting, so I locked him in place again.

"For starters, why did you try to purchase that necklace? Someone like you oughta be able to buy jewelry from any number of reputable sources. And it makes no sense for you to lock Laura up in that theater basement. Someone like you would normally keep a girl in a hotel or a California penthouse, take them out on the town decked in furs and diamonds. Why that necklace, that theater, and Laura?"

As I spoke, I nudged his heart. I didn't have time to slowly thaw the thing for him. I'd expected it to feel like ice from the North Pole, but the reality was somewhat different. It was certainly cold, and covered in a hard shell, but the inside was still surprisingly soft, almost like a young boy's heart.

Diefenbaker's square jaw stiffened and then relaxed. His pale blue eyes looked at me as if seeing me for the first time. He blinked.

"I wanted to be a comedian," he said, his voice low.

"A comedian?" I echoed, despite myself. "Like a stand up? Or more the juggling type?"

"All of them. Standing in a spotlight, bathing in the laugher and applause, singing merrily, doing tricks..." Diefenbaker let out a long sigh. "But I couldn't. My father and grandfather would never allow it. We started calling ourselves Diefenbaker when my great-grandfather made all the right moves during the Great Depression. Our name was originally Byrne."

"Byrne?" That sounded familiar.

"One of my ancestors founded that theater," Diefenbaker—or rather, Byrne—said. He groaned. "My grandfather and father both despised that sort of thing. Said it was foolish. Uncouth. I couldn't argue with them. Had I not been cursed with this fortune, and the burden of being their only heir, I'd have run away from home, pounded on audition doors like so many other young men and women.

"I did try once, when I was sixteen. I put on a disguise, left the house, and went to the back door of a theater. *That* theater. Another person owned it, but it was the theater my ancestor had founded. Of course, my father and grandfather caught me. Before I even had a chance to knock on the door, my father and his secretaries pulled up in a limo and dragged me away by my collar."

He buried his face in his hands, like he was sixteen again.

"I can still see them, the dancing girls in their colorful costumes, filing out of the dressing rooms. My father, yelling as he pushed me out the door. Most of them ignored me, but one girl at the back of the line shot me a quick smile. Her face glittered in the lights, shining with excitement. She was blonde, with red lips...

"They packed me off to a boarding school, and later I got my MBA in economics. I was never allowed to go anywhere near show business again. Even after my father died and I took over the company, I was so busy with work I never had time to dream. Only now that I'm old—"

"You found Laura?" I said, softly. He seemed to be sinking deeper into memory. "I heard you keep her photo in your wallet."

"No, that's not her," Diefenbaker said, frowning.

"There's certainly a picture in my wallet but not one of Laura. It's the one picture of a stage dancer that escaped my father's purge. The one memory I have of that day, a photo I bought in the lobby of the Byrne Theater."

"Can I see?"

Diefenbaker took out his wallet and carefully removed a single worn photograph. It was an old, cheaply printed postcard, out of place in this obviously expensive leather wallet.

The black and white photo showed a smiling blonde girl wrapped in lace and feathers. She did look a bit like Laura; the round, childish face and slightly downturned eyes were close enough I could see why Jeffrey had made the mistake.

But it definitely wasn't her, and without that makeup the resemblance would be totally gone. This girl looked like that ghastly retro poster I'd seen plastered outside the theater. If you made Laura up to look like this postcard and took a photo, well, the resemblance would be uncanny.

"I found her doing prep for a party," Diefenbaker said, lost in his memories again. His eyes stared into the distance, dampening at the long-gone dream. "It was just like that day... Smiling girls, all so young and hopeful, their futures a blank page, the whole world in front of them.

Meanwhile, I'd grown old, chained to this company and fortune and sense of decorum. I was crawling to my grave, wearing a mask with a phony smile on it. The day my father dragged me away and threw me into that limo, I was so envious of those girls. I hated them more than you can believe. All the women around me were hyenas panting after my fortune. I couldn't stand it. I needed a girl like that. Needed the youth she had. The possibility. A future not yet written, that freedom, wings carrying her forward..."

"So why go and lock her up when you know it'll just make her miserable?"

"I don't know," he said, shaking his head. "I think it was a form of revenge. Against all sorts of things. Against fate, I suppose. I know it wasn't Laura's fault, but when she smiled at me the same way that girl had, I knew I had to make her mine. I know it makes no sense. But I felt like her potential, her world, her future were all things that should have been mine. I couldn't bear it. The girl who smiled at me that day got to have her future, while I was dragged away in a limo."

To him, the chorus girl he'd seen as a boy was the same as Laura: a symbol of his shattered dreams and the misery that lay behind his mask. Laura had just been unlucky enough to resemble the girl in his memories, a girl whose name he'd never known.

Perhaps some would see his unhappiness as a luxury of the rich, but none of us lead lives filled only with joy. I could sympathize with living in a dreary reality far from what I desired. I'd been the same way, both before I'd found out I was a faerie and after.

Neither life had worked out as I'd hoped, but the world I lived in wasn't that bad. My mother's endless conversations weren't exactly unbearable. The worlds I dreamed about didn't exist, but at least I'd found a place and could work to make things better.

"Why not buy that theater and start a charity show?" The idea suddenly came to me. "Rookies who want a chance to shine, amateurs who want to show off the talents they've developed for fun, all up on stage. You could welcome walk-ins, let old people and children who can't normally afford the theater in for free. Scouts looking for new talent will want to check it out. You'll have huge crowds, and nobody will notice if one or two of the comedians are getting on in years."

"You think?" Diefenbaker's eyes sparkled. "You know, that just might work... The company can run itself without me, and I already bought the building." Then a shadow passed over his face. "But what will people think?"

"To hell with it," I said. This was a certain, effective "spell" I'd used ever since I was little: to hell with anything not worth fussing about. What other people thought was always at the top of that list. "Your father and grandfather ain't around anymore, are they?"

"Naturally! They're both long since six feet under. I..." His eyes widened, as if making a great discovery. "I'm free!"

"Then you'd better start getting ready. That place is a mess!" I stepped away from Diefenbaker, as he looked about ready to hop out of his chair and begin tap dancing. Before anything else, I remembered the big reason I was here. "That jewel you were going to give Laura. How did you come by it? My client wants to know just who managed to steal it from him. And why did you want to give it to Laura anyway?"

"Hmm? Oh." He managed to pull his mind out of his glittering future, frowning. "Who was it? Hmm. Right. A lawyer, I think. One of my usual lawyers came down with the flu, and the one who turned up in his place brought the offer to me. Said it was a special necklace that could really develop an artist's talents. You know, I don't think I'd ever seen the man before. I normally wouldn't pay any attention to such a suspicious proposition, but he was very convincing. And, truth is, Laura's singing isn't very good."

He shrugged.

"I don't know if it's the stone in that necklace, but I thought if that could help her talent shine... And of course, I wanted to take care of her. I didn't know how else to do that but give her gifts. Honestly, I didn't have the faintest idea how to decorate the room I prepared for her."

"This room seems really nice."

"This is all the work of my interior designer. I have no eye for these things."

Diefenbaker looked depressed again. Well, at least now I knew why Laura's room was such an eyesore.

"And this so-called lawyer..."

Something was bugging me about this. A lawyer?

The only people who knew about the dragon egg were me, Lindel, and the alchemist behind the theft. Only the three of us—no, wait, one more. The man who'd passed Lindel's offer to me.

Dean.

The request itself had gone directly from Lindel to me, but Dean certainly could have known the details. After all, he was the one arranging things. If he pretended he was just figuring out how much to charge, I could see him gleaning enough information to guess. This was a case big enough to warrant personal involvement from an ancient mage like Echos, and everyone knew Lindel was the dragons' guardian. The stolen dragon egg and a request from Lindel—even an idiot could connect the dots.

I had a bad feeling about this. "This lawyer," I said, absently fiddling with my bra. The dragon egg pulsed against my skin. "Was this lawyer—"

"Jack!" a voice yelled from my phone.

No ring tone, no sampled voices. Forgetting to use his beloved Bogart's voice, Baron's scream came out like a burst of white noise.

"Jack, get back here now! Your office is trashed, and Larry and Jeffrey are gone!"

9

I DID SOMETHING I RARELY DO. I jumped fully into the faerie world, knocking stunned faeries out of the way as I raced through the forest, and landed in my office. Usually I stayed out of the faerie realm because time flowed so differently there, but I had more important things to worry about right now.

I was standing on pieces of a broken plate and some leftover pizza. Fragments of crockery with congealed cheese stuck to them, a spray of brown on the wall where a can of soda had slammed into it. The couch had flipped over, a brown puddle of spilled soda spreading like a bloodstain behind it. A bag sporting a game store logo— Larry had used that money on a new game after all—had been flung to one side. The Nintendo was on, its light blinking furiously. Two controllers lay on their sides like dead mice. The game's title screen was displayed on the TV, the words "Press Start" blinking futilely.

"Larry," I whispered. Then I screamed, "Larry!"

No answer. I forced down the rising panic, checking every room, opening every door.

"Larry! Jeffrey! Larry, Jeffrey, where are you? Where are you?!"

Silence. Sickening silence.

My toe bumped something. I picked up a Yankees cap, the one piece of clothing Larry'd managed to keep after transforming in the theater. It lay wrong side up like an overturned turtle.

"No use. He's gone." Baron's voice issued from the phone in my pocket. He'd calmed down enough to use Bogart's voice again. Had I ever seen Bogie acting this upset? Not worth thinking about right now. "As soon as they left the place, he used some concealment alchemy. I've got everyone looking, sent copies of myself out everywhere, but they're coming up empty."

This was my office. Nothing could ever set foot in here that I didn't let in myself. That's why I paid such high rent.

The only people who could get in here were me, Larry... and Dean. My business partner.

He didn't directly visit my office all that often, but it had been known to happen. As my business partner, my security would let him in. If he wanted, he could step into my office whenever he liked.

Even when he intended to kidnap my brother.

"We'll expand the search. Hold on."

The Baron vanished. The BGM from the TV was making me fret. I turned, and the zombie lurching across the logo melted away. A text message replaced the title screen, white letters on a black background:

I've got your puppies and the bitch. If you want them back:

Bring the item to Great Hill in Central Park.
Don't use magic getting here. I'll know.
You know what'll happen if you don't show up.

The glowing letters flickered and then slowly faded. I stared at the screen, paralyzed. Only when they'd completely faded did I yell and throw Larry's cap. It bounced off the LCD display and fell to the ground. The TV shut off, and the screen went black.

The room was dark. I realized the sun had set. This was why I hated going through the faerie kingdom. It'd been early afternoon when I'd jumped here from the Plaza Hotel, but now it was a pitch black, New York night.

Maybe jumping here had been less of a drain than taking the subway or a bus, or glowering at traffic from the back seat of a cab, but it felt like I'd wasted a huge amount of time. That killed me.

Larry. The one person like me, really like me. When I'd decided to stay in the human world, he'd grumbled about it but come along. My twin brother, always acting like a kid, always making me look after him. If it weren't for him, I'd be truly alone. Neither my human parents nor my faerie parents had ever really felt like family. For all his griping, Larry was always at my side, ever since he'd knocked on my window that evening and shown me his wolf ears and fangs.

I couldn't just sit here, I had to go, and now. But how? He'd insisted I couldn't use magic to get there. And I was up against Dean, an alchemist and a traitor. He was well aware a faerie like me could hide until I was right on top of him, so he'd be ready with detection spells. Maybe he'd even left a trap behind in this room. I quickly heightened my senses and looked around, but I was too upset to do a proper investigation, much less release any traps.

Should I ask other alchemists for help? No, that was a bad idea. I had to assume he was monitoring my actions. If I didn't show up with the dragon egg as directed, if I did anything suspicious, Larry, Jeffrey, and Laura would absolutely be in danger.

"Jack, you there?"

A knock on the window. I jumped to my feet, nearly tripping as I made my way across the darkened room. Staggering, I opened the window and saw a young, tanned centaur with dreadlocks. He looked at my face, looked at the state of the room, and his eyes widened.

"What the hell happened? A tornado hit you?" he asked.

"Vince," I wailed, holding fast to the window frame to keep myself upright. Even by the glow of the headlights and neon signs, I could tell my fingers were horribly pale. "Vince, I got a job for you. Rush delivery."

The words were out before I'd consciously thought it through, but as I spoke I realized this was the best approach.

"Can you give me a ride to Great Hill in Central Park? Fast. ASAP. A bad guy kidnapped Larry and my client."

Jeffrey wasn't technically my client, but I didn't have time to explain the complexities.

"If I don't go to him, three lives are in danger. Please, Vince!"

"Hmm. I dunno about that, Jack," Vince said. He clearly knew I was desperate, but he scratched his chin and glanced at the delivery bag on his shoulder. "You know I'm just the postman. Others handle the taxi service. If I step on their turf, it'll really piss 'em off."

"This is a personal favor. Just think of me as a package. You deliver things that live, talk, and think all the time, right? What's the difference if the sender herself is the cargo?"

"I don't know if the taxi folk'll see it that way..."

"I'm not kidding, Vince. This is serious."

"Sorry, but rules are rules, Jack. Ask your house automousebile. I'd love to help, but—"

Vince was already backing away.

"Vincent McNeill-Windrunner!" I roared. At his full name, Vince froze, his hindleg still raised. I ran to my desk, opened a drawer, and pulled out a white envelope. I dumped out the Linden leaf inside and thrust it under Vince's nose. "How about this? The express fee and the charter fee upfront. You get a penalty from the taxi people, you can pay 'em off with that. I'm in a hurry. Get me to Central Park, now! Please!"

"Whoa!" Vince grabbed the leaf the dragon aerie mage had sent, his eyes nearly popping out of his head. "You give me something like this, I'd have to be your personal taxi for the next year."

"I don't have time for chit chat! Hurry! Central Park!"

"Aye aye, boss."

I clambered out the window and heaved myself onto the centaur's back. As I did, Vince kicked the wall, and we rocketed like a bullet across the New York evening.

"You said ASAP, right?" Vince moved his leather bag to his back and glanced over his shoulder. "This might get a bit intense. You ready for it?"

"Go for it, Vince!"

"Roger that!"

His speed increased dramatically. The view around me blurred, everything melting together, the lights turning into lines as they sped past us.

I was getting a sound lesson in just how fast a centaur could run if they wanted to. This was like a top-speed roller coaster, except we bounded this way and that, making sharp turns and sudden drops that sent us slamming into the ground. The wind was so strong I could barely breathe. I gritted my teeth and held onto Vince's back for dear life, but it felt like my organs were being shaken so hard they'd never go back to their original locations. His bead necklaces thrashed like mad things, and the silver bits and feathers in his dreadlocks clattered wildly.

"Is that you, Lady Agent?" said a voice at my ear.

I forced my eyes open. A gentleman skeleton in a top hat floated next to me. Despite our blinding speed, he was easily keeping up with Vince without even ruffling his collar.

"Those uncouth men came and took Laura away. They were quite rough with her! I thought you should know. They may be plotting something dastardly!" Roderick cried.

"They are." I nearly bit my tongue trying to talk. The roaring winds snatched my voice away. "They took my brother and Jeffrey hostage and are trying to get their hands on that jewel you saw—the dragon egg. I've got the necklace right here. They failed to get it from me, so now they've resorted to kidnapping."

"Gadzooks!" Roderick's teeth chattered, and he raised a fist in fury. "Such evil is truly beyond the pale. If it's not too presumptuous, allow me to rally some support. At this time of night, there should be no issue with any number of us leaving our positions. I'm familiar with most of the local residents. One word from me and we'd gather quite a crowd."

"That would help! Please do. I've got to get to where the villains are, pronto."

"I shall soon return, my lady."

Roderick touched the brim of his top hat and vanished. I was left behind in the rushing wind, pretty convinced my stomach was about to force itself out my throat. What was Roderick's last name again? Roderick... Roderick Byrne?

"Yeehaw!" Vince howled. We'd already torn past the Empire State Building. He raced up a slanted, mirrored roof and leapt off the tip. I think that was the Bank of America building. Had anyone inside seen a centaur running up the windows, a faerie riding on his back?

Trees surrounded us. We were in Central Park now. People out for a midnight stroll or jog were scattered here and there. We raced through the rustling trees, headed north. Great Hill was in the northwest corner of the park.

"Here's good, Vince," I said.

I had him stop near Park West and 103rd Street. I put my feet on the ground and staggered, feeling dizzy. Vince hadn't been able to cut loose like that in a while, and clearly it hadn't been enough to take the edge from his energy; his hooves stamped restlessly, and his tail flicked this way and that.

"One more favor: Let some alchemist leader know that Dean is trying to pull a fast one on everybody. You probably know who'll need that information. They'll definitely want to stay out of anything involving Lindel."

"Lindel?!" Vince stopped pacing for a moment, blinked a few times, and nodded. "Wow. No wonder that leaf was so powerful. Right, I think I know an alchemist who lives over on Gramercy. They find out, word'll soon spread to the other alchemists."

"Thanks. I'll go face down the bad guy."

"Careful, Jack," Vince said, bending down. He pulled me in for a rare hug. "I mean it. You watch your back."

Vince turned and dashed off into the city again, the treetops thrashing in his wake. I took a deep breath, waiting for my head to stop spinning, then turned toward the trees.

There was no one around. The alchemist must've been warding them off. Even the lights outside the park seemed dim and the air oppressive. I figured I'd have to search for Dean, but as I took one step forward, a threatening voice emerged from behind a tree.

"I said not to use magic, Jack."

"I didn't. I just got a ride," I said, trying to sound dignified.

Evan Dean stepped out of the darkness, surrounded by gangsters in black suits. Bound, gagged, and blindfolded, they shoved forward Jeffrey, Laura, and...

"Larry!"

A silver cord bound his feet together. They'd gagged him, but my brother was here. He'd clearly tried to change into wolf form and fight, but they'd pinned him down. That silver cord must've sealed his faerie magic.

His eyes were closed, and he wasn't moving. I felt tears welling up. How horrible!

"You brought it? Let's see it," Dean said.

"Hell no. Release the hostages first."

I folded my arms and stood firmly, legs apart. Inside, I desperately hoped my backup would arrive soon. Either Roderick's ghost army or a group of flustered New York alchemists would be just dandy. For now, I had to buy some time and wait for my chance to teach this disgusting dirtbag a lesson. The leather pouch burned against my skin.

"I should have realized why you were so insistent about me handing the dragon egg over, Dean. You heard about the egg and planned on using me to make off with it yourself. You pretended to sell it to Diefenbaker, gave Jeffrey the fake, and when you learned he'd made off with the real one, you had me fetch it, planning to slip away with it once I delivered. You think you could fool Lindel? Or were you planning on telling him I'd screwed up and failed to recover it?"

"Stop running your damn mouth off, halfling," Dean said. Even in the dark I could see the sweat pouring down his face. "I never liked you two. You're just changelings, but you waltz around like you own the place! 'Jack the Flash'? Gimme a break. I'm done being yanked around by everybody! They can all go to hell! If I've got that egg, I can be the most powerful alchemist on earth! Lindel? An old mage holed up at the edge of the world? What can he do to me? Now gimme that egg!"

"Come and get it, if you can."

"I'll shoot them!" he cried.

"Then I'll throw this egg so deep into the faerie realm even I won't know where it is. It'll be somewhere untouchable, packed with the kinda faeries that swarm around sleigh beggy. They'll take it away where you can never get it."

His underlings definitely looked nervous. Several had guns but seemed unsure where to aim. Dean had clearly hired them without explaining anything about magic or alchemy. Given what he was trying to pull, he didn't have much choice.

"Um, Mister," one said, unable to wait any longer. "Would you mind explaining just what's going on here?"

"Shut up!" Dean snapped, veins in his neck throbbing. He waved a hand, and the speaker reeled backward as if punched in the face. The guy slammed into a tree and didn't move again.

"Stay still!" he yelled, when the rest of them began backing away.

He looked at me again, his eyes bloodshot.

"Gimme that egg. *Now*. Give it here before it's too late!"

"Too late, how? Hell, it doesn't matter, because I'm not ever giving this to the likes of you."

I pulled out the pouch and knelt down. It spun at the end of the glittering gold thread. "You come to me."

Dean howled. He lowered his head like a wild thing and charged. Magic energy rose up within me, crumbling his spell. Dean's chant became a roar, spell after spell growling like thunder, the magic stitched together like a quilt. The spell shattered, vanishing into the earth.

Dean knocked me aside. Naturally, he'd cast faerie wards on himself. He tried grabbing me, but I ducked under his hand and jumped backward. I looked for help from the spirits in Central Park, but he must have driven them off beforehand since none were in sight. Dean knew well enough that the spirits of nature would take my side.

I jumped and swung from a tree branch, concentrating my magic in the center of his goons. They were already shifting on their feet, and this knocked them down like bowling pins. Trussed up, Jeffrey and Laura collapsed to the ground.

"Jeffrey? Laura!" I cried.

The ropes around them fell away. They were fine; still breathing but unconscious.

I looked at the giant gray wolf lying next to them.

Larry's eyes were closed, and he wasn't moving. I tried reaching out but winced at the pain, like an electric shock. The silver cord gleamed, writhing in a threatening way. It reacted to faerie magic, absorbing and reflecting it back at us.

"Larry! Larry!"

Enduring the tingling shock, I shook the wolf's head. Dean had bespelled his gag. It felt like touching dry ice barehanded, draining all the heat in my body, sucking my magic as well as Larry's.

"Jack," he groaned, his eyes opening. The golden fires in his gaze had dimmed, nearly going out. He could only open his mouth a little, and a weak boy's voice emerged. "No. Too dangerous. Run..."

Something shot past my face as I turned. Larry let out a shriek, and his head flopped to the ground again.

His fur turned red, his blood dripping onto the ground.

The gunshot seemed so drawn out. Behind me stood a man with his back to a tree. Broken sunglasses hanging off his face, he held a gun in shaking hands.

"You idiot!" Dean shrieked. "Don't make her mad! If you do that, she'll—"

Me?

What *about* me, asshole?

I think I turned around. Probably.

It felt more like the world spun in place around me, like I was standing between two funhouse mirrors. Dean's tense face occupied the center of that world.

An incredible wind blew in my ears. The sound of my magic faerie blood ran wild. My twin was injured, and part of me screamed with pain and terror. The pain Larry felt, the chill of the blood leaving him, gripped my heart like a vise. The dragon egg that dangled between my breasts still burned with a powerful heat.

"How dare you?" I whispered. "How dare you!"

Dean screamed something, holding a hand out toward me. Too late; I'd totally lost control. An incredible amount of magic rushed out of me, all of it directed at Dean. The air swirling around me was as cold and sharp as a razor blade. The trees shuddered, swaying to and fro erratically. My hair stood on end, the fangs in my mouth sharpening. Goosebumps covered my skin; a golden sheen coated me. I was sure my face no longer looked human.

The silver cord that bound Larry thrashed, snapped, and disappeared. His gag vanished as well, unable to absorb the sheer quantity of magic my anger had unleashed. The man who'd shot Larry screamed and threw his gun away. It turned red on the grass, melting to nothing in a matter of seconds.

But something was odd; Dean continued screaming. He should have long been vaporized like the gun, the full force of my anger trained on him. Naturally, he'd chanted a spell to fight it, but against this much magic he wasn't nearly powerful enough to stay standing.

I realized that something was rapidly draining my magic—something other than the cord that had bound Larry. As my anger raged, I tried to see what was absorbing my power. Something close to me, right next to me. Something warm, small, pulsing...

Something floating in the air, tucked into a leather pouch around my neck.

The dragon egg.

Despite the powerful magical dampener on it, the egg shone so bright I could see it through the thick leather pouch. I tried controlling the flow of magic, but I couldn't stop it. The edges of the pouch began peeling back.

The robin's-egg-sized opal inside was like a beating magical heart. It was an ancient crystal of power.

I saw an entire world within its depths, a world teeming with magic. Memories woven through an eternity of experience swirled within it, taking form and unfurling.

Without thinking, I reached out my hand. The dragon egg hovered over my palm, its light blinding as it slowly changed shape.

Tiny, thin, rainbow-colored wings, transparent as soap bubbles, unfolded. Droplets of light scattered all around as a narrow head reared, delicate as a baby bird.

Its eyes were like two night skies, each containing the full breadth of the universe.

It looked up at me and opened its still-soft beak.

"Jakku?"

Suddenly, the sky fell.

I lost all power and fell over backward. Dean pounced on top of me. I struggled and tried to kick him, but was too weak. My body felt sticky. My physical strength had drained away with my magic. Gravity pinned my limbs with ever-greater strength, and I tasted blood.

"Jacqueline. Jacqueline, Jacqueline." Dean smiled, or maybe his face was just so twisted it only looked that way. Grinning like a broken man, tears flowing from both eyes, he put his hand around my neck. "It's all your fault... You ruined everything!"

I stared down the barrel of a gun, much like I'd done just the other day. But last time, an ugly, ordinary man had taken aim at me. Now it was Dean, and he looked grotesque. Hideous. His face was twisted with hatred, racked with despair. Yet he still smiled—I'd never seen anything so monstrous in all my life.

His finger tightened on the trigger.

"Die," he said.

Several things happened at once: a gust of wind knocked Dean over; a gunshot echoed; a hot burst of air rushed past my ear.

A moment later, the Central Park night gave way to light and voices. I heard screams. Alchemists dressed in dark suits wrestled with Dean, who struggled in vain.

"Jack! You okay?"

"Are you quite all right, Lady Agent?"

Two voices. A pair of strong arms cradled me. I forced open my heavy lids and found Vince supporting me. Roderick, top hat in hand, peered down at me with concern written on his bony face.

All manner of ghosts were chasing the gangsters, looking like they'd slipped out of a horror movie. Roderick's ghost army, frightening as could be, waved claws, groaned spookily, showed off the bullet holes in their chests, or cradled their own heads under their arms. A bride in a mud-covered wedding dress revealed a mouthful of rotting teeth and leaned toward a gangster's throat while laughing maniacally.

"I do apologize. I'd hoped to get here a tad earlier, but that man had cast a very strange spell on the area," Roderick said.

"It took the alchemists a while to break through it. Yo, you're bleeding! You okay?"

Vince touched my cheek, and I flinched. His heat and magic slowly seeped into my frozen body.

They must have used some binding spell on Dean, because he was standing in a very odd position. The remaining gangsters had mostly fainted at the sight of the ghost carnival. The alchemists' leader waved his arms. Those gangsters who were still staggering about collapsed onto the ground. The ghosts all grumbled, deprived of their "dance partners."

"Jack," Larry said. He was still stuck halfway between wolf and boy as he walked barefoot across the grass to me. He looked the same as the day he'd first tapped on my window. Blood mingled in the fur on his chest. He had a hand to his neck, a look of pain on his face.

"Larry! You got shot?" I cried.

"It's okay now. Just haven't washed off the blood yet."

He pulled his blood-covered hand away. There was just a faint wound from where the bullet had grazed him.

"Um, Jack? I, uh..."

I took a few unsteady steps and more or less fell on him. "Whoa!" He staggered, but his wolf strength kicked in, and he managed to catch me.

"I'm sorry, Larry," I whispered. My nose was buried in his pointy wolf-ears. My brother's hair smelled faintly of the forest. "I'm sorry..."

Larry put his arms around me and gave me a comforting pat on the back. "Don't worry about it. We're twins. Changelings. But..."

"But?"

"I'd really like the money to buy another jacket."

Vince and I both busted up laughing. Roderick looked back and forth at us, confused. He quickly summoned the most mischievous look his skull allowed and clapped his hands dramatically.

"Jack the Flash," said one of the approaching alchemists. He seemed like the leader. Didn't look any different from your average human, but he'd clearly been dragged out of bed and was both sleepy and grumpy. "One of our number was behind this mess. Based on the contract in place, our college and the mage Lindel will handle the rest. As for you..."

I just walked away. He gaped after me. I stood in front of Dean, who glared sullenly back.

I swung my arm.

There was a loud *thwack*. Dean's head rolled back, his nose bleeding. The alchemists holding him had to adjust their grip.

"Like I said," I hissed. "You call me Jacqueline again, I'll knock your head off."

The sounds around me faded. Warm darkness hovered on my periphery. Vince and Larry ran over as my body sank. I smiled and closed my eyes.

"Jack! Hey!"

"Jack the Flash...at lightning speed."

Super cool.

10

"JACK!" Larry wailed. "He ate all the sesame seed balls! I only got three!"

"Is that any way for a big brother to talk?"

"I never agreed to be this thing's brother!"

I sighed. A bundle of crow feathers lay spread out on the desk before me. As I undid the dried grass and waggled my fingers, every feather morphed into a pale, crow-shaped shadow. Sparkling, they flew out the window. Twilight had already come to New York.

Next, I touched my fingers to a stone, one swirled through with blue light and brown storm clouds. The storm was released; a dust-and-dry-leaf-scented wind brushed past my nose, and the stone spoke in a creaky voice.

I opened a box filled with stationary, my letterhead stamped on every page. I began taking a brandy-colored piece of amber out of the box but thought better of it. No need for me to stoop that low. Instead, I selected a piece of pale pink rose quartz and tapped it lightly to the stone. The quartz sparkled faintly, the rose-colored light permeating the stormy depths. When I pulled it away, the storm stone was entirely pink, with a six-pointed star indicating apology and friendship floating on the surface.

I headed over to the windowsill, intending to leave the stone there so I'd remember to send it off with Vince, when something landed on my head. Something about the size of a large pigeon, only light as a feather.

"Hey!" I scratched his throat. "You stuff yourself like that and you'll get a tummy ache, little one."

"Jakku."

His supple tail tapped my shoulder affectionately. The creature stretched out his neck, peering into my face. He had a sesame seed ball clutched in his mouth, and as I watched he tossed it into the air, caught it, and swallowed it whole. Dark eyes ablaze with the light of universes stared back at me.

Ultimately, I never got my special bonus. Evan Dean—that villain—must have decided there was no point in handing such treasure over to the otaku faerie he planned on killing anyway. He'd sold the pamphlet for chump change at a comic shop downtown.

Lindel and the alchemists offered to buy it back for me, but after a lot of soul searching, I refused. I'd managed to solve the case, but every time I'd look at the pamphlet and the characters' adorable, smiling faces, I'd remember Dean. I didn't need that, and taking a bonus for a job I hadn't exactly wrapped up would hardly make me the most honest faerie around.

However, I couldn't call the job a total failure either. Richard Diefenbaker—or rather, Richard Byrne—had properly apologized to Laura Winfrey, paid her a substantial amount for her distress, and released her. He'd done the same for her boyfriend, Jeffrey Chandler.

He'd offered both of them jobs at the new theater he planned to open, the Byrne's Family Theater. They'd declined, electing to return home to Kansas.

"My great-uncle Henry needs more hands on his farm," Jeffrey said, as I saw them off at the bus terminal. He'd gotten himself a respectable haircut, replaced the punk band T-shirt with an open-collared white one, and definitely cleaned up nicely. Laura had ditched the poisonous lipstick and pancake foundation for some pink lip gloss and a few light touch-ups. She was wearing a blue sundress and flats with straps, seemingly so happy she looked like a different person altogether.

"He's ninety-two, and his back can't even handle riding around in a tractor anymore. Great-Aunt Susannah's arthritis is getting pretty bad, so they're only too happy to have some young folks come help out."

"We both decided New York just wasn't for us. Thanks to you," Laura said, bashfully.

"This wasn't exactly the emerald city for us, but at least there was a wizard here. A real one. I know we'll think of you any time we see that movie."

"You could have taken a plane, you know," I said. I was a faerie, not a wizard, but I didn't bother correcting them. There was little point in explaining the distinction to two kids in love. "I'm sure Diefenbaker gave you enough to cover the tickets."

"Yes, but we wanted to take the bus. Take our time. Honestly, if we could, we'd love to walk home, savoring every step."

They looked at each other and giggled, as if sharing a secret.

"But it's a bit too far to walk. At least buses stay on the ground, so we'll take the journey to free ourselves of everything we've picked up here and think about how to move forward."

"Together?"

"Exactly."

Their fingers twined, and their hands clasped together. I felt sure they'd make it work. That required no magic. Love was all the magic they needed.

"Shame the road isn't paved in yellow bricks," I said.

"But we aren't going anywhere but home. Back where we came from. To Kansas!"

Laura looked up at the clear blue, May skies, smiling. She spread both arms out as if trying to hug the world.

For an instant, I was incredibly jealous. I felt like I understood why that old man had wanted to grab her and lock her away. They had something I didn't—a home. People to call family. A place where they really belonged.

As a changeling, I barely had any of those things.

"I don't think New York's an awful place," Laura said. "This is my Oz, I suppose, the magic land at the end of the rainbow. So many strange, enchanting, surprising things here, but, in the end, the fields and pastures of Kansas are where I belong."

"Right." If only I could say anything with such confidence. Ignoring the thorn prick in my heart, I wished them well. They'd return home, where they belonged. Meanwhile, I was caught between the faerie and human realms, with nowhere to go.

"If you want to go home—"

"Then close your eyes and tap your heels together three times."

"And think to yourself, there's no place like home."

All three of us tapped our heels together, and the bored crowd on the benches around us looked surprised and then laughed. The bus arrived. Laura cried a little, there were hugs all around, and the two of them were off on their long road to Kansas, trailing exhaust fumes in lieu of a wedding veil.

The Baron was in a deep sulk. Dean had placed jammer devices all around our meeting place to keep the electric loa out, so, as a result, the Baron had missed the entire climax. He'd compared it to having a main course taken away and being forced to make do with a single sardine.

But he admitted I'd had no way of knowing what Dean had done and that this wasn't my fault. He was pissed someone else's cavalry had hogged the limelight, but at least he understood he couldn't take it out on me. Currently, he was hellbent on figuring out how to keep his network going through any and all types of jammers. I guess that meant we were even.

Vince had really enjoyed getting to use his top speed and asked if he could be my personal taxi for the rest of the year. I politely turned him down; riding a roller

THE ANCIENT MAGUS' BRIDE

coaster with no seat or safety bar across the New York skyline was a once-in-a-lifetime experience. Instead, he offered half the usual rate on express parcels and his messenger service. This was far more useful.

Roderick was delighted, too. His descendant had had a change of heart, refurbished the theater, and brought in staff and customers for Roderick to look after. Given the chance to be the power behind the scenes again, he was positively giddy.

"I may be getting on in years, but you're never too old for the arts!" he'd declared when I stopped by to thank him.

His theater had been beautifully renovated, polished up, and given a sign that proclaimed Byrne's Family Theater.

"I'm over 200, you know! Yet I'm as fit as a fiddle! My descendant certainly has a great deal to learn about the arts, but..."

He glanced over at Diefenbaker, who was clumsily practicing his juggling.

"That's life for you, my boy! Welcome to the stage! I salute you!"

Parts of it had turned out well. The rest...not so much.

Lindel sat across from me in my office. I wanted to run for it.

"Hmm." Technically, he was a projection. The real Lindel was back in the dragon aerie in Iceland. "Oh, dear," he sighed.

The source of Lindel's consternation was happily sitting on my head, his wings spread, his belly flat against me, his head raised—a favorite pose.

The joints on his wings boasted small claws, which allowed him to get a firm grip on my hair. His neck and tail were long and supple, tracing graceful arcs. His tiny head had golden horns and a beak like a songbird's. In the midst of all this glittering gold, platinum, and rainbows were two incredibly deep, black eyes, always looking around with innocent curiosity.

"I'm sorry, Lindel," I said, feeling like a kid brought before the principal. "Um, I never thought this would happen. I can't believe the egg actually hatched. And the hatchling, um...saw me as..."

"Oh, that's fine, don't worry. I'm well aware you're not to blame," Lindel said, rubbing his temples. "If someone like Dean had hatched the egg, it would have been far worse. One reason this type of dragon is so rare, Jack, is that they have a particular quirk."

He pointed his wand at the top of my head.

"They're heavily influenced by the source of magic closest to them during incubation and are born with a very strong connection to it. Most of the time the mother dragon would be in that position, of course. And, obviously, dragons are usually untamable by any mage, alchemist, or even faerie. But that hatchling..."

The purring hatchling stared at the tip of Lindel's staff, his head tilted to one side like he was puzzled.

"As an egg, it spent a long time pressed against your skin, incubated by the magic you give off. That hatchling is now closely linked to you. I'm guessing Dean was hoping to do just that, which would have given him access to incredible magical power. But because he pissed you off, you ended up forming a bond with that dragon first."

"I'm sorry," I said, thoroughly cowed.

"So, little one." Lindel held out his hand to it. "Could I ask that you come stay with me? There are many of your kind here, including your brothers and sisters. Your current home isn't the safest place for a dragon. I know you don't want to leave Jack's side, but I'll do what I can to help. What do you say? Any interest in a peaceful, quiet life, somewhere safe with others of your kind?"

The hatchling lifted his long neck. Six hatchlings—his siblings—gathered around the projection, sitting with Lindel.

They were each much bigger than this hatchling. Compared to the large-ish, pigeon-sized creature on my head, they were already the size of calves. Their bodies were more bronze than platinum, and the rainbows on their wings less vivid as well. The dragons seemed to recognize their youngest sibling and called out to us like a chorus of low-pitched bells echoing in a distant valley. It brought tears to my eyes.

The hatchling seemed like he wanted to answer their call. He opened his mouth, raised his head, widened his eyes, and took a deep breath.

But no voice emerged. He shut his mouth, blinked, and buried his head in my hair again. His little claws clutched me tight.

"Jakku."

"Sounds like a no," Lindel said, lowering the staff with a sigh.

"Lindel, um..."

"This is a first," he said, shaking his head. "Perhaps I might have found a means of handling this in the information lost during the great war, but... Jack, I have no idea how to wean that hatchling off you or how it would affect him if I tried forcing you two apart."

"Right."

"But as the one charged with protecting the dragon aerie, all matters related to dragons are my responsibility."

"Right."

"Can I trust you, Jack?"

"Yes?" I said, surprised. "Um, you mean...I can keep him?"

"What choice do we have? Until we figure out a way to wean the hatchling off you without harming it, we have to leave it with you."

Lindel put both hands on his staff, looking me right in the eyes.

"My desire is that the dragons remain safe and free. It's been some time since they were safe in the world of man, but I have never once thought of the dragon aerie as the only place they could be happy. What's important is that the hatchlings live in peace and harmony. If you can treat it right and protect it, then it doesn't matter where it lives. That's what I mean when I ask if I can trust you."

"Of course. Um, I'll do everything I can, but...it's a big job."

"Naturally, I'll help in any way I can," Lindel said, giving me an appraising look. "Are you not sure you're up to it? Or is the responsibility getting to you? Well, perhaps the best plan is for you to move to the dragon aerie and remain trapped here until one of you dies. What do you say?"

A chill ran down my spine. He was smiling, but there was no mirth in those green eyes.

If he genuinely thought that was the best course of

action, he would have already taken the hatchling and me without giving either of us a choice. Lindel was the dragons' protector, their guardian; for all his talk of freedom, he could be incredibly stern, and he expected the same fortitude and responsibility from others. I had no idea how he'd become the aerie guardian, but, as a mage, he instinctively craved freedom. The decision to hole up at the ends of the earth must have taken more struggle and self-doubt than I could ever imagine, but he had persevered through that hardship and passed swift and decisive judgment on anyone who would interfere, be they human or faerie.

"I think I will trust you for now, Jack the Flash." The Icelandic chill vanished from his tone, and he leaned back against the rock as if exhausted. "I'll prepare a spell that will allow me to monitor the hatchling's condition at all times. That way, I'll know at once if anything occurs. Oh, and we'll need a plan to deal with anyone unscrupulous who makes a play for him. And a way for the hatchling to escape human attention in such a crowded city." He let out a long sigh, deflating. "My head hurts just thinking about it."

"Sorry."

I felt like that was becoming my sole response to anything. I glanced up at the creature on my head, and he looked back at me. I would love nothing more than to avoid shouldering a burden like this, would love to wash my hands of the whole thing. But once the dragon guardian made up his mind, I knew I couldn't refuse.

"Are you listening, Jack?"

"Yeah, yeah."

Larry was still griping about the Chinese delivery. I put the rose quartz back on the desk, closed the window, rubbed the hatchling's warm belly, and sat down in front of the steaming food. The hatchling flapped its wings and began wheeling through the air, waiting for his chance to swipe another sesame seed ball.

"No more!" Larry hugged the box of them to his chest, ready for war.

The hatchling thrashed his tail, annoyed. "Jakku."

"No fighting, kids," I said, getting a headache of my own. Was there anything we shouldn't let dragons eat? Onions? Chocolate? Or was that dogs and cats? Clearly, sesame seeds and mochi seemed to be okay. If there was a problem, we'd hear from Lindel soon enough.

"All right! You can have my annin tofu and some of my egg tarts. But only two! Not three!" I said.

"You oughta give me three, you miser," Larry sulked, glaring at me. "I'm the one who asked for sesame seed balls!"

"And I'm the one who paid!" I snapped, glaring back.

A silent war raged between us. I lost.

"All right! Three. But the cashew chicken and Sichuan crab are all mine!"

"Yes!" Larry yelled, his chopsticks already moving the food to his plate. The hatchling seized his chance and swooped, grabbing a sesame seed ball before flying away. He landed on my shoulder, nibbling on the ball like a squirrel with a walnut, and eyed Larry's seafood chow mein.

Larry's fluffy wolf ears twitched happily. Savoring the sweet and sour sauce on my chicken, I watched him eat his noodles. The hatchling lined up a new target now that he'd had his fill of sesame seed balls.

As I ate, a real feeling of warmth welled up. It was almost a ticklish sensation, like little bubbles rising up and popping inside of me. Larry used his chopsticks to keep the dragon away from his seafood and shot me a strange look.

"What, Jack?" he asked.

"Nothing."

My family, where I belonged.

Everyone should have a place like that. I was a faerie cast adrift in the human world, unable to ever truly fit into either realm.

But at the very least, right here, in this room, with these two bickering kids, I was at peace. Both of them called my name, fought over scraps, argued over how to split the egg foo young, squabbled over nothing... This was where I belonged. This was my family.

I kept myself going so I could live here with them.

Jack the Flash moves like lightning.

Super cool.

The End

Flightless Stars

KORE
YAMAZAKI

FIVE DRY COCOONS rolled across my palm.

"What's with these?"

Eugene, the well-built man seated next to me on the bench, folded the cloth bag that'd held the cocoons and laughed. He sounded proud of himself.

Helsinki in early October was a little chilly, but the trees in this seaside park hadn't yet changed color, and the sunlight warmed things considerably.

"Silkworm cocoons," he said.

"I can see that!" I glared at him, adjusting my glasses. "I'm asking why you have something like this."

My shoulders were half as broad as Eugene's, so no amount of glaring on my part would ever intimidate my friend.

Laughing, Eugene took a wallet from his backpack and counted his money. The man had never owned a credit card, so he always paid in cash. I'd have preferred he wire me the money—it was easier, and the fee was pretty cheap—but he was twice my age, and his lack of credit cards likely had something to do with his papers. That was a whole other mess.

"Don't get so upset, Jonathan. Few months ago, I stayed at an inn with...can't remember if he was Chinese or Japanese. Either way, an Asian guy gave 'em to me. Said these were rare cocoons, and if you spin 'em they'll shine like silver."

"Silver?"

He made a show of groaning and glaring at his wallet, looking from his backpack to the pile of receipts and the calculator. He could afford this amount, honestly.

"A different shine to 'em than your average silk."

"If these were that valuable, why give 'em to you?"

I shoved a receipt toward him. He scowled. His already narrow eyes narrowed further and then softened in relief. I guess he had enough.

"Well, he said he had no use for 'em. Didn't know how to reel 'em, and only had five. I thought they might be more up your alley, Jonathan."

"Well, if you're giving 'em away, I'll take 'em."

I glanced down at the empty cloth bag and carefully put the five cocoons back inside. I felt it would be wrong to treat them roughly, probably because they clearly still carried pupa.

Just as I'd finished putting the bag in my backpack, Eugene thrust a thick bundle of Euros into my hand. He then slipped a few bills into his wallet and returned the wallet to his backpack. Euros didn't need to be exchanged, which was helpful for life on the road.

"Well, my livelihood *does* depend on this sort of thing, but I've never reeled a cocoon before."

My livelihood? Yeah, that was the word for it.

I made a living selling special cloth to mages and alchemists. I'd occasionally finish the item myself and cast a spell on it, but it wasn't a common practice. It was easy to attach spells to the cloth I made, so I bought the vast majority of it as a material for subsequent use.

These backpacks were a major product of mine. With magic energy woven into the fabric, they could hold ten to twelve times more than their size suggested. Lots of magic folk lived on the road and needed to haul around research materials, essays, cursed items, etc. I myself used them to carry products, sewing machines, knitting needles, assorted looms, multiple types of thread, yarn, cloth of all colors. Other than how hard it was to find the one thing I actually needed, the packs were quite well made, if I did say so myself.

Eugene gripped his jacket with both hands and grinned proudly.

"Your cloth really is perfect for casting spells. Look at this jacket you tailored for me; I've been wearing the thing ten years, and it ain't frayed at all. I got stabbed the other day, and it straight up deflected the blade! You're a good mage," Eugene said.

"That's all I can really do though."

I ignored his alarming anecdote. Getting stabbed wasn't uncommon for anyone who lived in the world's back alleys.

"What are you talking about, kid? You ain't even fifty yet. You can try your hand at anything you want."

"It doesn't suit me, you know. Living for decades looking this young."

I glanced down at the cocoons in my hand.

I'd stopped aging around sixteen, or maybe eighteen.

No wrinkles or spots, no bony arms and legs. No need to worry about my eyesight or blood pressure. My father had had high blood pressure. My little brother and sister were just like him, so they might be getting real worried about it.

My brother married a girl from our hometown. When

I heard he'd had a grandkid, I stopped making yearly visits home.

Four years after I set out on my journey, the master who'd spotted my talent and taught me all manner of things vanished without leaving so much as a letter of explanation. By now, I felt sure he was dead.

Through no desire of my own, I was always left behind.

I sensed someone looking at me, and a few seconds later Eugene patted me on the back. I could feel the heat of his palm through my jacket.

"It ain't good to think too deep about these things. It's just what fate has in store for us," he said.

I didn't answer, but this didn't seem to bother Eugene.

If I lived as long as Eugene, maybe I'd come to see it that way.

I sighed. Eugene gave me another fatherly pat.

"Here, now, don't look so gloomy. Let's go down this hill, grab a bite at a stand somewhere. There's a festival on today! We can grab some meatballs, maybe some salmon cream soup or fried muikku. Good eats drive the bad things away."

This was a blatant attempt to cheer me up, but the corners of my mouth twitched anyway, and my stomach growled.

Even depressed, I still got hungry.

I didn't know whether to smile or feel sad about that. Either way, Eugene and I went down that hill together.

With his tab paid up and my purse full, I could have easily gotten a room.

But for some reason I felt hesitant to sleep in a comfortable bed, so I took a sleeping bag and passed the night in the woods near town.

Moss was soft on my back and under my head.

The city noises were faint on the night air. The chilled breeze carried the sounds of the surf from the Gulf of Finland. My bespelled sleeping bag kept the cold out, warm as a sauna. Soon, I felt very sleepy.

If my nights were too peaceful, I felt as if I wouldn't wake in the morning.

I opened my eyes and saw the stars twinkling.

Their hard light resembled the color of the cocoons I'd seen that afternoon.

I'd never reeled a cocoon; had barely seen one before. I couldn't be sure just how unusual the cocoons in my bag really were.

Even after nearly fifty years on this earth, I still knew almost nothing.

That fact came as a relief somehow. I closed my eyes

for good this time. Tomorrow I'd research how to reel silkworm cocoons.

Hurry.

For a moment, I thought I heard the stars speak.

The voice was faint but vibrant. There was something about it I couldn't ignore.

I stood, searching for the voice's source. It was closer than I'd imagined.

Like the stars above, a metallic gleam spilled around my feet...from my backpack.

I hastily bent down and scooped the light's source from the bag's side pocket.

It was the cocoons Eugene had given me.

Hurry, hurry.

Hurry, hurry.

As the voices whispered, the bluish light shimmered like smoke.

"What's the rush?" I said, lacing my voice with magic so the cocoons could understand me.

Hurry, hurry, hurry, hurry!

The cocoons began shrieking.

"Come on, work with me. Hurry to do what?"

Hurry, hurry.

Hurry, hurry.

Hurry and reel us.

I felt cold, smooth fingers brush against my face.

I jerked backward and fell on my ass. The cocoons seemed to calm down a little, as the shimmering slowed.

"You said to reel you? But..."

I didn't deal in weaving, sewing, and trading cloth for nothing. I may not know the exact process required to reel silk from a cocoon, but I knew how to pull the thread.

You put the dried cocoons in boiling water to loosen the threads, leaving the pupa inside.

Don't worry.

I could sense no sadness in the voice.

We know what will become of us.

Yes, yes, at last.

We must become that.

At last we've found a man who will turn us into thread.

The voices sang and laughed as the cocoons' light flickered. Something about the voices reminded me of a child's lullaby.

"Let me look into it."

I glanced at the phone by my sleeping bag and saw the time.

Both sleep and dawn seemed far away...

The world had certainly become more convenient, I thought, skimming the search results.

I found the recipe to make silkworm thread much faster than expected, but the work would be nigh impossible in the dark. I talked the cocoons down and waited patiently for dawn. The sky to the east then began turning slightly red. It was time to prepare.

I took a portable gas stove and pot from my backpack, poured in a bottle of water, and lit the burner. There weren't many cocoons, and the pot was small, so it would boil quickly.

Meanwhile, dawn seeped across the sky.

I won't be thread.

One of the cocoons suddenly called out to me. I squinted, wondering which, and saw the largest one twitching.

I'll lay eggs instead.

I hadn't asked if they were alive. All the cocoons should have long since been dead, but since they were talking to me I thought it best to listen.

"Then you sit here," I said, laying it on my sleeping bag, atop a pile of leaves I'd gathered from the nearby brush. The cocoon seemed delighted, but it may have been my imagination.

I heard the water start to bubble and lowered the gas so it wouldn't boil over. The rising steam soon faded into the cold morning air and the darkness of the woods.

Oh, oh, at last!

At last we can become thread! Oh, oh!

The cocoons' voices sounded like the residents of a snow-locked land greeting the arrival of spring.

I picked them up with shaking hands. For some reason, my throat felt parched. I gritted my teeth, shook the voices from my minds, and dropped them into the boiling water.

Plop.

Such a dull sound.

I could no longer hear the cocoons' voices. They were as quiet as they'd been originally. Nothing about them indicated they'd ever given off such a beautiful, bluish light.

I boiled them a while, turning them with a tiny broom made from fallen twigs. The sticky surface loosened. Threads began spreading out in the water, so I gathered those threads on a twig. As it was still fairly dark, this was easier said than done.

Groaning, I finally got all four. I pulled the threads, gathered them together, and reached for the empty spool. I spent quite some time simply winding away.

A cocoon could produce up to 1,500 meters of silk thread.

Between the water's heat and the tension, sweat ran down my brow and back.

"Why did you want to become thread?" I asked, without realizing I was saying it aloud.

That is what they want from us, a soft voice answered.

Not the vibrant voice I'd first heard at night. This one was more graceful, gentler.

Forgetting to watch my work, I looked toward the voice. Something silver lay on my sleeping bag.

A pair of feelers, like two combs, emerged; silver hair, and silver eyebrows. White skin, like cotton.

The eyes looked almost human but were a solid, glittering black. I saw no mouth.

Its clothes boasted large, fluffy sleeves. The entire outfit appeared to be made of fur, with shining silver flecks dancing all over it—were they scales?

Its belly looked swollen, like it was pregnant.

"You're that silkworm?" I asked.

Please, keep working.

I remembered I was supposed to be winding thread and quickly looked back to the pot. If I boiled them too long, that would be awful. I only had these four cocoons.

Thank you for hearing our request, traveler from the far, far west.

"I just boiled all your friends to death."

The silkworm laughed softly.

Our insect lives ended long before you boiled them. But this is their proper destiny, just as mine is to lay these eggs.

"But why?"

I spoke to the cocoons. This time, I didn't stop my hands... No, that's not right. It wasn't that I didn't stop them; I couldn't. It was like someone else was moving my hands for me.

We are born of human hands.

The silkworm laughed. It seemed to do that a lot.

Because we are boiled and turned into thread, our numbers increase. We are venerated, and we are valued.

Wind, wind, wind. The spool turned.

If we do not become thread, we can no longer be ourselves. If we do not leave children behind, we can create no more thread.

A gust of salt-tinged wind darted between my hands, and the winding threads wavered.

"Even if that's true," I gasped, the words forcing themselves out of me. "If you want to live, you can eat mulberry leaves, become pupa in your cocoons, then emerge from them. Isn't it scary to have someone else decide who becomes thread? To have that choice taken from you?"

Someone had decided *I* should be like this.

I'd never wanted magic talent, to have that potential.

All I'd wanted was to stay in my hometown, be normal, put down roots, live with family and friends, and grow old.

Perhaps we felt that way once. Perhaps even now.

The silkworm didn't seem upset. It spoke with a soft, musical voice.

We consume mulberry to live, weave cocoons to live, emerge from them to live, and lay eggs before we die.

The silkworm didn't move at all. Its unblinking eyes stared fixedly at the pot. I could feel its gaze even as I reeled in the thread. Those eyes showed no pity, no sadness, no anger—just joy.

Human hands changed us. Though we can no longer live without human hands, we go on living. Even if our lives can only be fulfilled like this, we continue as long as we can.

The thread wound on, turning, turning, and turning some more. I'd lost all sense of time.

We know, and we remember.

Beyond the forest depths, I glimpsed growing trees I'd never seen before.

Somehow I knew they were mulberries. I strained my eyes and could faintly make out strange wooden houses. Between the mulberries, people went to and fro, clutching large bundles of leaves. Sweating, laboring, smiling... *Oh,* I thought.

This is where these cocoons came from.

Human houses are warm, comfortable, free from predators.

It was warm inside those wooden boxes. The silkworms would never freeze. They were fed all the mulberry leaves they could eat.

There were many delicious mulberry leaves. From time to time, a large cat would look in, eyes gleaming.

The cats would catch the awful rats.

Gnarled human fingers touched us gently, carefully.

Hands that reeled so much silk they changed shape, turned red.

So very warm.

The silkworm never moved, yet I felt it looking up at the sky.

Ah... I hear the sound of flutes.

In the distance, a ship bound for foreign lands issued a steam whistle.

That's the festival song.

Around us, the trees rustled in the wind.

Spring comes, bringing warmth. We hatch, our children hatch.

Behind me, cloth rustled. Was the silkworm dancing? Or was it crying, crying while smiling?

Sleep, sleep, green, green, soft leaves...

Before I knew it, I'd reeled all the thread.

If I left it like this, the threads would stick to each other. I needed to re-reel them on the spinning wheel. Where in my backpack had I put it? I'd made enough stock that I hadn't touched it in a while. Worried, I turned toward my pack.

The humanoid silkworm was gone.

A dead silkworm remained, fully emerged from the cocoon, its wings outstretched.

Not one egg had hatched from its large, glistening belly. And without mating, the eggs wouldn't live even if released. Even if the worm had mated, there was no mulberry here for them to eat.

Silkworms cannot live without human hands and homes.

Moaning, I took the pupa from the bottom of the pot, dug a little hole at the base of a tree, and buried them. I tried convincing myself they'd been dead long before I boiled them, but even if that were true, boiling them had killed them once more. No matter what anyone said, I had boiled them. I had turned them into thread.

I buried the silkworm that had rested on my sleeping bag in the same hole.

I filled in the dirt and patted it firm.

The burial complete, a noise escaped me.

Even if our lives can only be fulfilled like this, we continue as long as we can, it had said. It had smiled. Yet it hadn't left the eggs it wished to. Not here.

"I have to reel it."

I searched my backpack and drew out a small spinning

wheel. The thread probably required a proper machine, but this was all I had with me. I had to re-reel it quickly.

I had to give meaning to them.

Applying just a little magic so the thread wouldn't snap or tangle, I spun the wheel. There should've been far more thread than this, so if an ordinary human had tried, it would've been ruined almost immediately. Without magic, I could never have done it.

It's just what fate has in store for us.

As my mind spun, Eugene's words from yesterday flooded my head. Oh. That was right. I felt like laughing out loud.

The past thirty years of drifting had led me here. I'd left my family, my friends, lost my master. Because I couldn't use suggestive magic or transformative magic, I had no home, and drifted from town to town, country to country.

To save silkworms that wished to fulfill their purpose.

I was sure, almost sure, that was why.

"You're right, Eugene."
The wheel spun on, as if my words had spurred it.

The thread came along. It did, indeed, gleam like a sil-ver star.

I'd gathered only a small amount. I wondered what I should make from it, my head hazy from lack of sleep. Buy a little extra silk, weave it on a loom? Use it for embroidery? Weave it into an accessory? Even though I hadn't asked for the responsibility of reeling them, I knew the final result had to be something good. That's just how I was.

"If I didn't think like that, I could never live an unend-ing life."

I chuckled. There was a desperation to it that surprised me.

Being forced into an awful role for thirty years was hardly pleasant. Yet the morning had brought a beauti-ful blue sky. I was starving after my sleepless night, and my rumbling stomach thought that coffee and cinnamon rolls sounded very appealing.

When I finished this work, I'd return to the harbor.

Maybe I'd find Eugene snoring in front of the Havis Amanda, having been unable to afford a room for the night. Maybe I'd kick him in the ass and force him to buy me breakfast as punishment for foisting all this work on me. Who cared if he refused?

I spun the wheel faster, relying on the magic.

In the bright morning light, the thread glittered like laughter.

The End

Author Biographies

Yuichiro Higashide (scenario writer, novelist)

MAIN WORKS: *Fate/Grand Order* (Aniplex), *Fate/Apocrypha* (Type-Moon)

"I barely scratched the surface of *The Ancient Magus' Bride's* setting. A bit of a gruesome piece, but I hope you enjoy it."

Megumi Masono (novelist)

MAIN WORKS: *Gyokuyo Kitan* (Tokyo Sogensha)

"Nature's bounty, the shifting seasons. Life abounds, and bonds grow between them. Sensing the beauty of *The Ancient Magus' Bride,* I wrote what I wanted and what was fun for me. Thank you."

Chikashi Yoshida (novelist)

MAIN WORKS: *Joko no Teikoku Naishinnou Nako-sama no Seisen* (Shogakukan), *Totsugeki Houki Shoujo Maria* (Shogakukan)

"It's an honor to be a part of the world of *The Ancient Magus' Bride.* The characters, time period, and tone in my story are quite different from what the other authors submitted, but I hope you enjoy it."

Sako Aizawa (novelist, manga writer)

MAIN WORKS: *Shosetsu no Kamisama* (Kodansha), *Torino Hatsu no Jikenbo* (Tokyo Sogensha)

"England, faeries, inhuman creatures, and magic—all things I love. I've added servants and mysteries, another two of my favorite things. I hope you enjoy!"

Yoshinobu Akita (novelist)

MAIN WORKS: *Sorcerous Stabber Orphen* (Kadokawa Shoten), *Blood Blockade Battlefront: Only a Paper Moon* (Shueisha)

"I live deep in the mountains these days, but all living things possess skills I can never begin to understand. Like how ladybugs get into the house. It's like magic!"

Suzuki Ootsuki (scenario writer)

MAIN WORKS: *Kuro no Dansho* (Abogado Powers),
Sabae no Ou (Lost Script)

"Kind of an *Ancient Magus' Bride* and Cthulhu crossover. Hey, even the actual series goes straight to that well in the first volume, so! That's all from me."

Yuu Godai (novelist)

MAIN WORKS: *Guin Saga* (Hayakawa),
Paracelsus no Musume (Media Factory)

"Continued from the first part in *The Golden Yarn*. This story turned out to be quite different from what I've written before, but I hope you all enjoyed it. Thank you!"

Kore Yamazaki (manga artist)

MAIN WORKS: *The Ancient Magus' Bride* (Mag Garden)
Frau Faust (Kodansha)

"I've always found silkworms fascinating, both their lives and their appearance. Getting to write about a very human mage was also fun. I bet there're lots of them working part-time jobs and backpacking around."